JILLIAN'S WILD HEART

Ladies of Munro, Book 4

Elizabeth Donne

ARE YOU SIGNED UP FOR DRAGONBLADE'S BLOG?

You'll get the latest news and information on exclusive giveaways, exclusive excerpts, coming releases, sales, free books, cover reveals and more.

Check out our complete list of authors, too!

No spam, no junk. That's a promise!

Sign Up Here

www.dragonbladepublishing.com

Dearest Reader;

Thank you for your support of a small press. At Dragonblade Publishing, we strive to bring you the highest quality Historical Romance from some of the best authors in the business. Without your support, there is no 'us', so we sincerely hope you adore these stories and find some new favorite authors along the way.

Happy Reading!

CEO, Dragonblade Publishing

Additional Dragonblade books by Author Elizabeth Donne

Ladies of Munro Series
Sophia's Letter (Book 1)
Ellena's Secret (Book 2)
Verity's Choice (Book 3)
Jillian's Wild Heart (Book 4)

Dedicated to my sons

PROLOGUE

Munro House, late September 1814

THERE SHE WAS again. Miss Jillian Kinsey. Best friend to the bride.

Lewis had first noticed her at the wedding, where she had been throwing rose petals from a basket with the gleeful energy of a lass much younger than she was, golden hair streaming down her back despite being a grown woman who should have been wearing it up.

Should have. How often he had heard that expression applied to him. It wasn't that he was a disappointment to his parents. Heavens, no. It was good to have a "spare to the heir." He had followed the rules: he was usefully occupied as a barrister, did not get in his brother's way, and generally toed the line.

But, at thirty, he *should have* been married by now. *Should have* made more friends among the *ton*. *Should have* been, well, less himself.

His sister had not cared for the rules. She had taken all the risks necessary to free herself from their parents' expectations. In a way, she had been Lewis's salvation. She had shown him it was possible to be true to yourself and survive.

And that was, quite simply, why Lewis had remained unmarried. If he was going to spend his life with someone, he wanted a wife with whom it was safe to express odd opinions. To avoid the trappings of high society. To break the odd rule when it made no sense. Such a lady was rare, indeed.

Yet here he was, at the wedding celebration of his dear friend, Viscount Howell, staring unabashedly at just such a woman.

All right, so she was a groundskeeper's daughter, Howell had mentioned. His mother would have been crimson with rage if she'd known he was even *pondering* a woman of such low station. But if Miss Kinsey was good enough to be a loyal friend and companion to the new viscountess, who was a baron's second son to judge her worth?

Besides, if he was going to annoy his parents, he should at least meet the young lady properly.

Lewis drifted in Miss Kinsey's direction. He was obliged to stop and make conversation every few steps, yet he was making steady progress. Her laughter tinkled up even from a distance, her face radiant with unbridled joy. Lewis was finding it hard to focus on whatever was being said to him, his gaze constantly drawn to the golden-haired nymph. The nearer he drew to her, the stronger he felt her pull.

He had reached a space mere yards from her when the bridegroom found him.

"It's been a while since this house has seen so many people," the viscount said with what Lewis could only guess was regret that it had not remained so.

"You've never been one for crowds," Lewis agreed, frustrated that he was unable to see Miss Kinsey over the viscount's tall shoulders. "But I warrant marrying Lady Howell has been worth the temporary discomfort." He tilted his head to try and catch sight of Miss Kinsey in case she moved off in a different direction.

"A hundred times over," said his friend, stepping to the side. "Is that better? Is the view improved?"

Lewis felt his cheeks grow warm. "Er… yes, thank you."

Lord Howell followed his line of sight and nodded. "Miss Kinsey is quite lovely and, as I'm sure you've noticed, disarmingly natural in her manner. Would you like to be introduced?"

Lewis cast a wary glance at the viscount. "It's not like you to play matchmaker."

"Good grief!" cried Howell. "That was *not* my intention. I merely thought, since you and Miss Kinsey are close friends of ours, you will find yourselves frequently in each other's company and an introduction would be called for. I do *not* thereby suggest any sort of match between you! It is hardly a suitable one for either of you."

"Hmm," answered Lewis vaguely, for his heart was already well on its way to being smitten.

"I should warn you," the viscount added, "she is a bit... much. She does not appear to have a filter of any sort."

Good, thought Lewis, but he said nothing. Lord Howell liked everything to have its place. It was part of the role he had been raised to play. But Lewis was only a second son. A nobody, as far as upper society was concerned. A bit of plain talk would not bother him. In fact, it would make a refreshing change from the formality of the law courts and his parents' stern upbringing.

He followed the viscount as he cleared the path to Miss Kinsey, who stood next to the bride, encircled by a gathering of slightly stunned listeners. Lewis grinned to himself. Clearly, they had not been warned by the viscount.

The small crowd parted as the bridegroom approached, the murmur among them subsiding. But Miss Kinsey's eyes shone, and her smile remained broad and welcoming as she addressed her host.

"Lord Howell! Ellena has been wanting to introduce me to your friends. Alas, as she has met none of them before today, it has been an impossible task. How genteel they all are, though! Such excellent manners, letting me gabble away about my home and family and the exciting journey we have had all the way from Ermenbrough just to attend your wedding. And what a splendid ceremony it was! With the most beautiful bride Munro has ever seen. And a husband who, I can clearly see, appreciates her. Good for you! That will be your best quality, of which Ellena tells me you have many."

The new Lady Howell slipped her arm through that of her friend's and said in a half-whisper, "Catch your breath, Jilly dear. His lordship's friends are not accustomed to such abundant speech all at once."

As it was, the viscount's friends had used the distraction of his arrival to melt away into the nearest pockets of more sedate conversation, where the pace and content was better suited to their taste. All of his friends, that is, bar one.

Lewis waited patiently for the promised introduction.

"Bradford," Lord Howell said quickly, before she could set off again with her tireless chatter, "may I introduce Miss Jillian Kinsey of Ermenbrough? Miss Kinsey, this is Mr. Lewis Bradford of Oakwoods."

Instead of resuming her lighthearted chitchat as Lewis had expected she would, Miss Kinsey stared at him in awed silence before declaring, "Oh my, Mr. Bradford, you have the most beautiful dark-blue eyes! Just like the wings of a kingfisher."

As she'd said it, Jillian knew she had gone too far. Ellena's sharp intake of breath confirmed it.

After a brief, shocked pause, Lord Howell cleared his throat and said, "Do you know, Bradford, the lady is quite correct. I had never noticed before. They are, indeed, a remarkable shade. Quite enviable, I should say. Well spotted, Miss Kinsey."

Ellena was right about the viscount, mused Jillian. He was a most thoughtful man, trying to save face on Jilly's behalf. This infernal urge to blather when she was nervous was bothersome, to say the least. What must Mr. Bradford think of her?

And yet Mr. Bradford did not appear troubled. A slow smile crept across his features. "That is the best compliment I have received by far," he said. "Possibly because it was sincerely meant," he added. "Allow me to return the favor, Miss Kinsey, and tell you what a pleasure it is to meet a lady who is utterly without pretention. You are a rare find, indeed."

"Oh," said Jillian, truly speechless now. And again, "Oh." She turned to Ellena for assistance. Ellena, however, was sharing a look with her brand-new husband that Jillian could not decipher. There was definitely an edge to it.

By contrast, the expression on Mr. Bradford's face was familiar and inviting, his jaw slack, his eyes focused, his tongue wetting the inside of his lower lip.

In Jillian's experience, honest feelings did not need to be uttered, even though she was inclined to do so in heaps. She was good at reading the unspoken truths in the countenance of others. She knew when a man had seen something—or some-one—that pleased him. She recognized in Mr. Bradford's face what his words did not say.

He liked her.

Jillian considered him more closely. He had well-defined cheekbones, well-tended eyebrows, and perfectly-proportioned ears. All elements of a man's appearance that Jillian believed were too often overlooked.

She could like a face like that.

Far, far more important was the comfort of his stance. He did not fiddle with his cravat or look down at his fingertips in an effort to disguise his dismay at her awkward manners. He was looking straight at her, seeing her properly, and not disapproving. In fact, quite the opposite. Mr. Bradford was, bless his heart, quite obviously taken with her.

She could love a man like that.

"What a lovely thing to say," she answered at last. "If that is truly your opinion, we shall fast become friends."

"I am delighted to hear it," he replied. "Shall we promenade about the room and share stories of the bride and groom that they absolutely would not want us to know?"

Jillian laughed loudly, causing several heads to turn in shock. Mr. Bradford, she noted, only smiled more broadly.

She had, in the few hours she had been in Munro, become painfully aware that she did not belong, although the viscount's friends had been very polite about it. Small wonder, for when had she moved in such circles before today? Ellena's parents were the nearest she had come to engaging with gentlefolk, and they had stoutly disapproved of her being in their daughter's life at all. But Mr. Bradford… He simply let all the expectations of his class roll right off his back.

Jillian slid her arm through his and declared, "I shall like getting to know you very much, I think, Mr. Bradford. Shall we?"

The gentleman threw a glance over his shoulder. Jillian could have sworn he winked at his friend. The earlier look between husband and wife was repeated. Jillian discerned an element of concern in their unspoken thoughts. Before they could act on their shared musing, however, Mr. Bradford and Jillian had fallen into step.

And thus it remained the rest of the day. Though they sat at opposite ends of the dining table, their eyes were ever upon each other. If Jillian felt a chill, Mr. Bradford arranged for a footman to collect her wrap. If her hands were empty, he supplied her with an interesting book from the library or a glass of refreshment.

Their world had shrunk until it was just the two of them.

It was the most complete Jillian's world had ever felt.

CHAPTER ONE

Munro House, one year later

J ILLIAN KINSEY FLEW down the stairs, her dress billowing behind her, her feet nimble and light. Her long, golden tresses streamed in a rippling wave, wild and free except for a ribbon that tied a few strands away from her face.

On the landing below, a footman carried a tray with elegant decorum, his uniform starched, its buttons shiny. Like everything else in Munro House, he was the very picture of order, a perfectly suitable element in the home of Viscount Howell and his good lady.

Jilly reined herself in, her feet slowing to something nearing an acceptable pace. She must not embarrass Ellena. It was a privilege to be a houseguest of the viscountess. But it was so hard to behave! Sedate walking. Quiet speech. How did the servants manage it all day long?

Jillian missed the freedom of Trenton Grange and its nearby village, although her friend Ellena would have scowled at such a thought. For Ellena, the years in her childhood home had offered little latitude. She had been raised to become a lady, every day a lesson in refinement, and her marriage to Lord Howell had been the very triumph her father, Henry Trenton, had craved.

Jillian, unbound by such expectations, had offered the master's only child a little balance to her restrictive life, orchestrating escapes when Mrs. Trenton's back had been turned. She and

Ellena would sneak off to the meadow, where they were not curbed by the rules of men, and could run, barefoot and breathless, or braid flowers in their hair, laughing with abandon.

For Jilly, this was the only life she had ever known. As daughter to the Trentons' groundskeeper and sister to three rambunctious younger brothers, her only tasks had been to help her mother in the home or keep the boys occupied while Mum had worked unhampered by their tireless presence. It was a simple life, and she'd desired nothing more. She had never imagined herself an honored guest in the home of the most powerful man in Munro. Nor how lonely it would make her feel.

Throughout twenty-one years, and despite the Trentons' stout disapproval of the mismatched friendship, she and Ellena had remained loyal to each other. And when, a twelvemonth ago, Ellena Trenton had transformed into Lady Howell, Jilly had become a frequent visitor at Munro House for weeks at a time, bringing the comfort of the familiar as Ellena adjusted to her new role.

Jilly, however, had not adjusted. The two worlds were too different. Even descending a simple flight of stairs could be a challenge. Mostly, she could manage, if she forced herself to remember what was expected in this great house.

But today, all caution had been thrown aside. Today, she *needed* to race to the door! Mr. Bradford was waiting. Lovely, lovely Mr. Bradford—a blessed solace in this confusing world among the gentry and nobility of the great northern city of Munro.

Jillian took another dainty step. Bother! There were too many of them between her and the foyer. Each one proceeded with painstaking self-control. And there was always another just ahead. This home was too big. And her room was on the top floor of the stately, triple-storeyed residence.

Ahead of her, the footman descended with steady grace. Jilly followed with mounting irritation.

She had negotiated two flights of stairs with some success

when the sound of a humming baritone vibrated up toward her. Her heart swelled at the unmistakable rendering of their favorite song. Mr. Bradford would sing it to tease her if they ever had a moment alone before Ellena and her husband joined them in the drawing room. In particular, he loved the lines:

At ball or play, she flirt away, and ever giddy be;
But always said, I ne'er will wed, no one shall govern me.

"Wild thing," he liked to call her. It was said with affection. And some envy, perhaps. Jilly took no offense, for it was an apt description. She was not sorry for it. As much as she admired Ellena and enjoyed the privileges of their friendship, she could never exchange spontaneity and naturalness for the stiff, staid life of society's upper crust.

Jilly turned the corner at the last landing. And there he was! Dear Mr. Bradford. Her toes curled with pleasure. As always, his dark-brown hair was combed back so that nothing concealed his clean-shaven face with its perfectly straight nose and defined cheekbones. His shapely lips, so often pressed into a thin line from his habit of fretting over things he could not control, were pouting as he hummed. They were begging to be kissed. One day, she would throw caution to the wind and do just that.

Sixteen steps to go. But they no longer mattered, for she could see a smile spread up into the dark-blue eyes of Lewis Bradford as he caught sight of her, his humming ceasing so that he might say, "Good afternoon, Miss Kinsey. How well you look! The color of your dress suits the flush of your cheek. I wish more young women would exert themselves a little if this is the pleasant result."

"Do you, indeed, Mr. Bradford?" Jillian remarked as the last few steps disappeared behind her. "Is it not enough that *I* should catch your eye in this fashion? It seems you would have all of England emulate me. Then the little I have with which to recommend myself would no longer be a novelty, and I shall fade into the background once more."

Mr. Bradford barked a laugh. "It is quite impossible to imagine you fading in any form or manner. You exude life, Miss Kinsey. You need nothing else to recommend you."

A heavy tread announced the approach of the master of the house. Lord Howell, tall and broad-shouldered, stepped into the foyer from the passage that led to his study.

"You should not give Miss Kinsey false hope," the viscount admonished his friend. "She has had a difficult time of it, trying to find her way through all the senseless rituals that define the lives of nobility. It is bad enough that we who are born into it must endure it. To tell her it has been unnecessary because she can simply be herself would be a cruel blow after the effort she has made to accommodate us. Sadly, a woman's enthusiasm alone can never be enough to grant her entrance into society. More's the pity."

"Who said I *wanted* to enter society?" Jillian retorted. "It has very little to recommend it, as you have said yourself on several occasions. Back home, I am every bit the nymph of the fields I have always been. And I regret not one minute of it."

"What do you say to that, Howell?" Bradford grinned. "Come now, be honest. Would you not far rather live like Miss Kinsey, free of care and bursting with energy?"

The viscount shrugged. "I do not deny it has a certain appeal. But we do not all have that choice. Some inherit a position that is more demanding, and we accept it. Living such a life well carries fulfilment of its own."

Bradford pursed his lips in the now-familiar show of discontent. "Ah, now you sound like my brother. Ever complaining about the burdens of the firstborn son. And yet it is he who will receive our father's barony and continue to enjoy the lifestyle in which he grew up. Meanwhile, I must plead cases in court and earn my way in life, *sans* your privilege or Miss Kinsey's freedom."

"Poor Mr. Bradford," said Jillian, slipping her hand through his arm. "We must amend this at once. What say you to a long walk in the sunshine? The colors of autumn are upon us and flocks of birds announce their departure overhead. Some brisk exercise and the sights and sounds of the outdoors have always lifted my spirits, and they are bound to do as much for you."

"You cannot keep stealing Bradford away, Miss Kinsey," said the viscount, "even if it is with a lady's maid in tow. We have business to discuss. And when that is done, *I* would enjoy the company of my good friend. I so rarely have time to socialize with those whose company I actually enjoy. You are not alone in finding the elite of Munro tiresome."

"But the evenings are chilly of late," Jillian countered, "and the shadows lengthen earlier. Let me take Mr. Bradford on an excursion around the grounds while it is pleasant outside. Then you can be formal and serious indoors when we are done. And if Mr. Bradford stays for supper, we may all join in the conversation at the table. No one shall be denied their pleasures. This must surely be amenable to you. Is it not a worthy compromise?"

His lordship looked helplessly at his friend, causing Mr. Bradford to laugh once more.

"You know you can't argue with such excellent reasoning, Howell. You might as well tell Mrs. Anders right now that I am staying and to organize an extra seat at the table. I think a spot of fresh air is exactly what I need to cleanse the palate of my mind, so to speak. I will be better able to give you legal advice when I have tossed away the cares of the day."

Jillian cocked her head and pouted her lips teasingly at the viscount. "Oh, do not take it so to heart. You are master of this house in every way. I have merely suggested *how* you might master it."

"It is dizzying, the speed at which you rearrange my day, Miss Kinsey," his lordship replied. "Even my wife is not as adept at twisting me to her will."

"But it is all for a good cause, else I would not dream of taking such liberties," Jilly assured him.

"I have known you a year," Lord Howell pondered aloud.

"One would think I should have grown accustomed to being maneuvered in this way by my favorite houseguest. There are very few people who may say they can best me in negotiations. Perhaps your power lies in the reasonableness of your arguments. As such, I concede willingly. But I will send *two* maids with you. One alone will be too easily bewildered by your wiles. I shall not have you running off to the woods to braid Bradford's hair. The man's dignity must be protected."

"Spoilsport," Jilly grumbled, though a smile played about her mouth. "Well, then, let me fetch my wrap. I'll be back in a minute." She turned and made to race up the stairs, two at a time, when she heard a meaningful cough behind her.

Lord Howell gestured to the footman who had opened the door to Mr. Bradford and now stood waiting with the gentleman's hat and coat. "Have someone fetch Miss Kinsey's wrap for her, will you? And these"—he indicated the hat and coat—"might as well be returned to our guest. He'll be needing them, after all. Oh, and while you're at it, fetch Clark. He'll be joining you on your walk."

The footman handed the items back to their owner, then began to tread the steps in a dignified manner that did his uniform proud.

Jilly slunk down the handful of stairs she had climbed, her tail firmly between her legs, reminded once again that she did not belong in an environment where she could not scamper like a goat.

"Do not worry, Miss Kinsey," Mr. Bradford said softly. "We shall soon be beyond sight of these walls. Then you may dash about as much as your heart desires."

Jillian caught the rolling of the viscount's eyes, but he said nothing. He knew she made a constant effort not to let him down. When they were in company—other than that of Lewis Bradford—she really did try very hard to do all that was expected of her. And the viscount and Ellena, bless their hearts, asked nothing more.

In fact, Jilly had been spared much of the darker side of Munro. She had seen snatches of it at dances, where gossiping and sniping and condescension were rife. But dinners were only ever attended at Munro House and invitations to these were limited to a very small selection of guests. Anyone who might treat Jilly with disdain—whether or not they felt entitled to do so—were not considered welcome. Indeed, this was the norm even when Jilly was not visiting. The viscount and viscountess did not tolerate arrogance or any similar meanness of spirit. Their friends were few and dear to them. And they all adored Jillian.

She had been given a great deal of grace and was grateful for it. And yet, she still yearned for her life back home, where cows stuck their velvety noses over the fence, her father grew endless beauty from the wholesome soil, her mother could turn the humblest of ingredients into something delicious, and Jilly's brothers would caper about her like puppies demanding her attention.

When she and Ellena were alone in one of the many rooms of Munro House, they recaptured some of the lightness of their childhood escapades, but it was mostly in conversation. Lady Howell could not be seen galivanting with abandon about the house and garden. And now that Ellena had a newborn to care for, her responsibilities had increased even further. Her husband fussed over her, scarcely allowing her to move from her bed. He would not have her exert herself. She must rest to recover more fully from the strains of childbirth, especially since she had refused the services of a wet nurse.

The past three weeks had therefore been particularly dull and solitary, since Jilly had scarcely even been allowed to hold the baby. She sometimes wondered if it was necessary to be here at all. She would be of much greater use to her mother, who had no servants to assist her as Ellena did.

During this period, when Jillian mostly sat with Ellena in quietude, save for the happy gurgles of little Christopher Howell, Mr. Bradford had become her salvation. He alone now welcomed and encouraged her lightheartedness. It was as if a secret part of him sought it for himself, and Jilly was more than happy to share it. He visited Munro House more and more often and his excuse for doing so grew increasingly vague, until it became clear he was there for Jilly.

And always they made an escape to the grounds beyond the house, Jilly relieved to move and laugh, and Mr. Bradford grateful to be away from the rigors of life in front of judges and magistrates. Their rambles about the estate had become something of a game, seeing how quickly they could elude poor Ingsley, only to reappear behind her and pretend they were chaperoning *her* walk.

Today, however, Lord Howell had undone their mischief. Two maids were too hard to evade. Unless she and Mr. Bradford split up and circled 'round individually. Jilly grinned within the privacy of her thoughts. Yes, that might work very well. She had to hide her gleefulness at the idea. If Lord Howell suspected, he might withdraw his chaperones altogether, and then the walk could not take place.

He really was very serious about protecting her reputation, bless his heart. It did not matter that her father was a groundskeeper, and that she could run wild back home. At Munro House, she was a companion to the viscountess, and that meant playing a role in the public eye. Lord Howell relented a little within the privacy of their home, but only a little. Stolen moments with Mr. Bradford were just that: moments.

Today, however, she would foil the viscount's efforts to rein her in. She hugged her little plan to herself until she could whisper it to her accomplice.

As soon as Ingsley had arrived with her wrap, Mr. Bradford took it from her and placed it about Jillian's shoulders, his warm hands resting a moment upon her arms. Jilly felt the heat seep deeper into her body. She reached across and touched his hand with her fingertips—gently, so that he would not think she wished his hand to be removed.

A buzz of current ran between them. Jilly wanted to step

back, fully into his arms, to feel his chest against her back, his lips against her hair.

Instead, it was Mr. Bradford who stepped back abruptly. Jilly turned, disappointed. Mr. Bradford was looking down, pulling his gloves from his pockets and then tugging them over his fingers. Why he needed them, she could not understand. His hands had been warm enough and the day had not yet turned cool.

Ready at last, he offered Jilly his arm. She took it with a little less enthusiasm than she had felt but moments ago. They fell into step together. Behind them, the two footmen did the same.

"Be back in an hour," Lord Howell commanded. "I cannot have you so tired that our business cannot be concluded, Bradford. And I am sure my wife already misses Miss Kinsey's company."

The two nodded in unison. Jilly brightened at how quickly they became one. Despite their differences in gender, age—though what was nine years when they were both still young?—and background, their connection was undeniable. If only more could come of it. But even impetuous Jilly knew she could not broach such a topic. Not unless Mr. Bradford did so first.

Today, then, this would be a walk shared by friends. Dear friends. Friends whom she wished could be so much more. Perhaps, if she were patient…

"You are far away in your thoughts today," her companion noted.

Jilly tried to shake her daydreams from her mind. After all, an hour with Mr. Bradford all to herself was not to be wasted. Except they weren't alone. Not really. Which reminded her…

Jilly lifted her chin toward his ear. "I have an idea," she whispered.

MISS KINSEY'S WORDS breathed warm and moist into his ear.

Lewis felt a shiver of delight thrill down his spine. She always had this effect on him. It didn't matter what she wore or what she said or did. Miss Kinsey was like a beam of light that shone straight to his heart.

And his heart could be a dark place.

Being a second son had not merely been an accident of birth. It had bled into all aspects of his life. Although he had moved in social circles with other nobility, he had always been counted among the lesser order, the ones who would have to marry into other noble families to maintain their status.

When his brother, Philip, traveled to London, he took a carriage and servants, enjoyed a generous allowance, and visited the homes of the upper echelons. Lewis had been given his mother's maiden name as his Christian name, a reminder that he would inherit very little from his father. When he studied at university and later at the law inn, his finances had been more limited. After all, he did not have to maintain the lifestyle of a future lord. In every sense, Lewis was reminded he was less, simply because he'd been born second.

The only advantage to this position was the freedom to make somewhat riskier choices. He did not have to be quite as proper or move in all the right circles or maintain quite the same degree of perfection to which a firstborn son was bound. The result of mixing with other lesser mortals was that Lewis was kinder, more down-to-earth, and automatically the brother more likely to befriend Viscount Howell, who detested pretentious behavior of any kind.

This friendship had, to Lewis's immense delight, also led to an introduction to Miss Kinsey. It did not matter that she was of humble origins. He had no need of rank or money. He earned enough, and he had experienced firsthand how nobility—and the subsequent lack thereof—could affect the dynamics within a family.

Besides, the viscount had married a country gentlewoman without prior status and see how happy they were! Lady Howell had risen to the role of viscountess with ease and had not compromised her good nature in the process.

Certainly, Miss Kinsey was not genteel by birth or upbringing, as the viscountess was, but she would not be hosting dinners on an estate. Lewis could be satisfied with a comfortable home, the minimum of servants, and a few good friends if Jillian Kinsey filled each day with her sunshine. No title or money could buy that kind of happiness, and he was determined to claim it.

This was the business he wished to discuss with his friend Howell. He needed advice. Despite his bravado, he suspected his parents would not be pleased with his choice of bride. He needed to know he at least had the viscount's support. If he did, the Bradford family would be less likely to protest. After all, a guest at Munro House was a rarity, and Miss Kinsey was akin to a sister to her ladyship, her visits frequent and lengthy. If she was good enough for the viscount and viscountess, who were his parents to judge her insufficient?

Right now, however, such serious thought was difficult to sustain. Miss Kinsey was whispering her little plot into his ear, her voice tickling his senses and doing funny things to his self-control. Thank goodness propriety required him to wear gloves. If he should touch her with his naked hands, feel the smoothness of her arm, the fine details of her fingers, he would be quite undone.

With each visit, he had found it more challenging to resist her lips, her neck, her curves. It was just as well Miss Kinsey had been assigned two chaperones. If they had evaded the previously singular chaperone, Lewis would not want to circle back as their usual game required. He would want to linger alone with her, and… No, a lady's maid should definitely remain with them!

"And so," whispered Miss Kinsey, as if reading his mind, "if we head in separate directions, we can easily elude them, as we have done before, and meet up at that tree." She pointed to a large oak that stood out among its kin. "We shall be able to watch them as they search for us. Then we shall jump out and surprise them! It will be terribly fun."

It was all very well. They had done this sort of thing many a time. But today, Lewis knew that if they were to be alone, he would not wish to be found again. He would want to pull Miss Kinsey to his breast and kiss her mouth, her eyes, her shoulders, until she groaned with pleasure. She would say they should stop, then beg him not to.

And he had no right to any of it.

Not until they were betrothed.

He would go down on bended knee this minute, in sight of both footmen if need be, but he didn't want to rush into it. Howell knew her better, would have a clearer sense of her thinking. There was risk in both Miss Kinsey's possible answers to his proposal. If she rejected his suit, it would make things dashed awkward between them. And if she agreed to be his wife, there was no going back. Not without considerable consequences, which he did not wish on either of them.

He wanted to make her happy. But she was not like other women. He would not manage it with dresses or jewels or a house in the fashionable district of Munro. She needed regular visits to her family and lots of space to roam like the wild thing she was. He had enough funds to arrange travel and a home on the outskirts of the city, where she might have her own kitchen garden for vegetables and herbs, and a shaded lawn for their children to play. He had even considered the merits of keeping their own chickens, though he knew nothing about the feasibility of such an idea. And he had ideas aplenty. A barrister was never short of studied arguments in his client's best interest. Here and now, however, he was the undecided party seeking counsel.

He considered the supple arm of Miss Kinsey once more. It was quite delectable. And she smelled wonderful. His mind began to wander into dangerous territory again.

"Er… I think perhaps we should take pity on the servants, just this once," he said. "I cannot imagine they relish their roles as your chaperones. Let us not make it more burdensome for them."

"Oh," said Miss Kinsey, her bright eyes clouding over. "You don't want to play?"

A growl of desire rose in his throat, but he swallowed it down. He wanted to play very much. But not this game.

"I would rather spend my time with you than seek ways to evade our watchers by separating."

"Oh," said Miss Kinsey again, though this time her lovely neck became pink and flushed. "If that is what you want…"

"It is."

"Well, if we are not to play hide and seek with my chaperones, what shall we talk about?"

Lewis looked ahead toward the path as it shrunk into the distance, but his thoughts went even further, into a future he had yet to tread. He pictured Mrs. Jillian Bradford standing in the doorway of their home, a row of cheerful flowers lining the path that led to it. He tilted his face toward the object of his hopes and said, "Tell me what you know about chickens."

CHAPTER TWO

WITH THE SCENT of Miss Kinsey lingering upon his arm and a plethora of new knowledge regarding the keeping of chickens filling his mind, Lewis Bradford entered the study of his friend, Viscount Howell.

"Take a seat," said the viscount, gesturing to a plush leather armchair at the side of the room. He took up position at an angle to Lewis, half-sitting against the edge of his desk so that his tall frame still towered over his guest.

Lewis did not take offense at this seemingly ungenial stance. It was merely force of habit. Lord Howell was a formidable man of business, a tyrant in negotiations, so opposite to his more benign nature in private. His imposing stature, supported by the fact that he preferred to stand, made it clear who was in charge of proceedings. It was intended to put the opposition on the back foot and secure his advantage from the start. He tended to forget that such machinations were not required among friends and they had learned not to pay it any mind.

"I shall save you some time," Howell said as Lewis lowered himself into the comfortable chair. "Your idea is a terrible one, and you should discard such thinking with immediate effect."

Lewis froze in the middle of settling himself, his features unmoving except for his eyebrows, which shot upward and remained there. "I haven't said anything yet," he protested. "How can you reject a subject that hasn't even been raised?"

"You want to marry Miss Kinsey. And you want my opinion. I have given it to you. Now you may begin your arguments, as I am sure you have many. I shall hear them patiently and show you the flaw in each, one by one."

"I feel perhaps I should stand," said Lewis, feeling a tad ruffled, "if this is to take the form of a court case. Though I have to wonder, if you are to be the opposing counsel, who shall be the judge?"

"Common sense shall prevail."

"You seem to think you have a monopoly in that commodity. But I have thought this through for some time. My plans are practical. Common sense has been applied at every juncture."

The viscount looked up as if considering an argument written on the ceiling. "That may be true," he conceded, "and yet common sense did not rattle around in your head by itself. There would have been a stout measure of other less sensible thoughts, nay, *feelings* that colored your views."

Lewis felt the heat of his embarrassment rise in his neck and color his cheeks. "Well, you should know," he countered weakly. "You have been in this position yourself."

"Which is why I can say with confidence that your situation is worse. More fluff and less logic."

"You do not wish me to be happy?"

"That is exactly the sort of nonsense to which I am referring. Happiness does not come from the desiring of it. The match must be able to stand the test of a lifetime."

"But I don't have nearly as many factors to consider as you did," argued Lewis. "You are Munro's foremost citizen, a viscount needing an heir, which your fine wife has provided you. I am but the younger son of a baron. I can marry purely for happiness. And I intend to. Enough of my life has been made up of duty without much in the way of reward. Miss Kinsey offers me a lightness of being I have not felt before."

"And what do you offer her?" asked his friend.

"Why, everything! My heart, my home, the security of a sound income."

"Can she be happy in the home of a gentleman? You see how she struggles in Munro House. She bears it for Ellena's sake, but she is always relieved to return to Trenton Grange."

"Our abode will have nothing like your estate," Lewis said with confidence. "There is no comparison. She will be able to do some gardening without folk questioning it. I'm certain our blooms will be the envy of all Munro if she has her father's skill. And we can keep chickens. I will try my best to include the reminders of her childhood home in our own."

Lord Howell tweaked his mouth into a restrained grin. "Chickens, hey? You really do love this woman if you are talking of poultry running about your grounds. Whatever will your parents say?"

"They will just have to endure it if they choose to visit. Their home is run as they choose. It shall be the same for mine."

"And when Miss Kinsey—I mean Mrs. Bradford—desires to run about, as she is wont to do, where will she find an outlet for this urge?"

"I hope to have a large, shaded lawn where she can do as she needs within the privacy of our property."

"Hmm, too small for her levels of energy."

"Then… Munro Park. It is certainly large and varied enough."

"Not private enough. Even the wife of a barrister must maintain some decorum in the public eye."

"We'll take the carriage and go for a picnic farther afield," said Lewis with some exasperation.

Howell looked at his friend with squinted eyes. "Not so easy to accommodate her after, all, would you say?"

"We'll figure it out," Lewis insisted. "Everything is new in the beginning. Within a year, it will be so familiar as to no longer require thought."

The viscount focused his unflinching gaze upon Lewis. "If you are so confident, why do you seek my advice?"

There was a pause. It was but a moment, but it was enough.

"It will be challenging to blend our worlds," Lewis admitted. "But I am determined to manage it. I had hoped that your experience with Lady Howell, who was herself no part of the *ton*, would give you insights you might share with me. I had thought you might advise me how to proceed to attain success in this venture. I did not expect you to discourage me."

Howell shook his head. "Ours is too great a friendship for me to withhold hard truths from you. I fear the challenges you will meet will not be as easily overcome as you surmise. We would not want Miss Kinsey's vivacious nature to suffer. If she were to marry a farmer, she could continue as before. But as *your* wife, even though you are a mere gentleman and not titled, she would be expected to maintain the very lifestyle she finds so uncomfortable during her visits here."

"I think you forget that we may dictate the way we live, as you have. You are highly selective of your visitors and intolerant of arrogance and airs, even in public spaces, ignoring whoever dislikes your stance in this regard. I would choose to do the same."

A deep sigh answered this bold statement. Lord Howell looked at his friend with downcast eyes. "I wish it were that simple. My position grants me certain privileges with which to counter the loathsome expectations of society. Regardless of what people think of me, they are forced to show respect, at least to my face. And I am not fully at liberty to do as I please, either. There is a minimum of taste and propriety I must uphold. As with you. A barrister cannot do entirely as he wishes. His clients want a man who carries himself with dignity. Knowledge of the law must be paired with a solid reputation. And your wife, whether you like it or not, shares in the burden of that responsibility."

"Are you saying Miss Kinsey is not up to the task?"

"I'm saying it might be hard for her, even if she were willing to try."

"Should I not give her the opportunity to decide for herself?"

"My dear Bradford, I fear the young woman is as smitten as you are. There is every likelihood that she will say *yes* to the idea of marriage simply to be with you. But the reality might be a blow from which neither of you can recover. I should hate to see two of my dear friends made miserable by their pursuit of happiness."

Lewis tapped his fingers on his knee, his lips pressed together. "You seem to have a rather lower opinion of us than I gave you credit for."

Howell lowered his lids and shrugged. "I merely speak from experience. I almost threw away my own joy by letting my feelings run away with me. You will remember the course of events, to my shame."

"Our situation is not the same! You had barely met when you were married. I have known Miss Kinsey for a year. We are no longer strangers to each other. Our weaknesses are already known and have not affected the fondness we share."

Lord Howell lifted his seat from the table's edge and resumed his full height, indicating the meeting was at an end. "Look, Bradford, you seem determined to pursue this matter, despite my words of caution. I can only hope that Miss Kinsey shows more sense. Unfortunately, thoughts of romance and marriage are rarely swayed by logic and wisdom. If I cannot persuade a sensible man like you, the artless Miss Kinsey is unlikely to fare any better."

"So that's it?" Lewis could not hide his displeasure. "We are to proceed without your blessing?"

Howell stepped forward and patted his friend's shoulder. "You don't need my blessing, old chap. You don't even need the permission of Miss Kinsey's father, as she is of age. As two adults, you can do as you wish. We will all remain friends whatever imprudent action you might take. But you must promise me this: do not expect her to change once she is your wife. That is the way of madness and the fastest route to misery. Celebrate what you have in whom you have. Then you may yet prove false my concerns about this match. And remain a man of honor in my eyes."

Lewis cast his gaze to the lushly carpeted floor. "I suppose this is the best you have to offer, little though it is. I had thought your own happy ending would cause you to welcome mine. But I see I was mistaken."

"Oh, do stop sulking, Bradford. Keep your promise, and there will be cause enough for celebration. Until then, you have heard my reservations. They have been uttered in love and should not be written off just because they are not what you wished to hear. Come, raise yourself from your doldrums and that chair. The ladies will be expecting us. Ellena has been clamoring to eat with company again. She is quite done with the four walls of her room. You shall have the privilege of being our first guest since we became parents. Besides Miss Kinsey, of course."

"Well, I suppose that is something," murmured Lewis, not quite ready yet to cast off his earlier disappointment.

"It is more than just something, old boy. Don't be such a wet blanket."

Lewis shook himself mentally. His friend was right. He was behaving like a spoiled child. Why he should do so was a mystery, as he had certainly not been a spoiled child in reality. But that sort of thinking would only worsen his mood. He must discard the frustrations of the past and move firmly into the future. A future with Miss Kinsey would be a much brighter affair than the circumstances life had dealt him so far.

The promise of her imminent company cheered him considerably. The thought of a lifetime with her... Well, she must still accept his offer. Despite the viscount's gloomy summation of their differences, Lewis still wanted her to say *yes*. He would not wait long. It was never known how long Miss Kinsey would stay at a time. But he would travel all the way to Trenton Grange if necessary to ask for her hand.

Tonight, they would dine together as friends. A few days hence, they might do so as a betrothed couple. In as little as a month, they could be married. It was all Lewis could do to stop himself from taking the stairs two at a time—just as the vital Miss Kinsey was wont to do—to fall to one knee and beg her to be his. It was only his respect for his host that prevented him from doing so.

Just a few days… Perhaps the longest days of his life. But he would bear them with fortitude. She would say *yes*. She *must* say *yes*. The wait would be worth it. He could finally slip his fingers through her golden hair and cup her waist with his arm, drawing her closer, closing the distance, until nothing stood between them, and the rest of the world became a distant memory. There was much he wished to leave behind. Miss Kinsey, he was certain, was the means to do so. Her sparkle was a seed that grew in his heart. Together, they would grow ever brighter and happier. Just a few more days…

CHAPTER THREE

THE INTIMATE MEALS in Ellena's room the past three weeks had been informal. There had been no need to know which cutlery to use or what the fancy French name was for the wobbly thing they had for dessert. Jillian did not have to wipe the corners of her mouth daintily. She could giggle and jump up suddenly to demonstrate a part of the story she was telling.

In contrast, any dinner served in the vast dining room at Munro House would feel a little stiff and awkward, no matter how delightful the company they were hosting. The dinner with Mr. Bradford as guest, however, did not even offer that delight. What should have been a simple meal seasoned with lively conversation instead felt strained and uncomfortable.

Mr. Bradford shifted restlessly in his chair and kept throwing glances her way that confused her, his expressions doing a dance of wrinkling brows, quirking lips, and self-conscious smiles. She could not fathom his thoughts at all. To make matters worse, their host appeared to understand all too well what had come over his friend and all but glared him into submission. Lord Howell was not a jocular man, but he usually had an ease when among his friends. However, it was noticeably absent that night.

Even at their parting, Mr. Bradford remained fidgety and on edge. Curious how a day that had started with such high hopes, flowing into a treasured afternoon excursion, should end in an odd sort of silence. There was mention of another visit later in the week, but the viscount's gruff response had discouraged further talk on the subject. The great oak door had closed. Ellena and her husband had bid Jillian good night, leaving her standing alone and confused in the foyer.

Had the two friends had a falling out? Surely not! They had known each other most of their lives. Jillian had never heard a cross word spoken between them. But there was definitely something in the air. If only she could find out what had changed since that afternoon. But that was quite impossible. Despite his generous nature, Lord Howell was not a man she felt she could interrogate. All Jilly could do was hope that he would confide in his wife and that Ellena would share the details with her.

Alas, the next day came and went without even a mention of Mr. Bradford. Ellena ate an early supper in her room once more with Jilly for company while Lord Howell tended to matters of the estate. The conversation circled around neutral topics. That was, until—after they were quite satiated and Ellena relaxed against her chair's backrest—the viscountess commented in an offhanded manner, "I suppose you miss home."

"No more than usual," replied Jilly. "I am always grateful for time spent with you."

Ellena traced the pattern of the ornate armrest with a distracted finger. "You have been with me six weeks already." The finger ceased its exploration. Ellena stared at it as if making a decision, then looked up abruptly. "Your presence has been a great comfort to me as I have ventured into the newness of motherhood. However, I feel I am selfish in keeping you here. I am becoming quite well adjusted to my new routine, and my body is healing well. I feel stronger and ready to resume my responsibilities within our home." The corners of her mouth turned down. "I would have been running the household already if Dominic had not been insistent that I continue to rest."

Jilly recognized the determined glint that flashed in Ellena's eye. She knew it all too well.

"The day is fast approaching when I will be firm about getting my own way," Ellena declared. "And dear Dominic has learned that I can be just as stubborn as he."

A pang of sympathy sounded in Jilly's heart. The viscount really didn't stand a chance!

"I think it is time I released you to return to your family," Ellena continued. "I am certain they miss you as much as you do them."

Jilly cocked her head to the side. "I do not want to outstay my welcome. But I have visited longer than this before and you have not said anything."

"And that was greedy of me. Dominic and I understand your discomfort when you are in Munro. We enjoy your company tremendously, but we know it comes at a cost to you. You need time to miss us again, preferably from a joyful place among your family and the amicable sort of bustle that village life provides."

Jillian's heart ached a little at these words. It was true. She was ready to return to Trenton Grange, where the fall blooms would be on full display, the harvest underway, and preparations started for Mell Supper to celebrate the cutting of the last sheaf of corn. Her mother would want help readying the winter preserves and would appreciate the presence of another woman in the cottage. Meanwhile, her brothers were growing up, the eldest already eleven and learning his father's trade. She was missing their childhood and the way they doted on her in an almost feral way.

"If you are sure…" Already, Jilly pictured the hearty embrace of her father. She was ready to pack her things at once. Except… An image of the delectable Mr. Bradford surfaced in her mind. It was getting harder to leave him behind each time her visits came to an end. She wished they could at least write to each other. Society had so many silly rules.

"Absolutely!" said Ellena, cutting short Jilly's thoughts, which was probably just as well. "It will give me an excuse to dust off my letter-writing skills," continued Ellena, "for I rarely write to anyone but you."

"Your mother seems to enjoy receiving your news."

"Ye-es," came the cautious response. "But I must speak of any private thoughts and feelings obliquely in case Father reads our correspondence. You know how intolerant he is of sentimentality. It is hard for her to please both his needs and mine. And being under his roof obliges her to accommodate *him* for the most part."

This was nothing new to Jillian. She had often marveled at how well Ellena had turned out—able to find joy in the little things, show love unequivocally, and draw people to her—when her examples had been a cold father with a mind only for profit and a mother who hid her fondness for her only child for fear of provoking her husband's ire. Mr. Trenton had been of the opinion that his daughter should not be mollycoddled, and even simple shows of affection had been categorized as an indulgence. Mrs. Trenton had only been allowed to show interest in Ellena if it in some way furthered her daughter's chances of finding a promising match. For many years, the two women had conversed almost entirely about suitable attire and proper behavior. It was only now that Ellena had gained independence from their home and assumed the power that was hers as a viscountess that she could claim her mother's affection without risking too much of her father's habitual interference.

Jilly fondly recalled the way her own father patted his belly, which persisted in its roundness thanks to his wife's baking prowess and despite the hours he spent sweating under a blazing sun or fighting against wind, rain, and hail to protect his precious plantings. As a little girl, she would curl up against him and lay her head upon his belly-cushion, his mighty arm swooping 'round and gathering her in its protective arc.

He had taught her to read, just as the vicar had once done for him. It was a skill that had helped him secure the position as groundskeeper, as he would need to keep an inventory of equipment and take copious notes for landscaping. He knew his bright daughter would master reading and writing with ease, making her a better suited companion for Miss Trenton, since they had insisted on being friends. Jillian had known such patience and encouragement from her father that it was no wonder she had taken the lonely daughter of the master under her wing despite her being no older than little Miss Ellena.

Indeed, until the age of ten, she had been an only child and had had her parents' warmth and affection all to herself. Now all three of her brothers would clamber up and perch on and around whoever was sitting nearby. Personal space was for the wealthy, in houses where there were more chairs but emptier arms.

"Perhaps it will be different now," Jilly mused aloud. "You outrank your father both in affluence and status. He has no power over you, for you are married and have borne the heir to the entire Howell estate and title. I imagine that if you ever do visit Trenton Grange, you could say and do what you like, and your mother would be able to express herself more freely with you."

Ellena pressed her lips together. She did not seem convinced. "It would be preferable if Mother could visit me at Munro House as you do," she said. "But Father always has need of her. She keeps the household running smoothly, and he does not tolerate domestic distractions."

"Will you take little Christopher to visit her at least?"

"He is too small for such a long journey. And I am in no hurry to be under my father's roof again."

Pity filled Jilly's heart. They had grown up very differently. Still, the times they'd spent together had been happy for them both. Maybe a little more of that was just what Ellena needed. "I could look out for you like I used to when it grew unbearable for you," she said. "We could take Christopher for walks by the river. Maybe, if your father is sufficiently distracted, we could even invite your mother along."

A grin displaced Ellena's glum expression. "What a lark that would be! After all those years of Mother trying to keep the two of us apart lest I should fall under your supposedly uncouth influence, it would be you, the very instigator of all my favorite mischief, who offers her respite. The irony will not be lost on her."

"Perhaps, at last," commented Jilly, her voice uncharacteristically somber, "she will understand that I intended only to rescue you from a fate similar to hers."

"No doubt," Ellena replied with equal earnestness before sucking in her breath and announcing, "So, then, we are in accord. You will return to Trenton Grange and begin corresponding with me at once so that I shall not feel your absence too much. Ingsley can pack for you and Dominic will arrange for the carriage and footman. This time tomorrow, you can be back in the bosom of your family, no doubt sampling something exceedingly tasty from your mother's skilled efforts."

"Tomorrow?" Jilly drew back. "Why so sudden?"

"Why not tomorrow? We are agreed your return home is overdue. Besides, the sooner you are home, the sooner you may yearn again for the gloomy halls of Munro House." Ellena pinched one eye shut in a wink.

"Oh, you! It's not as bad as all that! Not all of your great estate is daunting to me. I love the ballroom, though you don't use it nearly often enough. The nursery is particularly splendid now that it has little Master Christopher in it. And the kitchen is filled with goodies that Cook tries to hide unsuccessfully."

"But there aren't nearly enough arms to welcome you here," said Ellena. "It is time to get your fill of the most important things in your life. I am happy to step into the background for a few months."

"Oh!" Jilly cried, her eyes flying open at a sudden thought. "Mr. Bradford was going to visit later this week. I should like to say goodbye to him in person before I leave. I could wait a day or two. It would make no difference." *Except to me*, Jillian thought. One more visit with him mattered a great deal to her.

"Or we could explain the circumstances to him," Ellena countered quickly. "He will not begrudge you time with your family. He knows you miss home."

Jilly felt her ears grow warm. "Oh, I don't mind a short delay. I had not even thought of leaving until we started this conversation. It would be worth postponing my plans to have one more walk with him."

Ellena tapped one fingernail on the polished armrest. "I am not certain that is such a good idea, Jilly."

"Why, what do you mean?"

"Your fondness for Mr. Bradford might be misunderstood."

"As what?"

"As…" Ellena hesitated. "As putting yourself forward for consideration."

Jilly's laughter sounded out like the tinkling of a silver bell, all mirth and unfettered delight. "How serious you look! As if the union of two of your dearest friends was not greatly to be desired!"

Ellena's expression, however, remained unchanged, her mouth a straight line and her eyes unlit from within. "We are, of course, very pleased that our friends should find each other's company agreeable, but anything more than that is simply not plausible."

Jilly's smile disappeared. "Why do you say that? Mr. Bradford and I must have similar good qualities for us to be frequent guests in the very well-guarded sanctuary of your home. If we have your approval as individuals, why would we not have it as a pair?"

Ellena's face softened. "You both have impeccable character and generous spirits, but the truth is that your paths would never have crossed if it were not for the very sanctuary our home offers. You can be yourself here, Jilly. The rest of Munro, of England, of human nature, is not as accepting."

"And what must they accept?"

"Come now. You are being intentionally obtuse. Society does not welcome a mixing of classes. You would be the object of spiteful gossip. I do not wish that for you."

"You and Lord Howell are also mismatched, if it comes to that," Jilly protested. "You have endured meanness from people who disapproved of a viscount marrying a merchant's daughter. Yet you are happy."

"Dominic holds much power in Munro. Many have ceased their ill-mannered speech to maintain healthy relations with him. And they have found me equal to the task of being his wife. After all, that is what my entire childhood trained me for. But, Jilly dear, Mr. Bradford does not wield such influence, nor have you had such an upbringing. The naysayers would remain opposed, and you, my all-too optimistic friend, would find yourself in over your head. Don't let the *idea* of a match blind you to its reality. I would not see either of you hurt."

Jilly fell silent at these words. Ellena had convinced herself of the worst possible scenario. Jilly would forgive her such negative ruminations. After all, the Trenton household had not been a happy one. There had been little opportunity for dreaming. But Jilly was not bound by such a dark way of thinking. Her life had been very cheerful, free of any trouble at all. Even illness and poverty had eluded them. She was not in the habit of expecting the worst. Things had a way of falling into place. Why would a proposal from Mr. Bradford change that?

Ellena seemed quite determined that it would. In fact, she appeared to have given it some thought.

A realization landed with a thump in Jilly's mind.

Ellena would only have pondered the consequences of a match if the possibility of one actually existed. Had Mr. Bradford given them some indication of this?

Jilly's thoughts returned to the perplexing behavior at last night's dinner. Their host had been almost stern. And Mr. Bradford had fluctuated between highly attentive and withdrawn. Had the gentlemen, too, had a debate about the practicalities of a match between Mr. Bradford and herself? Had Lord Howell expressed similar dismay at the idea?

A cold fist twisted in her stomach. Was this why Ellena had

suggested her departure with such urgency? That would explain why she would not want Jilly to bid Mr. Bradford goodbye in person. Was a proposal imminent?

For a few brief moments, Jilly bristled at the interference of her best friend. Who was she to chase Jilly home to avoid a match that would make her friend happy?

Yet the anger dissipated as quickly as it had formed. Jilly was not one to cling to unpleasant thoughts. Besides, Ellena had no reason to wish her anything but the best. Her friend's concern was misplaced, certainly, but it came from a place of love.

Of course, that did not mean Jilly had to agree with it. If Mr. Bradford—that most wonderful of men—was considering making her his bride, Jilly had no intention of dissuading him.

A plan, delicious in its simplicity, took shape in her mind.

"I suppose that's that, then." Jilly shrugged.

Ellena, who had been leaning forward, possibly to better reason with her friend, stopped mid-motion. "Really? You understand my concerns?"

"Oh, absolutely." Jillian nodded. "You have made some very good points. I would be a fool to ignore them."

A wrinkle of worry puckered Ellena's brow. "You are not angry with me?"

"Of course not. You mean me no harm. I shall write to Mr. Bradford and apologize for not waiting for his visit. Then I will send for my travel trunk."

Ellena folded her hands together. "I'm sorry, Jilly, but a letter is quite out of the question. You are both unmarried. It would be unseemly. People have been forced into a betrothal for less."

"Ay, yes. And a betrothal is exactly what we *don't* want." Jilly tapped the side of her nose twice.

"Er, yes." Ellena hesitated. "You are taking this very well, I must say."

"I would not waste our last evening together arguing. But I will admit that I am a little tired. What time do you expect the carriage will be ready tomorrow?"

Ellena thought a moment. "I should like to have breakfast with you, so it would be a late-morning departure to make sure you are home before dark. I will send a letter to be given to Father, asking for the usual courtesy to be shown our groom and footman and your borrowed lady's maid. They will rest at Trenton Grange before returning the following day."

"A sound arrangement," agreed Jillian. "Then I think I will make an early night of it. I would like to be well-rested for the bumpy journey ahead. Packing can wait until morning. I don't have that many possessions."

"Jilly." Ellena reached across and touched her hand. "I *will* miss you."

"And I you," answered Jillian, rising and throwing her arms around Ellena's shoulders. "I'll be back before you know it." She paused, then added, "You can count on it."

She slipped from the room before her friend should say anything more. Ellena's guilt for manipulating Jilly to leave the house was unmistakable. Too bad. Jilly was playing a game of her own with no feeling of guilt whatsoever.

In anticipation of her little scheme, she would have taken the stairs two at a time, for there was no one to see her. But she was only a few doors away from Ellena's rooms and had no need to use the stairs. Not yet. Instead, she skipped lightly on her toes, her excitement needing an outlet without her heels thudding her secret joy along the echoing corridor.

Once in her room, she closed the door and leaned back against it, her heart pounding, her broad smile radiating all the way to her eyes. She squeezed her shoulders to her ears, very satisfied with herself, indeed.

Right. First things first.

Pushing herself from the steady wood of the door, Jillian strode purposefully to the writing desk that had been provided for her. She settled herself with pen and ink and began writing at once, her thoughts clear, the sentences tumbling easily from her. Having a gentlewoman for a friend had definite advantages.

Expressing herself well was one of them. And the confidence that she gained from the certainty of her goal lent further eloquence to her words.

Ha! Ellena thought Jillian would make a poor gentleman's wife! What did she know? Jilly had a gift for fine speech—some might say far beyond her station. A few fashionable dresses and a lady's maid like Ingsley who had a skilled hand for hair, and Jillian would fit right in! They wouldn't be able to help themselves. After all, everyone commented on how likeable she was. And they wouldn't bother to compliment her just because she was Ellena's friend, would they? Of course not! They would merely have politely avoided her. Especially when she became "chatty," as Ellena called it. An unfortunate habit, to be sure, but not a disaster. It was simply a way to deflect her own nervousness. Sometimes, she filled the silence when the listener was more nervous than herself, this being far more likely, as Jillian was too brazen with the *ton*, according to the viscountess.

Well, she had no desire to mix with anybody who didn't want her, so that was the end of that matter. She would lavish her good nature on those who deserved it and simply disregard the rest. Mr. Bradford would not object. He was of a similar opinion.

Jillian lowered her gaze to the letter, a golden curl slipping from her shoulder down the length of her arm. She pictured Mr. Bradford brushing it back, then cupping her cheek with his hand. She could almost feel the skin of his palm—smooth, as a gentleman's hand should be—against her own. If they were wed, his hand would slip down the curve of her neck and the rounding of her shoulder, drawing the puff of her sleeve with it. And then he would...

There was a soft knock on the door.

"Who is it?" Jillian asked, a tad more sharply than she usually would have, flipping the letter over so that the blank side was displayed instead.

"It's me, Miss Kinsey. Ingsley. The mistress said you'd be wanting to get ready to sleep. May I come in?"

"That won't be necessary. I will undress myself tonight, thank you."

There was a pause. Jillian could imagine the maid's conundrum. Whose wishes should she respect? Would she be in trouble either way? Bother these stupid rules!

"I can manage on my own," Jilly repeated. "But I'll tell Lady Howell how helpful you were. Good night, Ingsley."

She could almost hear the relief on the other side of the door. The servants had long hours. While dressing someone was some of the lightest work there was to do in a house of this size, even lady's maids would not mind an early night. Besides, it was a ridiculous task to begin with. If it weren't for all these silly fastenings and falderals they insisted on adding to perfectly sensible clothes, she would have no need of assistance in the first place.

Jillian waited until Ingsley's footfalls grew faint before turning the letter back over again. One of the words had smudged a little, but it was still legible. Good enough. She folded the page into a self-concealing design as Ellena had taught her, addressing it with painstaking accuracy. This was one item of correspondence that absolutely must reach its intended destination without delay. She blew on the wet ink, then waved the tightly folded and tucked letter gently to and fro until she was satisfied it was thoroughly dry.

On tiptoes once more, she left her room and crossed to the staircase, which she descended with greater-than-usual care. Any stomping would give her away utterly, as she was the only person in this household who ever did so.

At last, she reached the foyer. Given the hour, and the fact that no one was expected, there were no footmen about. But a faint light shone down a side corridor from the viscount's study. Jillian listened for any indication that he was moving about. Nothing. In all likelihood, he was elbow-deep in paperwork.

Within a few strides, she was at a side table, upon which rested a silver tray. A small heap of correspondence lay on display. Lord Howell would be adding to it before morning if the lamplight in his study was any indication. She drew her own letter from her pocket and slipped it in at the bottom of the pile so that it did not catch the viscount's eye. First thing in the morning, all these little sheets of writing would be spirited away and delivered by hand to local addresses or the post office. There should be ample time for her mission to succeed.

With a final act of self-restraint, Jillian climbed the stairs as silently as she could, entered her room, and clicked the door shut behind her. Released from the necessity for composure, she launched herself onto her bed, shuffled up to the head of it, and threw herself back so that her tresses splayed out like a golden fan across the goose-down pillows.

So many times, she had lain in this way in the daisy-dotted field near Trenton Grange. No four-poster drapery then shielding the view. Only sun and clouds and the passing of birds like fish in the current of the sky. She could see herself sharing such moments with Mr. Bradford. Not in his barrister's wig, of course. Odd little accessory of his profession that it was. He would have no need to wear it when with her. When they were together, it would just be their simplest selves. Their hands would reach for each other's, fingers intertwining. The sun would warm their faces. Their children would bound about, their laughter rounding off the perfection of the day.

Jillian closed her eyes. Her hand slid to the side, her fingers reaching. No answer yet. But it was so close, she could sense it. His touch. Just one question and they could have it all. If Mr. Bradford was lucky, she would even allow him to finish asking before she said *yes*.

CHAPTER FOUR

L EWIS SIPPED HIS coffee in silence. He fought the urge to slurp a little, or even a lot, just to annoy his father. It wasn't a very mature approach for a thirty-year-old barrister, but he was tempted nonetheless. It was the only way to get his father's attention. Philip was not there—probably off riding. If so, there was a very good chance he was meeting up with the Sangford sisters, who enjoyed a bit of morning exercise within Munro Park, along with many other of the city's riding enthusiasts. Miss Irene Sangford, the elder of the two, had caught Philip's eye, and both sets of parents heartily approved the match. Lewis could not think of anyone more opposite to Miss Kinsey, who was all light and laughter. Philip was welcome to Miss Sangford—her money, her status, and her joyless personality.

Mother was never at the breakfast table. She preferred to take a tray in her room, where she sat under the heat of several layers of coverlets for her legs and a thick, woolen shawl for her shoulders. Downstairs did not warm to her liking until at least noon.

He had no idea where Penelope was. His younger sister was the only salvageable element of their family, himself included. He was painfully aware of his status as the spare, and the bitterness it had bred in him. Pen, as he liked to call his younger sibling, was even worse off, being born a girl. But she could not be bothered in the least. She happily denounced every suitor, knowing full well she would lose her independence to her husband, and was perfectly content to embrace spinsterhood, consequences be damned. It would be just like her to run off and seek her own fortune if her family did not wish to take care of an old maid. It must have been the sheer magnetism of her temperament that prevented their parents from making a marriage arrangement on her behalf. Perhaps they, like Lewis, suspected she might very well cut her hair and go to sea if they forced her hand.

That being the case, Pen had tremendous freedom within the grounds of the barony. Provided she toed the line in public, they gave her a very long leash in private. Which was why, at this moment, she could be anywhere on their vast estate.

In many ways, his sister and Miss Kinsey were alike. That was probably at least half the reason he had been drawn to the lovely friend of the viscountess. Penelope's willful insistence on being her true self had shown him a different path than the one his parents desired for him was possible. And Miss Kinsey would walk with him on such a path.

He could picture them being the best of friends, if only their parents would allow such a friendship. It would be good for Pen. Despite her independent streak, he often wondered if she was lonely. Her self-imposed exile from the marriage mart meant that much of her time was spent roaming the estate by herself. Miss Kinsey would make the perfect companion, being unafraid of whether such random activity was suitable or not. It was a pity that the rules of society should force such exceptional souls from each other's company.

Lewis eyed his coffee once more. His father was making his way through the morning post, his head slightly bowed so that the baldness at the top of it was exposed. Lord Bradford had a ring of hair about his head, feathering upward to soften the expanse of pink flesh where baldness had won. The effect of this style mimicked the laurel wreath commonly associated with Julius Caesar.

Lewis very much wanted to shoot a paper pellet at the fleshy target. It reminded him of his days at university, a time when he'd been able to lark about as much as he liked, provided he passed his exams and didn't embarrass Philip, whose years of study had overlapped with Lewis's. Growing up had come with an expectation of more sober behavior yet no matching privilege, save the respect he had earned from his fellow intellectuals at court. It was small compensation when all Philip had to do to inherit the advantages of being a future baron was to exist.

"Ah, Lewis, one for you," his father said suddenly, handing a letter folded into a complex self-locking design to the footman standing nearby, even though Lewis sat but one seat from his father. The footman took the letter with a small bow, turning in mid-bend and handing it to Lewis before straightening again. Lewis rolled his eyes. The manners of the aristocracy were very questionable. He could just imagine what Miss Kinsey would say.

He looked down at the address. Munro House. But it was not the handwriting of Lord Howell. How curious!

He fought with the letter somewhat, not wanting to tear the paper while pulling apart the tightly folded form. With one deft tug, he managed to release the full page and searched at once for the signature.

Miss Kinsey.

The urge to turn his back to his father so that he might not see who had written had to be overcome, for it would draw attention to the very thing Lewis wished to hide. Miss Kinsey was not *au fait* with the finer etiquettes, but even she should know it was a terrible risk to her reputation to write directly to him. What could she possibly need to say that could not have been communicated via their mutual friend the viscount?

He had scarcely read the first line and managed to suppress an involuntary cry of surprise when he decided quite suddenly this letter was best read elsewhere. He tucked it into his pocket, placed his serviette on the table, and stood.

"If you will excuse me, Father."

"Hmph," said Lord Bradford.

With the usual minimum of parental acknowledgement, Lewis made his way to the library, where he quickly opened the letter once more, his eyes darting across the page and growing wider as they did so.

He looked at his pocket watch. Almost ten o'clock! He considered his attire. Hardly the right gear for riding. But a carriage would take far longer to ready than a horse. He rang the bell pull more savagely than it was designed for, and a footman appeared in an awkward dance between haste and decorum.

"Tell the groom to ready my horse. At once. Go!"

The footman obeyed and disappeared at as close to a run as possible without actually breaking into one. Lewis tore upstairs to retrieve his overcoat from his wardrobe, then circled round to the bricked courtyard where a stablehand was assisting the groom in the final adjustments to his horse's bridle and stirrups.

"Make haste!" he shouted somewhat unfairly, since they were clearly working as fast as they could. Lewis felt the minutes slipping away. It was half an hour to Munro House by carriage. He could do that in a quarter hour on horseback. Miss Kinsey said she would be leaving late morning. How late was "late"? Ten-thirty? Eleven-thirty? If it was the former, he was cutting it very close, indeed. Unless Miss Kinsey had found a way to delay her departure.

Five minutes felt like hours, but Lewis was finally on his mount and away, the ground disappearing beneath his horse's hooves as clods of mud spat up behind them. He half-expected to have to chase down the Howell carriage en route to Trenton Grange. But when he had conquered the country miles and the long drive to the main entrance of Munro House, the viscount's carriage still stood at the entrance. Two footmen had just lifted a trunk onto its roof and now wrestled with leather straps to tie it down. The step had not yet been lowered and no one stood impatiently by the great oak door, waiting to enter the carriage cubicle.

Lewis scarcely slowed, jumping from his horse and throwing his reins at the footmen. He bounded up the steps and... stuttered to a halt. He could not enter the company of ladies looking as disheveled and flustered as he did. Lewis tugged at his sleeves to smooth the creases, patted his cravat, and ran his fingers through his hair. His hat! He had forgotten his hat! No matter, he would not need it inside the house, anyway. He puffed out a few slow breaths to settle his booming heart. Gripping his lapels, he maneuvered his neck until he felt that all sat upon him as it should. One more deep inhale. And exhale.

Lewis rapped on the knocker, the sound pulsing through the thick wood that sealed the entrance. The butler appeared, quickly swallowing his initial surprise at seeing Lewis there.

"His lordship was not expecting you, Mr. Bradford. Miss Kinsey is departing this morning, and they are busy with their farewells."

"That's all right, Branson," Lewis replied, stepping past him into the foyer. "I am not here to see him." To the waiting footman, he said impatiently, "You may take my coat."

The unusually wide-eared footman glanced at the butler, who nodded. Lewis offered his back and the footman slipped the warm outer coat from his shoulders. "No hat, sir?" asked the footman.

"No, no hat," said Lewis without further explanation. "Branson, please let Miss Kinsey know I have arrived."

"If you would be so good as to wait in the drawing room, sir, I shall inform the young lady."

Lewis knew the way and showed himself through. However, once he'd entered the room, he was at a loss as to what to do with himself. He had evaded disaster and made it to Munro House in time. But now the moment for which he had raced like the dickens had finally arrived. And suddenly, Lewis was nervous.

It was silly, really. Miss Kinsey would not have reached out to him in the forthright manner she had if she were not of the same thinking as he. Still, she could have changed her mind. *They* could have changed her mind. So, he stood and waited. He paced. He stared out the window. He paced some more.

Where *was* she?

Just when Lewis thought he could bear it no longer, a light step approached the door. He knew that sound. Only one person walked as if the world were an open field and she must fling her arms open and spin until she tumbled, breathless with laughter, and watch the colorful blur of it settling upon her vision.

The steps paused. Another set of feet were catching up, feminine but more assertive, as though the hallway and the ground beneath belonged to her.

"Please, Jilly, think! You cannot change your mind without bringing shame on both households. Once it is done, it cannot be undone!"

"Good!" said the determined voice of Miss Kinsey. And she stepped into the drawing room.

Lewis sucked in his breath. This was it. She had wanted him here. And he had come. But there were unspoken things…

"Mr. Bradford!" cried Miss Kinsey as she entered the room alone. In a trice, she had crossed the space between them and looked about ready to fling her arms around him when she pulled up short and sat down quite suddenly.

"Ellena says I am too graceless to mix with your sort of people. But, as you can see, I am perfectly able to restrain myself, even in circumstances where the lack thereof would be quite forgivable."

Lewis allowed himself a moment to process the series of emotions that had just bombarded his senses. Where to start?

"I see Lady Howell shares her husband's reservations about… our, er… mixing company," he began.

"Needless to say," Miss Kinsey answered matter-of-factly, "it is not an opinion with which I agree. They are very sweet to worry, but their thinking is rather dull. I suppose it must be, when all day one weighs up matters of great importance." She blinked twice, then her mouth made a shocked "o." "Not that *your* work isn't meaningful. Goodness! I would never want you to assume I do not understand its worth. But you have wisely chosen to leave those dusty, old law books at the office and let yourself live a little. Lord Howell never laughs, you know. Well, not that *I've* seen, at any rate. What a waste, when the world is full of things to be joyful about. Although why I should tell you this when you and I are so like-minded that there is no need to explain… It's only that their thinking is so very different and yet they are comfortable imposing their thoughts upon us as though they were the only ones worthy of consideration. Do you see?"

"Er…" said Lewis.

He had only witnessed this once before. This chattiness of Miss Kinsey. It had happened when they had first met, a year ago. She had been new to the city, the estate, the complexities of etiquette. And it had made her nervous. She had gabbled away in this seemingly easy way, but, really, she had just been covering herself in words like a protective blanket.

"Miss Kinsey," he said, both to stem the tide of her words and to rescue her from the need for them, "let us speak plainly."

"Oh." She sat a little straighter, her hands clamped to her knees. "Yes." She nodded briskly. "I am ready."

Lewis suddenly felt quite out of his depth. This was not like a courtroom, where everyone else was either an opponent to be defeated, a witness to be summoned, or a judge to be convinced. The many years of study had given him little opportunity to consider marriage before now. No practice having been possible, nor, indeed, likely, as these things tended to be a once-off affair, Lewis considered himself wholly unprepared for this moment. Under different circumstances, he would have mulled it over more, practiced the wording of his case before presenting it to Miss Kinsey.

The young lady in question waited, her head tilted up expectantly.

Lewis sat down opposite her. He steepled his fingers, his wrists on his knees.

"Miss Kinsey."

"Yes?"

Lewis cleared his throat and looked up into her lovely face. Saints above, but she was beautiful! He wished this awkwardness was behind him and he could claim those lips, those eyes, the soft skin inside her wrist…

He cleared his throat again.

"Your letter—for which I must thank you, as it was sent at great risk—was very, er… *thorough*."

Miss Kinsey shifted happily in her chair. "Oh, good! Ellena was totally against any correspondence between us, of course, but then I wouldn't have seen you for *months*, and some grand heiress might have caught your eye."

Lewis tried to hide a smile that was itching to surface. "I assure you, Miss Kinsey, no one else can catch my eye while you exist."

"Oh, well, that's all right, then." Miss Kinsey beamed.

"It seems, however, that our friends do not share our enthusiasm when considering a match between our houses."

Miss Kinsey giggled. "Is this your barrister voice? It isn't half funny! I can just picture our crowded, little cottage wed to your parents' fancy home." Her eyes looked up to the side and were joined by a tiny frown. "Actually, I can't imagine it all. I have no idea what their estate looks like, having never visited."

"We shall remedy that soon enough, if this conversation has a satisfactory end."

Miss Kinsey returned her open gaze to Lewis. "Never you mind Lord and Lady Howell and their opinions. They have said their piece. They get to live their lives according to their hopes and expectations. I would rather hear what *you* have to say."

"I… I… It is no secret that I am very fond of you." Lewis knew he was blushing. He only hoped it made him seem endearing rather than foolish.

"Is that all?" Miss Kinsey's face fell.

"Oh, no! That is to say… I did not want to overstep the mark. I would not want to startle you by saying too much too soon."

"Mr. Bradford." Miss Kinsey folded her hands and huffed impatiently. "I have seen pigs give birth. I am not so easily startled."

"Ah." Lewis was momentarily put off his stride. "That is… useful to know."

"I am *very fond* of you too," Miss Kinsey declared. "Though I haven't exactly made a secret of it. You know me to be a forthright sort of person. What these Munro ladies call 'subtlety,' I call 'an outrageous waste of time.' Which is why I spoke so plainly in the letter."

"Yes. Yes, you did." Lewis faltered. He felt he was losing the initiative. "I suppose the only question I must ask is…"

"Yes."

"I'm sorry?"

"Yes, I will marry you."

"Oh, er… that is good news." Lewis was now quite flustered. "What I had meant to ask was whether you could bear to live in Munro. But the, er… other question…would have followed."

Miss Kinsey waved a hand about nonchalantly. "I don't mind the city so much. There is so much to do. I would be able to move more freely as a married woman than I do now as Ellena's companion. We could attend more theater. I love the theater, but Lord Howell rarely takes us to a show. And our home would be less of a mausoleum than Munro House. Besides, you would not begrudge me a visit with my family if I missed them, would you?"

"Certainly not," said Lewis, glad that the conversation was righting itself. "I would very much want for you to be happy. Of course, a certain measure of formality would be required when hosting the occasional dinner. But, by and large, the basics of decorum would suffice."

"Like not running barefoot?" Jillian offered a lopsided smile.

"Exactly. Servants do need to respect their employers, or they will talk out of house. But that is not to say we could not go on a picnic and kick off our shoes…"

"That sounds fair. And we can host dances? Not a ball, of

course. That would be too formal and we would not have the room for so many people. But a gathering for friends with music and some country reels."

"Absolutely. Though perhaps you will want Lady Howell to assist you with the planning, at first. I believe there is much to organize before the music can begin. My mother rarely hosts a ball anymore for this very reason."

Miss Kinsey clapped her hands. "I can't wait! I shall write to my parents at once! After all, I cannot leave Munro now when you and I have so much to discuss What date shall I give for the wedding?"

"Miss Kinsey…"

"Oh, but you must call me 'Jillian' now. Or 'Jilly.' And I shall call you 'Lewis.' Dear, dear Lewis. And you must kiss me. Goodness, how I have waited for such a kiss from you!"

She tilted back her head and pouted her lips in readiness for said kiss.

Lewis stared at her. They were betrothed. How, exactly, it had occurred was a bit of a blur. He hadn't actually asked for her hand. Not that he hadn't planned to. It all seemed a little back-to-front. This was not how he'd wanted their lives together to start.

"Miss Kinsey. Jillian."

"Yes, Lewis?" she answered, her eyes still closed, her lips returning to their puckered form."

"Please open your eyes."

She complied, her chin dropping, her eyebrows lifting in a question mark. "You do not want to kiss me? Are things done that differently in the big cities?"

"All in good time, my love."

He slid down from the chair onto one knee, his hands cupping hers.

"Miss Kinsey, would you do me the honor of becoming my wife?"

"I thought my answer was obvious."

"Humor me."

"Oh. Well, then, yes. Will you kiss me now?"

"It will be my pleasure…"

He rose to his feet, pulling Jillian up by her hands until they were both standing, face to face, a few inches apart. Then he closed the distance.

His hand slipped across the small of her back as he drew her toward him, their bodies crushing against each other as his mouth sought hers. His passion awoke, heat searing through his core as he pulled her ever tighter against him. She answered his touch with equal fervor, wrapping her arms around his neck, her fingers pushing through his thick hair.

Lewis lowered his lips to her chin, her neck, his tongue wetting her smooth, feminine skin, while Jilly—his own hot-blooded Jilly—did likewise with the shell of his ear, teeth gently tugging at his lobes until he was forced to pull away.

"Merciful heavens, woman, you will undo me!" he cried, only to draw her back into a deep embrace. "Was that what you wanted, my love?" he whispered into her hair. "Was it the kiss of your dreams?"

Jilly lifted her chin, her cheeks flushed with exertion, her eyes dancing. "It ended too soon," she said, and she placed her head on his chest, where his pounding heart struggled to slow.

"I suppose we should tell our friends the good news," Lewis murmured.

"Not yet," said Jilly. "They will only spoil it with their disapproving looks."

"I think they worry for us. But when they see how happy we are, they will share in our joy. We will show them it is not a fleeting whim, but a lifetime of bliss, just like their own."

Jilly pulled back quite suddenly. "We *will* have the wedding in Ermenbrough, won't we? I don't want it here, where people like the viscount and Ellena—and maybe even your parents—will mean well but will wish to add excess to the event."

"You want it at your village church?"

"Yes, among people who don't care about silverware or who

is wearing the latest fashion. I want to be married in a place where no one will shame my family, with simple folk who only want to celebrate our special day. I don't mind if that means only our families attend, or whether I am holding a posy of wildflowers instead of an arrangement from an expensive florist. None of those things matter."

"Then that is exactly what we shall do." Lewis tucked Jilly back into his arms.

But she extricated herself again and added, "When shall I meet your family? I think I shall love Miss Bradford—or Penelope, I suppose I'll be able to call her—most of all. After *you*, that is. The rest shall have my respect as long as they are kind to you. I shall be quite the tigress in your defense."

Lewis tucked a golden curl behind Jilly's ear. "I can see I shall have to make arrangements at once. And while I am at it, I shall write to the vicar at Ermenbrough and have the banns read beginning next Sunday. For it seems you will not stand still in my arms until we are wed."

"Oh, I think we could sneak in a little something before that," said Jilly as she climbed back into his embrace. She nestled there as if it were her home, and Lewis felt his heart beat more evenly, as if he had found his home too.

CHAPTER FIVE

THE BRADFORD HOUSEHOLD had a strict rule about Sunday dinner. Regardless of Philip's privilege and the accommodations made for Penelope, all were to be present at what was often the only meal the entire family shared in a week. It was therefore the ideal opportunity for Lewis to announce his news.

He waited until everyone was seated and the footmen had served the soup. Talk had already begun, though it wasn't conversation as such. Lewis considered these meals to be his parents' way of eliciting a sort of report on their lives, a means of establishing whether their adult children were progressing as they should.

For a while, Pen had always fared the worst in these assessments. Her obstinate refusal to consider marriage had put her at loggerheads with both their mother and father, who could not fathom how they had raised such a foolhardy child. They had threatened to cut off her pin money if she did not marry, only to find her the following week—after great consternation by Mother and an extensive search by all the servants—at the docks about to board a boat to America, having sold some jewelry to pay for the ticket.

After this incident, Lewis would have thought their parents might have tightened the constraints even further where their daughter was concerned. But he had underestimated how great the impact of possibly losing Penelope would be on them. Perhaps they truly cared. Maybe they feared a scandal. Whatever the case may have been, an understanding had been reached. Lewis suspected that his mother held a secret hope that, one day, a gentleman would prove so irresistible that Penelope would throw all caution to the wind and choose marriage after all. So far, such hope had come to nothing.

As far as Philip was concerned, his life followed a predictable and pleasing path. He attended all the right functions, shook all the right hands. He was expected to propose to Miss Irene Sangford any day now. He said what he should, did what he should, and had few thoughts of his own. He was therefore, ironically, free to do whatever he pleased. If he gambled a bit too often or drank a little too much on occasion, well, it was all part of being a vigorous gentleman, was it not? Provided he did not shame the family name, he might be allowed some leeway.

And then there was Lewis. Their second son. Intelligent and successful, and friends with the most powerful man in Munro. And yet all of that did not seem to count for much. Lewis, as required, did not upset the apple cart. And as long as this remained the case, he was all but invisible. They neither worried about him nor commended him on his achievements.

Which was why, on this Sunday afternoon, Lewis's news caused more of a stir than he thought it would have.

Penelope had confirmed she was doing nothing by way of marriage or causing a fuss. And Philip had briefly described a pleasant ride with the Sangford sisters. Chaperoned, of course. Everyone had returned to their meal. Lewis had been discounted as unlikely to have done anything newsworthy.

That was about to change.

"Mother," Lewis began, "I should like to invite a guest to dinner next Sunday."

"Sunday is a family meal," Lord Bradford said firmly. "We do not invite guests. Choose another day."

"And if the guest is to become family?" Lewis asked, waiting for understanding to dawn.

"Oh, Lewis!" squealed Penelope, first to draw the correct conclusion. "Is it Miss Kinsey? Have you asked her? Did she say *yes?*"

"Who is Miss Kinsey, pray?" asked Lady Bradford, the tight line of her mouth matching the thin streaks of black and gray in her hair. "I am not familiar with the young lady. I do not recall you mentioning her before."

"Oh, Mother!" cried Penelope. "How can you say that? Lewis has spoken of almost nothing else these past months! I can't wait to meet her. She sounds an absolute delight."

"Who is her family?" their mother inquired. "Why have we not been previously introduced?"

"She is not a resident of Munro," Lewis explained. "Her family is from Ermenbrough, about four hours east of us by carriage."

"Then how did you meet?"

"We were introduced by Lady Howell. Miss Kinsey is a dear friend of hers. They grew up together."

"I assume she comes from a good family," said Lady Bradford, ticking along with her interrogation.

"They are very good people, indeed," Lewis said, feeling the first prickles of defensiveness. "I have never heard anything to the contrary."

"And yet she has escaped my notice," pondered his mother. "Is there something you are not telling us, Lewis?"

"I cannot imagine what else you need to know," Lewis said stubbornly. "Miss Kinsey is friends with the Viscount Howell and his wife. She has not created a reputation for herself by which you might be dismayed. Most importantly, she has agreed to marry me."

"What do mean, she has agreed to marry you?" Lord Bradford blustered. "We haven't even met the lady. What do you mean by proposing without our knowledge?"

Lewis clamped his mouth shut, lest he say something untoward to his father. He counted to ten. It didn't help. With barely restrained annoyance, he answered. "Father, I am thirty years of age. I am a man of independent means. And I have never done anything that warranted your attention before. I had hoped that my marriage might be a joyous announcement, but I owe you nothing more. I certainly do not need your permission to marry the woman I love."

"'*Love*'!" His father scoffed, his jowls billowing slightly. "What sort of foolish talk is this? A man of your standing must consider more than banal sentimentality."

"Why?" Lewis retorted. "Since when has my role in this family mattered? I have done all that I should. I have not hampered Philip's progress in society. I have not exposed Penelope to anyone of bad character. I have earned my independence, as a second son is supposed to. Further than that, you have seen fit to all but disregard my existence. And now you would claim rights over me?"

"Don't be churlish, Lewis," Lady Bradford scolded. "Your father is quite right to be concerned. You could yet harm your brother's and sister's prospects with a bad match. Why would you be so selfish?"

"'*Selfish*'?!" Lewis nearly choked on the word. "When have I ever done anything for myself? And why would Miss Kinsey, when she becomes the wife of a humble barrister, be a threat to them in any way? You haven't even met her, and already, you have decided she is not good enough."

"Well, is she?" Lady Bradford asked pointedly. "If she is such a prize, you would have brought her to our attention sooner."

"She is not *your* prize," grumbled Lewis. "She is mine. As for bringing her to your attention, I have done so on several occasions. You obviously thought her too unimportant to pay any mind to the mention of her."

"Hang on," Philip interrupted. "I remember now. Isn't Miss Kinsey the young lady who visits Munro House for weeks at a time? She was at the viscount's wedding. Do you recall, Mother, you commented on her country manners? Isn't she the daughter of the Trentons' butler or something?"

"Groundskeeper," corrected Lewis. "Though why that should matter escapes me."

"Does it, indeed?" Lord Bradford sat back in his chair, elbows out, his chest expanding like a bird displaying its plumage. "I would say, Regina," he said to his wife, "that we have stumbled upon the heart of the matter. Miss Kinsey is of the working class. An alliance with her family offers no advantage, only embarrassment. You knew this, Lewis. That is why she has never been a guest here before."

Lewis felt his hackles rise. His skin grew hot and irritable. A pressure, as of steam needing to be released, built up in his head. "Miss Kinsey," he said through gritted teeth, "is no embarrassment to me, and I shall have every advantage with her at my side. Her class is an accident of birth. Her parents are sound. Her father is no mere servant, and he has the full trust of his employer. Miss Kinsey herself has a fine enough character to suit the taste of Viscount Howell as a houseguest and companion to his wife. Who are we that we are above such things? And who are you to tell me I have no right to be happy in marriage because my siblings might choose an arrogant spouse? Why should their poor taste in partner trump my choice? If, for example, Miss Sangford does not wish to be sister-in-law to Miss Kinsey, I say we are better off without *her*."

"Now, just a minute!" cried Philip.

"No, Philip," Lewis bit back. "I'm sorry, but this is one matter in which I will not compromise. You have always had first choice in everything. Even when I desperately wanted that pony for my seventh birthday. You were frightened of the thoroughbred Father got you and insisted the little piebald would suit you better. The next thing I knew, they were both yours. It has been this way my whole life. I have had to accept it as an accident of *my* birth. I don't care what you tell Miss Sangford. Promise her she never has to mix company with me if that's what it takes. But I will not give up Miss Kinsey."

He looked from one person at the table to the next. They all met his gaze with their dark-blue eyes beneath brown-black hair—the only attributes they had in common. Lewis's glare softened when he looked upon Pen, her worried smile creating pity in Lewis's heart for the sister who would wish him well but who was so thoroughly outvoted.

His resolve firmed again when he settled his scowl upon his father. "You can welcome her into this family or reject us both," Lewis declared. "*That* is your only choice. Marrying Miss Kinsey is *my* choice, and mine alone. I will not be swayed."

Lewis panted a little when he had finished. The silence at the table was long and chilly. Lord Bradford cast his eyes to his eldest, as if considering what damage might be done him. Then he did the same with his daughter, though his thoughts there were clearly more fleeting. He splayed his fingers upon the surface of the heavy table.

"It seems our younger children are determined to unseat our peace, my dear," he told his wife. "So be it. Miss Kinsey may come for dinner on Tuesday. Sunday is out of the question. She is not yet family. We shall determine, from her visit, the extent of the damage you have done with your hasty proposal. But to say I am disappointed is a grave understatement, Lewis."

Lewis remained unmoved by this sentiment. "I can bear your disappointment with fortitude, Father. But I expect Miss Kinsey, who is an innocent party, to be treated with kindness and respect when she visits."

"Hmph," retorted Lady Bradford, the wrinkles about her mouth deepening as she pursed her lips. "She is hardly innocent. She knows full well what she gains from marriage to you. You have offered her a life beyond her wildest dreams. And she would be a fool to reject the opportunity you have thrown in her lap."

"See, this is exactly what I am talking about," said Lewis, his exasperation pitching into his voice. "Miss Kinsey does not desire a life of luxury. Quite the opposite. I had to convince her that we would live a simple life, for these are the things that bring her contentment."

As he said the words, Lewis realized he had made a mistake. But it was too late. He could only watch as his mother threw her hand triumphantly into the air.

"What did I say?" she all but crowed. "Did I not say it was a poor match? Simple life, indeed! What does she want to do, raise chickens?!"

Lewis wisely kept silent.

"If I may say something," came the soft voice of Penelope. All heads turned to her. Lewis once again marveled at the marriage of warm empathy and iron will that shaped his sister. "Let Miss Kinsey come and we shall see for ourselves what the truth of the matter is. From what Lewis has told me, she is a little unsophisticated, certainly, but not clownish in her behavior. If she is of good character, all other graces can be learned. I would even offer my assistance, should she want it. But we should not judge her for being unable to supply all we expect from the *ton*. Goodness knows, the upper class could do with a good shaking too, on occasion." She laid a persuasive hand upon Philip's. "Don't you agree?"

Philip pulled his fingers out from under his sister's and pushed his chair back to stand. He looked down at Penelope, both in stature and feeling. This was nothing new. Philip copied their father in every way, without the mitigation of parental attachment. Lewis despised his brother for it.

"I do not agree," Philip told their sister. "But then I don't even have to be here for the dinner, do I? Miss Kinsey is really coming to meet our parents. I will abide by their assessment of her. As should you both." He gave each sibling a pointed glance, then excused himself and left the room.

"Well," said Lewis, huffing a wry laugh, "it seems the family dinner is at an end. If you will excuse me, I would like to write to Munro House, letting my betrothed know about your generous offer to have her for dinner on Tuesday. Shall we say four o'clock?" When no answer was forthcoming, he shrugged his shoulders. "Four o'clock it is, then. I hope you will have had sufficient time to set your faces to the pleasant nothingness reserved for such gatherings with strangers. I would not like you to embarrass me. It goes both ways, does it not?" And he sauntered out of the room as if he had not just taken on both his parents and all of fine society.

By the time Lewis had reached his rooms, his legs felt like jelly. He dropped onto a chair and took a few measured breaths. But his hand still shook as he took up his quill.

Never in his thirty years of obedience stained with resentment had he spoken to his parents like that. It was not the liberating experience some might have thought. But it had been necessary. And it was done now. He must look forward. A letter had already been sent to the vicar in Ermenbrough. Soon, they would start calling the banns. Convincing his family to travel half a day to a quaint, little village to watch him marry a groundskeeper's daughter was a battle for another day.

First, they must overcome his parents' prejudice. Lewis was not convinced one dinner would achieve this. But they had to start somewhere. So, back to the invitation.

His hand was a little steadier now. With strokes as even as he could manage, Lewis shared the news with Jillian. He trusted that she would, in turn, tell her friend the viscountess, both as an outpouring of excitement and to procure the necessary transport to the Bradford estate for Tuesday. Lady Howell, he knew, would take Jilly under her wing. A suitable dress would be arranged. Some whispers of advice given. The fact that the viscount and viscountess's scheme to shoo her hastily back to Trenton Grange had failed would not stand in the way of the two women's long and loving friendship. Ellena would want to protect Jilly, and— heaven help him—she needed protecting.

A few weeks of this torturous confrontation with his family and they would be off to live their own lives. Lewis had already found a place that he was certain Jilly would love. It had everything they had talked about, right down to the flower-lined walkway. He couldn't wait to show her. It might be just the thing to soothe any ruffled feathers after the dinner.

He pulled the bell and handed the letter to the servant who'd answered the summons. Then he kicked off his shoes, removed his cravat, and put his feet up on the ottoman. Tomorrow, he was off to the law office again, preparing documentation for his next case. He might very well have dinner in town with a colleague and avoid any further debates with his family.

Lewis sighed out his gloomy mood. This was temporary. Everything was moving along. There was no need to linger on matters he could not change. His parents might come to their senses or they might not. But marry Jilly, he would. And that happy-ever-after was worth a month of temporary discomfort.

A small smile twitched at the corner of his mouth. Ah, Jilly. His woodland nymph. His own sweet love. His fingers lifted to his lips, a memory from the day before still playing upon it. Yes, indeed, she was worth waiting for.

CHAPTER SIX

Oakwoods, October 1815

J ILLIAN COMPLETED THE short journey from Munro House to Oakwoods, the Bradford estate, with her usual wide-eyed optimism. It was a pretty route, circling around the city rather than passing through it. The properties they passed were large, their drives long and winding, the homes deceptively small in the distance or hidden behind an avenue of trees.

She drank it all in—the afternoon sultry with heat, the kaleidoscope of autumn colors donning the trees and shifting steadily to the earth below. Her borrowed lady's maid saw none of it, the rhythmic motion of the carriage having lulled Ingsley to sleep. Jilly did not mind. As far as she was concerned, the viscount and viscountess could have given the poor thing the afternoon off. But propriety had demanded a suitable companion for the ride, especially now that she was betrothed to a gentleman. So, Jilly let her sleep.

As Jilly's eyes cast over the passing views of fields and sheep and crows on fenceposts, her thoughts replayed the contents of her mother's letter. It had arrived while Ingsley had been doing her hair and Jillian had been free to read it while the lady's maid had fussed over her. Her parents had been surprised at her news, which Jillian thought odd as she had been singing the praises of dear Lewis for months now and they had admitted numerous times that he sounded wonderful. Had they never considered that a match was possible, even likely?

At least they had not tried to talk her out of it, which made for a refreshing change. Instead, they were delighted that the wedding should take place so close to home. Travel was expensive, and her father would have struggled to take time away from his work at Trenton Grange to attend her nuptials if they had been planned for Munro.

There was more to the letter, and Jillian was excited to share it all with Lewis when she saw him. Not long now, for already, the carriage had turned from the road onto a private drive, passing a pond with ducks and a small bridge that offered a good spot from which to fish. Had Lewis and his brother played here as children? Somehow, Jillian found it hard to imagine. It sounded far too pleasurable an activity for a nobleman's son. More likely, there had been lessons in fencing and archery and—even duller— in Latin and mathematics. At least Lewis had put his Latin to good use as a barrister. As for the rest, Jilly did not understand why young boys should be tortured thus. Her own brothers had learned to read but also a multitude of other worthwhile skills and had still found time to just have fun. This was how she intended to raise her own sons. A bit of geography and an afternoon of three-legged races or hide-and-seek. An hour of astronomy and a night sleeping under the summer stars to see their studies come to life. Their scholarly exploits would not suffer, but she would see to it that they were given the chance to live life to the fullest.

With that thought in mind, she finally laid eyes on the great house. She hadn't known what to expect, but this was certainly not it. It was a monstrous thing, all ancient, gray stone in a hulking block. No romantic ivy. No classical statues adorning tall columns as with Munro House. Even the gardens were mostly lawn and hedges, with a pavilion off to the side and what looked like an herb wheel around a plain, circular fountain. The flowerbeds had not been planned as her father would have done—with varieties that bloomed at different times so that they displayed from early spring to late autumn. The plants looked spent. They had done their duty and would offer nothing further until the frost had withdrawn next April. Oakwoods was not a cheerful sort of place. It spoke of function and little else besides.

The carriage rolled to a halt and the sleeping maid awoke with a start. She tried to orient herself, her bewilderment touching a chord of pity within Jillian.

"Take yourself round to the kitchen for a plate of something hearty," Jillian told her. "Your services will not be required until I leave. Some lively chatter with other folk is just what you need." She looked up at the foreboding building. "That is, if chatter is allowed in a place like this."

Jillian made a mental note to keep a tight rein on her own tendency to talk too much. She had developed this unfortunate habit since visiting Munro, where her internal discomfort had often produced a relentless stream of one-sided conversation. This home did not seem to invite any type of excess, not even in a display of wealth. Perhaps when Miss Sangford became the lady of the house in years to come, she would put a more ostentatious stamp upon the dreary landscape.

The great door swung open, and Lewis descended the stairs with an enthusiastic pace. By now, the footman had lowered the step of the carriage and opened its door, but it was Lewis who reached in and drew Jillian out with a steady hand. The footman did the same for Jilly's maid, after which the two servants were both quite forgotten.

"Welcome to my home," said Lewis. "Quite the eyesore, isn't it? Do not be discouraged. This property is a reflection of my parents and not myself. Our home shall be a great deal humbler and have considerably more heart."

"I have every faith it will be so," Jillian said, tucking her hand around his arm. "How can it be otherwise when our love will be its heartbeat?"

Lewis lifted her other hand to his lips, pressing his mouth slowly to her skin. The touch rippled up through her arm and she leaned more closely against him. His bicep tensed to support her, and she was impressed with the power it radiated. It was masculine and attractive and…

"You must not do such things when I am trying to maintain my equilibrium," she scolded him unconvincingly. "I must be my most serene self, a picture of grace and decorum. It will not do if I am blushing every time you look at me. I will quite forget which is the salad fork and prove myself the country bumpkin your parents are expecting."

Lewis drew her hand to his chest. "You have nothing to fear. My parents may be stuck in their ways, but it is not them you are marrying. Whatever foolishness might escape their lips, you must remember that. You are my own sweet love, and soon you will be Mrs. Bradford. They will resist the idea at first, but experience tells me they will relent."

"Do you mean as they did with your sister?"

"Exactly. There were years of nagging, even the occasional threat. But now they just grumble under their breath. They can be noisy about their opinions, but they really are quite harmless. Just be yourself. They will come to love you. It is impossible not to."

Lewis kissed her hand again, lingering a little longer this time, so that she hastily withdrew her fingers before she should lose herself entirely to the moment. As far as she was concerned, there were simply too many weeks until the wedding. She could hardly wait to have *all* of Lewis all to herself. To follow such aching thoughts with a formal dinner seemed a rare punishment, indeed.

Up the steps they went, past the butler, who offered her tepid greetings, through the foyer—which was empty, save for a suit of armor that quite possibly had belonged to an ancestor—and on toward the drawing room. There were three very well-dressed people waiting, one smiling broadly as Jillian entered and rising to greet her warmly, the other two looking at each other, their mouths squeezed into disappointed moues, before both stood reluctantly. Had they hoped she might not come?

Jilly had no time to ponder this thought, for Miss Bradford had taken her other arm and led her to her parents, who barely bothered to rearrange their expressions into something more welcoming.

"Mother, Father, Miss Jillian Kinsey has come. Miss Kinsey, our parents, Lord and Lady Bradford." Miss Bradford patted Jilly's arm. "Excellent. Introductions are done." She eyed the bell ribbon and said impatiently, "Now can we eat? I'm starving!"

Lady Bradford watched as Jillian attempted one of her curtseys. Ellena always said Jillian looked like a drunk duck. Her friend had marveled that someone so young and fit could not manage to control her limbs for this simple task. Jillian wobbled a little, doubled her concentration, and managed to finish with more flourish than clownishness. Lady Bradford sucked her tongue on the roof of her mouth and heaved a sigh before giving a small nod in acknowledgement. Lord Bradford stood, unmoving, his hands upon a cane that Jilly could well believe had been used to prod people into compliance as much as it had assisted him in walking.

"You may ring for Giles and tell them we are ready," Lady Bradford told her daughter.

Miss Bradford did so, then returned to her position beside Jillian while the rest of the room was marked by awkward silence. Lewis had grown momentarily mute. But his sister stepped in to lighten the mood.

"Was it a comfortable ride to us, Miss Kinsey? Great improvements have been made upon the roads recently. I daresay your experience was better than it would have been even a year ago, when we were tortured by holes in the road, and loose stone clattered up under the poor horses' bellies. We must have had at least three misadventures with carriage wheels before the viscount took it upon himself to have the matter sorted. He's a good sort. Really cares about Munro. Better than most politicians, really."

Lord Bradford cut in. "Politics is not a suitable conversation for a young lady."

"But I don't want to talk about art or music or riding sidesaddle," Miss Bradford countered. "Besides, I can't imagine those things interest Miss Kinsey." She turned to Jillian. "Or do they?"

"I do not ride at all or play piano very well," Jillian answered honestly. "But I do enjoy visiting the museum of art in Munro."

"Do you, indeed?" said Lady Bradford with obvious surprise. "And which of the masters has caught your eye?"

"I don't remember the names," Jillian confessed, "only that they paint ever so well. My favorite display is the glasswork. Lewis says they make the glass soft with great heat and then blow into it like a bubble. He says he will take me one day to see it being done in Italy. Maybe we can bring something back for you. As a gift. Perhaps a vase? Or a fruit bowl?"

"That is… thoughtful of you." Lady Bradford seemed undecided whether to smile or maintain her firm resolve not to, resulting in a sort of pleasant snarl.

The butler arrived. "Dinner is ready, your lordship," he announced before giving a curious glance toward Jillian. She recognized the look. The servants at Munro House had done the same when she'd first visited. Now they had grown used to the way she stopped and chatted with them, despite the fact that both Branson, the butler, and Mrs. Anders, the housekeeper, complained when she did so. "Blurring the lines," they called it. Well, they were silly lines to begin with. People were people, no matter what they did for a living.

Lord and Lady Bradford now moved regally to the dining room, another lifeless space in terms of furnishings. However, it had a row of impressively large windows along one wall, letting in the afternoon sun along with the view of a rose garden that displayed late-season blooms in almost every color imaginable.

Miss Bradford caught her eye and nodded toward the thriving shrubs. "Do you like my roses, Miss Kinsey?"

"*Your* roses?"

"Yes, I persuaded our parents to plant them. It's a cheery

sight even when the sun is behind the clouds. And my room is just above, so I benefit from the scent when my window is open."

"How wonderful!" exclaimed Jilly. "Perhaps you would like to show me your varieties after dinner. I might not know the names of master painters, but I do know my botany. My father has been very generous with his knowledge."

"It will be dusk by then," answered Miss Bradford, "but you will come again and then we girls shall make a proper tour of it."

"I look forward to it."

"Miss Kinsey," said Lady Bradford, "please take your place here." She indicated the seat to her left. Miss Bradford took the place opposite Jillian while Lewis sat next to his sister. Lord Bradford had already lowered himself into his chair. Possibly his leg was bothering him. The seat to his right, opposite Lewis, was empty.

"Is your brother not joining us?" Jilly asked Lewis.

"Philip has other commitments," Lady Bradford answered for him.

Both Lewis and his sister looked directly in front of them and said nothing. Jillian understood all too well. The elder Bradford son would not condescend to meet her.

Jillian was not hurt by this. Not for herself. Ellena had warned her about this sort of upper-class nonsense. It was a reflection on *their* character, not hers.

But she knew it would sting for Lewis. This was yet another way in which his brother reminded him that he was discardable. The man's opinions and choices always carried more weight than Lewis's, even when it came to the common decency of meeting his brother's betrothed.

Jilly could not squeeze his hand to reassure him. Nor could she offer him a warm smile, for Lewis kept his gaze before him, his cheeks flushed and his lips pressed firmly together in his trademark expression of bitter frustration.

"That is a pity," Jillian remarked lightly. "It must be something very important for him to miss out on such a wonderful meal. Lewis tells me your cook is the envy of all Munro, second only to Lord Howell's. I cannot wait to sample her fare."

Lewis lifted his head. His mouth softened. His hand lifted surreptitiously to his heart and he blinked slowly, the combined gesture a salute to her handling of the obvious insult of his brother's absence. "I look forward to your mother's home cooking with equal zeal," he said, having at last found his voice again.

"Oh, that reminds me," Jillian said brightly. "Mum has promised her very best cake for the wedding tea. It will be filled with nuts and drizzled with honey—a decadent gift, indeed. I must remember to take a jar of honey to Trenton Grange when I go home. She will no doubt use up what honey they have with her generous endeavor. Perhaps I might supply a jar of candied orange peel to add the finishing touch to her efforts. A bit of color never goes amiss."

"Surely, you will use our cook for the occasion?" Lady Bradford remarked. "Why have your mother go to such trouble if they cannot spare the ingredients? And then to carry the cake tin upon her lap all the way from Trenton Grange... It seems an unnecessary discomfort."

Jillian was equally confused. "Why would she bring it here? The wedding is in Ermenbrough."

The atmosphere at the table thickened.

"Oh." Jilly realized too late. Her eyes swiveled to Lewis. "You have not told them."

He squirmed in his chair. "I had thought to have you all meet first. I would have discussed the logistics in due course."

"It is out of the question," said Lady Bradford curtly. "You cannot expect our family to go traipsing to some back-of-beyond village for a farmer's wedding." She fluffed out her serviette and drew it across her lap. "Giles, kindly serve the soup before I lose my appetite entirely."

The butler nodded at the footman addressed, who was startled into action. Jillian imagined he had been rather invested in the goings-on at the table and had forgotten his purpose there. From what she had seen thus far, this was not typically such an entertaining environment for the servants. Lord and Lady Bradford ran what appeared to be a tight ship in their home. Guests like Jillian would be about as rare as, well, anything that hadn't existed until now.

"Our family," Lewis said with dangerous calm, "need not attend if it is burdensome to them."

"Oh, don't be ridiculous, Lewis!" Lady Bradford cried. "That would be little better than an elopement. It will not do. Our family has certain standards to maintain. Reverend Keith will be expecting to perform the ceremony, as he has done for all the sons and daughters of Munro's aristocracy."

"Reverend Keith," replied Lewis, "is the last person on earth to begrudge someone happiness if they have a different parish in mind. Just because he has married the whole blessed lump of Munro noblemen does not mean he shares their superior notions."

"But it is expected! You will make us look quite the fools if you are married by some village vicar whom no one has ever heard of."

"Lady Howell has heard of him," said Jillian.

"What?" Lady Bradford swung her gaze irritably toward Jilly.

"He was her vicar. The Trenton household attended his services. They no doubt still do. And she would be attending the wedding without question if it weren't for her recent confinement."

"Hmph. The viscount has always had some strange notions. His wife is no different. It seems they have rubbed off onto you."

"Eat your soup, my dear," instructed Lord Bradford. "It's getting cold."

The soup, despite being of high quality and truly tasty, was eaten in a tense silence. The plates were removed and the fish served.

During this time, another footman entered the room and,

crossing the carpeted floor silently, whispered something in the butler's ear. Giles frowned, indicated for the footman to stay in his place, and exited the door in a hurry.

"It seems you are determined to have your way, regardless of our feelings," Lady Bradford said more quietly, poking at her mackerel in a desultory manner. Jillian wondered if the matriarch felt hurt as much as offended by the choice of venue.

She was tempted to reconsider her choice for the sake of better relations between them when Lord Bradford said blandly, "What does it matter, Regina? Philip at least will marry as he should."

The weight of this statement quashed any further attempts at reconciliation. Jillian watched as Lewis bristled under the implications of the words. She felt powerless to help him. Anything she said in his defense would only antagonize his parents further. Anything said to soften the experience for his parents would seem an act of disloyalty to Lewis.

"I think a village wedding sounds wonderfully intimate," said Miss Bradford out of the blue. "No stuffy pretense at joy, but the real thing instead. No soulless cake covered in marzipan and flowery loops like a thousand wedding cakes before it, but a one-of-a-kind creation made with a mother's love. Attended by village folk who've known you all your life and who don't need an invitation to turn up. I am quite inspired to get married so I may have a wedding exactly like that."

"Do not tease on that subject, Penelope," Lady Bradford said with an edge of bitterness. "You know it pains me that you refuse to take marriage seriously. But to taunt me with talk of you having a village wedding is too much. It would require you to marry into the working class. One such offspring is quite bad enough." She sniffed and pulled a face. "I do not need more of my children lowering themselves in this way."

It was very unfortunate that Miss Bradford's well-intentioned speech had led to such a visceral response from her mother. More so because Lewis now reached his boiling point.

He thumped his fist on the table so hard that even his father jumped a little. "There is *nothing* wrong with hardworking folk who were not born into wealth! If *you* were half as decent as the phrase 'upper class' would suggest, you *still* wouldn't hold a candle to Miss Kinsey!"

"Now see here..." Lord Bradford began, but Lewis cut him off.

"No, Father, *you* see. Miss Kinsey has come here as our guest. She has done nothing offensive since her arrival other than dare to be my betrothed and the daughter of a groundskeeper. Yet Mother has no qualms insulting her. It is disgraceful!"

Lewis was shaking now, anger roiling from him in waves. Jillian could only watch as he released thirty years of frustration in one fell swoop.

He pointed a furious finger at his father and mother in turn. "If you had spent but a moment trying to get to know her, you would have discovered what a blessed addition she is to our family. I now withdraw that offer. You don't deserve her. We will marry in Ermenbrough, where there is love for the both of us. And I will attach myself to her family, where I am welcomed and appreciated."

Lewis threw a quick glance at his sister. "I'm sorry, Pen. I don't mean you. You are the best of sisters." The corners of his mouth curled downward. "As for the rest of you...We will not darken your doorway again."

Lewis stood up so quickly that his chair clattered to the floor.

At this precise moment, the butler returned. Giles observed the overturned chair, saw the thunder upon his master's face, and decided to step out of harm's way. He took position beside Lord Bradford's seat, seeming to wait for an opportunity to speak to him when some measure of calm had been restored.

"Come, Jilly," Lewis said, reaching out his arm and gesturing with his hand. "I have let you down. I thought my parents could see reason, but I was gravely mistaken. They have not been kind to you. I should never have let you endure such mistreatment.

But it is done now. Here is the end of it."

Jilly sat, mute with shock. She was grateful for Lewis's protective nature, but this was not what she wanted—a family divided because of her.

"Lewis, I… Shouldn't we… Let's just catch our breath for a second," she finally managed to say. "I do not want you to lose your family over some…"

"Of course you don't," Lord Bradford said sharply. "You want to keep your claws firmly on the Bradford money. But if he marries you, he shall be cut off. There you have it. Do you still want him so badly now?"

"I never wanted him for his money!" Jilly cried in horror. "I *love* Lewis. Which is why I want your family to remain intact. Surely, you would not force him to choose between us? That will only lead to more bitterness and resentment. Do you really hate me more than you love your son?"

The poor butler, who had, as all good servants do, tried to remain invisible throughout the confrontation, could wait no longer and was forced to bend down to his master's ear and whisper an urgent message.

"What?" barked the baron. "The police, you say? What the devil do they want?"

A few more muttered sentences followed.

"No, I will not come to the door to speak to them. I have sat down for dinner and do not wish to disturb this bothersome leg. Go fetch them and show them in here. We have already been interrupted. Perhaps, while they are here, they can arrest my son for criminal insanity!"

Giles nodded and disappeared at once, while Jillian and the Bradfords remained frozen in suspended uproar. Less than a minute passed in waiting, but the tension only deepened in the silence. Lewis used the opportunity to walk around the table to stand by Jilly, grasping her hand firmly. Jilly could not discern whether he was offering support or needing it, or both. She returned the firmness of his grip in unspoken agreement that they were in this together.

And then the butler ushered the two policemen into the room.

The dynamic in the room was clearly not what they had expected. Perhaps they had assumed some surprise, even curiosity at their presence. But this space was awash with agitation. The constables looked at each other, uncertainty in their stance.

"Well, what is it?" demanded Lord Bradford. "I expect you have an excellent reason to disturb our dinner. Speak and be done with it, man! Don't dilly-dally. The butter sauce is congealing upon my plate."

One of the constables seemed to have the misfortune of being assigned the speaking role. He now pulled his cap from his head and scrunched it up in his hands, lowering his eyes to the floor.

"Your lordship," he began with great trepidation, "we are sorry to tell you, but there has been an incident involving your son."

"Do you mean Philip?" Lady Bradford asked, her voice tight, her body sprung with apprehension.

The constable turned briefly to his companion, who nodded. "Yes, milady, I believe that is the name we were given."

"What has happened?" cried Miss Bradford. "Is Philip all right? Where is he?"

The constable bowed his head, unable to look her in the eye. The grip on his cap grew tighter. "Your ladyship," he said in a voice solemn and low, "it pains me to say that Mr. Philip Bradford is dead."

CHAPTER SEVEN

"RUBBISH!" ROARED LORD Bradford. "My son? Dead? That cannot be! He is as healthy as a horse! Why, I just saw him a few hours ago, hale and hearty as always. He wouldn't just... He can't have..."

"I'm afraid they were unnatural circumstances, my lord," said the hapless constable. "A robbery gone bad. He appears to have visited a gaming hell of—shall we say—*lesser* repute, where he won a rich sum. It would seem he was followed and attacked for his winnings. He must have resisted. He was... er... well, I'm so terribly sorry... The wound to the head suggests he was hit with a hard, blunt object. No help could render him repair. Death was swift."

"Oh! My son!" wailed Lady Bradford. "My precious boy!"

Miss Bradford slipped from her chair and threw her arms about her mother, who began to sob into her serviette.

"There must be some mistake." Lord Bradford looked about him as if someone could explain the cause of such an error. "Philip would never enter a place like that. He could lay a wager at the gentleman's club if he wanted. There was no need to defile himself in this way."

"There are all sorts of entertainment at these holes, such as a young man might enjoy," the constable said grimly.

"Are you saying my son would seek such *entertainments?*"

blustered the baron. "He is..." He swallowed. "*Was...* a gentleman. He had money enough and was soon to be engaged. What could he want with such dross?"

The constable looked at his hands, which still clutched his cap tightly. "I cannot say, my lord."

"Where is he?" Lady Bradford's voice quavered. "I want to see him."

"He was transported to the undertaker's, milady."

"We must bring him home, Walter. I want my boy here, with me, where I can watch over him."

Lord Bradford said nothing, only staring ahead of him. Then, as if on a well-oiled axis, his head turned to Jillian and Lewis. As he spoke, bitterness dripped like acid from every word.

"How fortunate for you, Miss Kinsey, that I can no longer cut off my second-born. Lewis is now my heir." His eyes locked on to those of his remaining son. "You have new privileges. You have new responsibilities. Choose your actions wisely." His gaze flicked to Jillian and back. "More wisely than you have done thus far."

Lord Bradford rose from his chair with a struggle, the footman stepping forward hurriedly to bring him his cane. His lordship leaned heavily upon it, breathing slowly. He seemed to have aged twenty years in a matter of minutes.

"Make arrangements for the body to be prepared and brought home," he said as blandly as if he were tallying an invoice. "Spare no expense. We shall have the funeral on Sunday, our last family day together." He rubbed his brow with the back of his thumb. "Now, you must excuse me. I am tired."

A sob from his wife punctuated his departure. Her daughter stroked her hair and made soothing noises, but Penelope's own eyes remained dry.

Lewis stood unmoving. He had not reacted at all to the terrible news. He neither mourned his brother nor acknowledged his new position. Jillian knew it to be the shock of it all.

"Lewis," she said quietly into his ear, "let me arrange some tea. You could all use the comfort of something warm and sweet. And then, I think, I should go. Your family must process the loss together. If you need me, you know where to find me. But, for now, your attention should be here."

Lewis nodded. "I will see you out."

They walked, hands still intertwined, to where the butler stood. Jillian made the request for a tray of fresh tea to be brought at once, and the butler repeated the instruction to the footman, who disappeared to tell the kitchen staff.

Releasing Lewis for a moment, Jilly stepped across to his mother and hunched down before her so that she looked up into the sorrowful face. "I am so very sorry for the loss of your eldest," she said, her voice tender. "Please let me know if there is anything I can do."

A flash of fury burned in Lady Bradford's face. "You can leave my family alone for a start. Coming in here and ordering my staff about as if you are already lady of the house! That is never going to happen." Her voice pitched sharply. "Do you hear me? Never! I have already lost one son. I won't lose the other to the likes of you!"

"Mother," Miss Bradford said urgently. "You are upset. But none of this is Miss Kinsey's fault. Do not be unkind to her. Lewis will need her support."

Lady Bradford only hardened her stance. "Lewis needs the support of a woman of quality. It will be hard for him to assume the role Philip alone was raised for. He should not have to teach his wife the intricacies of a life of privilege. She will be more burden than help." She stopped and dabbed her eyes once more. "Philip had chosen well." She sniffed woefully. "Miss Sangford understands the duties of a lady. And she stands on her own merit. She doesn't have to rely on the reputation of her *friend* to be accepted in good society."

Lewis rushed forward and pulled Jillian up to her feet. "Do not make yourself small before such narrowminded hostility. You are worth ten Miss Sangfords, but my parents will not see what is right before their eyes. As for you, Mother, I hold my tongue for now, for you have experienced a loss no parent should have to bear, and I will not add to your misery. But I will say this. You *will* refrain from insulting Miss Kinsey. Carry whatever skewed views you have toward her in silence. Or you will have lost not one son, but two."

He grabbed Jillian's arm and ushered her from the room, while she looked over her shoulder at the broken scene they left behind.

"I'm so sorry, Lewis," she said. "My presence seems to have made a frightful situation so much worse."

"What are you apologizing for?" he snapped. "Have you done something wrong? Did you murder Philip? Did you teach my parents to be so outrageously arrogant? Of course not! They should be apologizing to you!"

"They are broken-hearted, Lewis. They say what they would otherwise have left unsaid."

"But not unthought," he replied, his lips drawn back in a snarl. "They had already crossed the line before the constables arrived. They did not have the decency to temper their speech for your sake or mine. And now"—he snorted his disgust—"they would remake me in Philip's image."

"Give them time. They may yet soften their approach. Especially when the reality of Philip's absence hits home more fully. They will not want to ruin their relationship with their remaining son."

"'Their remaining son.'" Lewis twisted his mouth into a display of disgust. "Ah, yes, the spare. How useful of me to exist."

Jillian drew the back of her fingers softly across his cheek. "Try not to think of yourself in that way, my darling. It does you no good. Besides, you know it isn't true."

"Isn't it?" Lewis huffed wryly.

"You know your worth. In court. Among your friends. With me. It is only your parents who have left this sour taste in your mouth. Why should their opinion outweigh those of so many others?"

"Because they are my family. And they should have loved me more."

Jilly grew quiet. There was not much she could say to counter such depth of pain. Instead, she leaned her head against his chest, curling her hands around his back, and gave him a little of the love he could not get from his parents.

"You know," she said, her head still upon his heart, "I think they love you very much, indeed. That is why I frighten them."

"They don't sound particularly frightened," grumbled Lewis.

"People who are confident in what they have do not need to protect their treasure with such vitriol. They are afraid to lose you. They think I will change you. They don't realize that this is who you've always been. They are close-minded and particular in their expectations, but they love you the best they know how. It's all wrong, I agree. But I am convinced their animosity toward me is borne of the realization that, if forced to choose, you would choose me."

Lewis wrapped his arms tightly around her. "And so I would."

"People who are afraid of losing someone are people who love. It is an insecure, possessive kind of love, and I have mercifully been spared such a miserable form of it. But I have seen it in our village. Even a seemingly tranquil place like Ermenbrough has its darker corners."

Jillian grew quiet, as if recalling these places and the ugliness that such relationships brought to them. Then she drew a breath and said, "The point is, you are not merely 'another son.' They were upset even before we heard the awful news. They are misguided in their approach, certainly. But you are valued nevertheless. Just as they sigh at Penelope for refusing any talk of marriage, yet they leave her be. Give them time. Our engagement has been a shock, followed by an even greater and irreparable wound. Let things settle. I can be patient."

Lewis nuzzled his face into her hair. "I wish they knew you as I did."

They stood in this way, two hearts united, until Miss Bradford found them.

"Mother is asking for you, Lew. I cannot console her. I fear it will be a while before anyone can."

"You are both so brave," Jillian said, squeezing Miss Bradford's hand.

The siblings looked at each other and said nothing.

"You do not have to be brave with me," Jilly tried to reassure them.

"It is not bravery, Miss Kinsey," said Miss Bradford. "It is an absence of connection. Certainly, we are sad. But Philip was not an endearing sort of brother. There was very little relationship to mourn the loss of. Our parents, on the other hand, had pinned all their hopes upon him. For them, it is a very real tragedy. Lewis and I, however, have always lived more along the periphery of Philip's orbit."

"I see," answered Jilly.

"I hope I do not shock you with my bluntness."

"No, I am not shocked, only grieved that this should have been the case. I cannot tell you what excruciating pain it would cause me to lose one of my brothers. The fact that such pain is absent here is a sorrow in and of itself."

"It is not absent in its entirety," admitted Miss Bradford. "No doubt the shock will release its grip within the hour and we will recall happier times. But, you will forgive me for saying, there were not many of these. It will be strange not to see Philip striding to the stables. His seat will be oddly empty at the table. But we never conversed warmly or laughed together or shared interests. Philip carried all our parents' hopes. They kept him upon a pedestal beyond our reach. He was not so much a brother as an example to us of what we should have been."

Jilly pictured the family dinner table at the Kinsey cottage. What Penelope had described was so alien to her, she could not transpose their image upon her own at all.

"It seems to me," she said, "that you have associated sadness and disappointment with him all your lives. There is hardly any room for more."

"Thank you for not judging us," said Miss Bradford. "We really do not deserve such grace when almost none of it was granted you today. Please know—though my views carry little weight in this house—I will be happy to call you sister soon. It may be small consolation for your mistreatment, but it is all I can offer."

Jilly felt her eyes prick with tears at these words. Kindness had a way of nudging open a heart that was trying to keep its pain firmly sealed. Jillian gave a few quick nods as both acknowledgement and thanks but dared not speak these sentiments aloud for fear of her tears flowing hotly down her cheeks. Her lips bunched into a tight clench through which she attempted a smile.

"Oh, Miss Kinsey!" Miss Bradford reached out and pulled her into a firm embrace. "You have been sorely wronged today. And you have borne it well. That is exactly the sort of quality a true lady should have. Our parents are such fools not to see it!"

Jillian wriggled free from the abundance of warm benevolence in Miss Bradford's embrace. She twisted quickly away from her. Her face, she knew, would be red and puffy. It always was when she suppressed her emotions, though she rarely had cause to do so.

"I must go." She began to stride toward the door. The footman stepped forward with her wrap, then opened the door to the front entrance, offering her escape. Jillian did a half turn. "See to your mother. I will be fine." Then she fled down the steps and, after a brief pause while another footman lowered the carriage steps, she climbed inside and hid herself in the darkness.

She had to wait while her borrowed maid was sent for. With every passing second, she prayed that Lewis would not follow her out. It would be so like him to do just that. He always thought of her needs. But today, he must not. She did not want to lose the tiniest bit of control to which she was clinging. Besides, no matter what else this family must overcome because of her engagement to Lewis, right now, they were in mourning and should be together. Without distraction.

Jillian tried to focus on slow breaths. A small semblance of calm returned. Just in time, too, for Ingsley clambered quite suddenly into the carriage, apologizing as she did so.

"So sorry, Miss Kinsey. I did not expect the dinner to end as quickly as it did. And then the footman told us the terrible news! The whole kitchen staff sat down in shock. Cook was crying into her apron. Mr. Bradford must have been greatly beloved. And to have such a tragedy at your first meeting with the family…"

"Yes, thank you. But I do not wish to discuss it further."

"Oh, of course." Ingsley folded her hands to resume a posture of humility, but the way she bit her lip told Jillian that the lady's maid was sorry to have to cut the conversation short.

Their nuptials would likely be postponed, Jillian realized. And the ceremony might need to be in Munro, a compromise for his parents, considering there would no longer be a wedding for Philip.

It was all so unfair! Jilly allowed herself a minute to sulk before guilt overrode her self-pity. How could she even think about weddings and her own preferences when the Bradfords had lost a son and brother?

And yet it was hard not to. She had been so excited. Now everything was tainted with loss. Not to mention the fact that Lewis did not have his parents' blessing upon their betrothal.

How cruel they had been! She could admit that now. Jilly had put on a brave face at dinner, hoping above hope that they would accept her as Lewis had promised they would. Patience and dignity. That was all she had believed necessary. But now the outlook seemed thoroughly bleak.

His parents had made no secret of it—they wanted nothing to do with her. And Lewis's loyalty to her would cause a rift in the family.

The carriage drew to a halt. The moment the door was opened and the step lowered, Jillian was out and up the stairs like a fox that had escaped a snare. She tore up the staircase, not caring who saw her undignified progress up the three flights.

She knocked briskly at Ellena's door and pushed it open as soon as she heard answer. Her friend looked up in surprise as Jilly crossed the thickly carpeted floor and threw herself onto the settee where Ellena had been occupied with some sewing. Jilly—the strength that had held her together now depleted—collapsed in a hopeless bundle, her head in Ellena's lap, tears at last wrenching from her, her shoulders shaking as Ellena put her arm around them in a maternal fashion.

"Whatever is the matter, Jilly?" she asked. "What has happened?"

But Jilly could not find the words to explain. She sobbed until her head ached more than her heart. Then, slowly, she sat herself up, fishing for her handkerchief and using it in a most unladylike fashion to blow her nose.

"You were right," she said dolefully. "They will never accept me."

Ellena shook her head. "That is not what I said. Though I am sorry to hear the dinner has not gone well. I merely indicated that they would struggle to understand Lewis's choice. Given time, they will make peace with it. You have taken on an unspoken rule of society, and those who choose to live by such rules will take umbrage at the challenge. If you are patient, and show them your best self, they will see that you are good for him. Since you are betrothed, they cannot undo the public contract between you without shaming the family."

"But they think that our union shames the family too. And now that Lewis's brother is dead, they will..."

Ellena froze. "What did you say?"

Jilly began to cry again, burying her head in her hands. "The constables came," she mumbled through her fingers. "It was awful, Ellie. He'd been murdered! And then Lady Bradford said I couldn't marry Lewis since he was their heir now. And his father wanted to cut him off even before that. And Lewis said he would disown them, and…"

"Take a breath, Jilly dear," Ellena said soothingly as Jilly hic-cupped between sobs.

Jillian obeyed, sucking in a lungful of air with a ragged stacca-to.

"And out again," urged her friend, guiding her gradually back to calm.

"Now," said Ellena when Jillian had regained some of her equilibrium, "start at the beginning, and tell me everything."

CHAPTER EIGHT

L EWIS RODE TO Munro House almost every day. It was an act of devotion to Jillian, but also a persistent need to escape his mother's obsession with Philip. While the entire household was numb with loss—even Lewis and Penelope had felt the strangeness of their brother's absence, memories surfacing now that held not only bitterness but scatterings of tenderness—the baroness had taken it the hardest. She had sat vigil with his coffin for two days before her husband had demanded she take rest. She had refused. The doctor had to be called to administer a sedative so that she could be carried to her bed. Never in all Lewis's adult years had their mother taken breakfast with them, always complaining about the morning chill upon her bones. But she sat beside the body of her firstborn right through the night, without a word of the discomfort she must have been suffering.

On Friday, she awoke to find the coffin gone. Lord Bradford had sent for the undertaker to collect and keep the remains until the day of the funeral to force his wife to sleep at night. Instead, she wandered the hallways like a restless spirit with nothing on which to focus her attention or help her sleep. Another doctor's visit. More sedation.

And then, on Sunday, she rose and called for her lady's maid, who dressed her with care so that she might look her best for the funeral service. Then she sent for Lewis and received him with a straight back and clipped tones that were reminiscent of the stern matriarch she had always been.

"It occurs to me," she said, "that Miss Kinsey may have planned to attend the service."

"She has," answered Lewis, wondering where this was going.

"And that she might intend to be by your side at the cemetery."

"That is so."

"You will tell her it is out of the question."

Lewis stiffened. "And why is that?"

"I do not want her there."

"But *I* do."

"You will do this for me. I want no distraction when I lay my firstborn to rest. There is no knowing what Miss Kinsey will do at such a solemn occasion. She is unaccustomed to it. This is not the time or place for country manners. I *will* have dignity at Philip's graveside. I want to grieve in peace."

"And who will support me in *my* grief?"

Lady Bradford pinned her son with a savage gaze. "I hardly know that you feel any."

Lewis jerked his head up at his mother's harsh words, ready to defend himself, only to find her eyes pooled with sorrow. His hackles subsided.

"No one can feel the same pain as a mother who's lost a child," he said, and meant it. "That does not imply that I feel *nothing*. You have Father to comfort you. I would like similar support."

"Your sister can play that role. For now."

"I would prefer the comfort of my intended."

"And you shall have it. But it will not be Miss Kinsey."

An increasingly familiar surge of outrage rose in Lewis's throat. "You are wrong, Mother," he said through tight lips.

Lady Bradford continued, unbothered by his response or the tone of it. "It was bad enough when you considered her a suitable bride for a second son, but it is quite impossible now that you bear the future of the barony on your shoulders. You will give serious thought to Miss Sangford."

"What about her?" Lewis was genuinely confused.

"Philip was on the cusp of proposing to her. Our families are well acquainted with each other. I believe she would be amenable to the suggestion."

"What suggestion? I don't follow your meaning."

Lady Bradford pinned him with a stern look. "Don't be obtuse, Lewis. I mean for you to propose to her, obviously."

In spite of the insult of the notion, Lewis gave a burst of laughter. "You cannot be serious!"

"But I am." His mother continued the discussion as if she were making the simplest of arrangements. "She was perfect for Philip and will be for you. It will ease her disappointment in losing Philip and save you having to search for a bride."

"'Dis… *Disappointment*'?" Lewis spluttered. "You think that is an apt description for her losing the man who would likely have married her?"

"Well, I'm not convinced they were in love. But they were well matched. And she expected to marry our heir. As far as that goes, she still can. And she would know how to play the role to perfection."

Lewis stared at his mother. He could hardly find the words. His mouth hung open and he blinked several times before saying. "It may have escaped your notice, Mother, but I am already engaged."

Lady Bradford waved a dismissive hand. "Oh, no one can take that betrothal seriously. It will be seen as a temporary madness— one quickly remedied by the better choice of Miss Sangford. Not only will your judgment be restored in the public eye, but the bringing of Miss Sangford into our fold will make perfect sense in view of the loss of Philip."

"It doesn't to me!" Lewis all but shouted.

His mother folded her hands in her lap. "Come now, my son, you are going to have a position of great importance. Miss Kinsey cannot possibly contribute to your public image, which will now be paramount."

Ah, yes. *Now* he was important. He, who was as nothing before. Still, he did not feel it was *he* who carried a sense of worth. He was merely a stand-in for Philip, fulfilling *his* role, *his* dreams. He was as good as rebaptized into the name and position that had belonged to Philip. Lewis was being all but absorbed into the life that had belonged to his brother. It was as if his parents did not see him anymore, but Philip reincarnate. Despite his new rank and privilege, he felt more invisible than ever before.

But he was not as impotent as they might have thought. Their desperation to bestow on him the status of heir gave him power he had not had before. Since they demanded he claim it, he would show them that he knew how to wield it.

"I have no intention of proposing to Miss Sangford, though I will offer her my sincere condolences. I am marrying Miss Kinsey. And that is the end of it. Feel free to disown me. I can make my own way. I don't need your money. I have no need of your title. And I have had enough years of being in Philip's shadow that I am accustomed to having no real relationship with you. Do your worst. But you will not shake me from my purpose. And if Miss Kinsey may not attend the funeral, then neither shall I. Society's opinion be damned. If they think something is amiss, they will simply have picked up on the truth. Now, make up your mind, Mother, and do it quickly. Do I fetch Miss Kinsey to join us? Or do I collect my belongings and leave?"

Lady Bradford glared at him. Lewis glared back. Her head vibrated slightly, as if she were about to burst with indignation. Then, all of a sudden, she twisted her face to the side and glared at the floor instead.

"Very well," she said.

"Very well *what*?" Lewis wanted to know.

Her gaze remained on the floor. "Very well, I will not speak of Miss Kinsey's presence again. You may do as you wish."

"Thank you, Mother."

Lewis stood to leave. His mother raised her sight to him. It contained little by way of love, but Lewis was undeterred. He had love enough with Miss Kinsey.

"Will you at least have the wedding in Munro?" she asked.

Lewis hesitated. This might have been an olive branch between them. A consolation for her having given in to his demands.

An image flashed through his memory. Jillian, at dinner, being offered no welcome, no respect. And another, but a moment ago—his betrothed all but discarded as if she were without worth or feeling. A wedding in Munro meant countless guests who were just like his parents, tittering and judging and finding his bride lacking.

"No."

He would offer no quarter. Jillian deserved better.

"You will not even consider it?"

"No."

His mother seemed to ponder another approach. "It would be a good way to introduce your wife to society. They may get to know her and see…" She paused, as if searching for something positive to say. "The goodness you see in her."

"Such as?" Lewis would have her say it. Anything good about Jillian. If she could get it past her lips, there was hope.

"I, er… She is…young enough to mold."

Lewis straightened his back. "I see. I think we have established that Munro society is not ready for her. I will not have the wedding day spoiled by the many who think as you do."

"They will still think it once you are married," his mother pointed out.

"When she has had time to acclimatize to her new position, we will begin our introduction to a select few. The rest can think and do as they wish."

Lady Bradford could hold back no longer. "But your position! One day, you will be lord of this estate. What does Miss Kinsey know of running a home of this size? Or hosting a ball?"

Lewis smiled wryly and shook his head. "Has it occurred to you that you might teach her? You could take her under your wing. You could guide her with kindness to be capable of all these tasks. Instead, you reject her at every turn, ensuring her failure. And for what? So that you can say, 'I told you so'?"

Lady Bradford threw a disbelieving palm into the air. "I will teach her if she will listen."

"But will you be kind? She is not used to the chilly instruction we have received."

Lady Bradford's voice rose. "And what does she give in return? Does she bring her country ways? I hear she visits the kitchen in Munro House *to chat*! Will she allow herself to be taught? Or will she turn our ancient and noble home into an oversized farmhouse?"

"We can always live elsewhere," he warned. "In fact, there is a lovely house I have had my eye on…"

"Lewis Bradford! You will draw the line at how you shame this family!"

Lewis bit his tongue. His mother had reached her limit. "Perhaps, then, as a compromise, we will stay in the summer cottage by the lake," he suggested. "Until such time as you feel my wife is worthy of the great house. It will be an easier transition for Jillian and you both. We will join you for Sunday family dinners and she can come to the house and see how you manage it as often as you are both comfortable doing so. We will still be on the grounds, with room enough for everyone to breathe."

Lady Bradford was quiet for some time. Then she rose, the rustling of her black skirt the only sound in the hard silence between them.

"You have shown me where your loyalty lies. I must now bury the son who did right by me. And then I will remain in mourning. You clearly do not feel the loss of your brother, so you must do as you wish. Marry Miss Kinsey. Take her to Ermenbrough, or the moon, for all I care. We will not be attending your nuptials. I shall not be staying in some village inn to watch you degrade yourself. When you return, the summer cottage will be ready for you with a complement of servants. Now, you will excuse me. You have made this day harder in every possible way, and I need a minute to gather myself. Some of us still wish to maintain a dignified air."

Her gown swept about her feet as she departed the room. Then the air was still once more. Lewis took a step toward the door and halted. His mother was wrong. She was wrong about so many things. He *did* mourn the loss of his brother. But he had been mourning it for years. He would have loved a closer bond with Philip, but his brother had been placed on such a high pedestal that Lewis could never reach him. Now the chance was lost forever.

As for the privileges of the firstborn, Lewis had taught himself not to think about them. It would have been unhealthy to crave things he believed he would never have. Now that they were his to claim, he might have done so with great gusto. There was much about the running of the estate he had wanted to suggest to his father but had never felt he could. Now they could work side by side to further the interests of the Bradford family. He would not need to spend long hours poring over thick volumes of law. It had been a worthwhile occupation when he had had to make his own way, and he would miss elements of it. But, Lewis admitted to himself, he was grateful that he could now allow himself the luxury of more private pursuits.

Instead, his parents had ostracized Jillian and turned the rights of the heir into a series of demands, some patently ridiculous. Marry Miss Sangford, indeed!

Lewis resumed his steps, quickening his pace at the thought of seeing Jilly.

With her borrowed lady's maid in attendance.

She was being courted by the heir to a barony, after all. Not long now and a chaperone would no longer be needed…

Lewis felt the first layer of frustration fall away. He pictured Jilly's full mouth. Her green eyes so often filled with mirth. More of his agitation melted and was gone.

He could feel the tickle of her hair, its thick cascades resting against his cheek as he reached in to kiss her, his hands growing warm upon her bodice.

Lewis was almost running now. How well he understood Jillian's frequent need to break free and do the same. When the heart was full, the body likewise was roused with energy. They were too old now for cartwheels and skipping, but the desire to run and jump and dance surfaced whenever he thought of her. That, and the more intimate exertion that would follow when she wore his ring...

Jilly would be his, all his. And all he had to do was love her. She had no list of rigid rules for him to follow. She did not ask that which he was unwilling to give. He would not delay the wedding for the sake of his family who had not done the same. If anything, he wanted to marry Jillian sooner.

Today, he was saying farewell to Philip and closing the door to his past. A few weeks hence, when the banns had been called thrice, he and Jilly would be married. And he would not look back. Nothing would come between them. Never, never, ever. And the certainty of it grounded him, while his hopes soared ever up to the heavens.

CHAPTER NINE

TWO WEEKS WENT by with surprising speed. The wedding drew nearer and with its approach, Jillian's excitement grew. A part of her felt guilty for having such feelings while the Bradfords mourned. Or, at least, Lord and Lady Bradford did. Lewis never spoke about his brother to Jilly anymore. He didn't mention his parents. He only repeated, at Penelope's insistence, how sorry his sister was that she was not allowed to come to Ermenbrough for the wedding.

Every time Jillian offered to wait a few months for his family's sake, hoping they would come around to the idea of her betrothal to their son, Lewis banned further talk on the subject. At first, she had insisted they discuss it, convinced he was denying himself a better relationship with his parents. But he was adamant that, if time should change anything, it might as well happen while they were married. He was done denying himself for their sakes. He would claim what he wanted, and now. He would debate it no further. Eventually, Jillian had relented.

Once the voice of concern had been silenced, they had let joy in. It bloomed as thoughts of her family and their enthusiasm were added to the image of the day growing in their minds... They could picture the villagers lining up at the church to watch their romance unfold and reach its natural conclusion—Lewis standing before her, holding her hand, slipping a ring upon her finger to bind them forever. A humble but cheerful feast would follow. All around them would be the smiling faces of people who wished them well.

And later, when they were alone, the chance would come at last to know him fully, to claim his body as hers, to let her fingers and lips explore, her skin reveling in his touch... The mere thought made Jillian shiver with delight.

One more week. Seven more days as an unmarried woman. But she would not be spending them here at Munro House. Today, she would head back to Trenton Grange. Lewis had offered that she return home even sooner than this to grant her more time with her family, but she could no more be parted from him than from her own breath. A week without him was about as much as she could bear.

It was time to say farewell to long stays with Ellena. The next time she was in Munro, it would be for good, and she would be living on the Bradford estate with her husband.

Husband... Ah, the word made her toes curl with pleasure. The man she loved would be hers for a lifetime. To have and to hold. She couldn't wait!

Only, he was not here today. There was a case in court that needed to be finalized. He may have been the heir to the Bradford estate, but he was still a most conscientious barrister. Jillian loved that he had not changed one bit in his principles despite his shift in rank. She only wished his noble work did not keep him from her. He had promised to follow her to Ermenbrough as soon as possible, but there was a chance he might be delayed until the day before the wedding. He could not even see her off, as much as it pained him. It was a terrible blow, to have four hours in the carriage with only Ingsley for company. And to barely introduce Lewis to her family before they exchanged vows was a disappointing development.

And yet... A familiar sound drifted up from the drive. Jillian's heart fluttered with hope. She ran across to her bedroom window and peered below. Here came the Bradford carriage! It rounded the bend smartly, the horses slowing as the coachman pulled deftly on the reins.

Jillian half-expected Lewis to come flying out of the carriage, pushing past the footman and tearing up the stairs to rush into her arms, showering her with kisses to remember him by on the long road ahead.

But the carriage door was opened with the usual formality by a footman, who lowered the steps and held out a gloved hand. A woman's foot appeared on the step, black skirts flowing around her ankle.

Jillian watched in confusion as Lady Bradford emerged from the carriage like a dark moth from its cocoon. Her ladyship walked to the front door with the sort of regalness that Jillian had come to associate with her. No doubt the butler had done his job, for the lady disappeared into the entry of Munro House.

Jillian was pondering whom it might be that Lady Bradford had come to see when the butler's steps sounded upon the landing. Jillian listened carefully to discover outside whose door his footfalls should cease.

It was her own.

A knock sounded on her door.

"Come in," she said to the butler, though her thoughts were with their visitor and why she had come.

"Lady Bradford is here, Miss Kinsey, and has asked to speak with you. She is waiting in the drawing room. Shall I tell her you will see her?"

"You may," replied Jillian, her voice lacking any enthusiasm.

Branson nodded and disappeared immediately. Jillian was less quick to follow. She checked her hair in the mirror. Ingsley had done an excellent job, as always. Her gown, however, was not her best, for she would be traveling soon and had opted for comfort over aesthetics. Should she change?

No. Her choice of attire was unlikely to adjust her ladyship's opinion of her. It was better to be accepted as she was, if she was to be accepted at all.

Jillian descended the stairs rather more sedately than usual. There was nothing to hurry for, nothing to pull her into the exuberant display that characterized her more typical movements. Instead, a seemingly endless following of the banister's curve brought her at last to the ground floor. Jillian inspected her dress. All was in place. Likely, her cheeks displayed a healthy flush. There was nothing for it but to proceed.

Lady Bradford was standing facing the doorway when Jillian entered the drawing room. It was not a conversational posture, nor did she appear to have come for a social call. She regarded Jillian as if she had caught her with her hand in the honey jar and was about to administer a stern scolding.

Jillian almost forgot to curtsey as she greeted the unsmiling visitor. She remembered her manners just in time. "Will you have a seat?" she offered. "I can call for tea." She indicated the bell pull.

"That is not necessary," Lady Bradford replied stiffly, though she did take the proffered chair. "I will not be staying long."

"I see," answered Jillian, though she honestly had no idea what she was supposed to see.

"I will come straight to the point," her ladyship said.

Jillian was only too grateful for it. If the mood in the room was any indication, the sooner this meeting was over, the better it would be.

"You are aware of my misgivings about your pending nuptials."

Jillian nodded. No surprises there, then.

"I have promised my son I would no longer discuss the matter with him. He has closed his mind to all reason."

Jillian could just imagine the conversation that had transpired between mother and son, if it could be called a conversation at all. She decided it was wise to make no comment. Instead, she waited for Lady Bradford to reveal her intentions.

"I am therefore silenced by my son in my own home. But I have made no such commitment to you."

Ah, so it was *that* sort of visit.

Lady Bradford folded her hands in front of her. "I understand you are leaving Munro today."

"I am hoping to spend some time with my family before I am married, yes."

"And they are satisfied that the wedding should take place?"

"Yes. They are very happy for us." Jillian let the words hang in the air.

"Why is that?" came the brusque response.

"Why are they happy for us?" Jillian found the question incredible. "They *love* us. What other reason could there be?"

Lady Bradford turned her head askew and looked at Jilly through one squinted eye. "But they have not even met Lewis. Why would they consider the match a favorable one?"

"I have written many letters praising your son's excellent qualities," she answered. "They have no cause to doubt my judgment. You must know what a fine gentleman he is."

Lady Bradford's mouth flattened into a line and her brows lifted with what Jillian took to be feigned curiosity. "And do those excellent qualities include his wealth and position?" she asked pointedly.

So, she would be crass enough to state her insinuation as bluntly as that.

"I have told you before," Jilly retorted. "Lewis is enough for me, regardless of his income, inheritance, or status."

"'Enough'?" Lady Bradford scoffed. "I should say so, indeed! *More* than enough, wouldn't you agree? But are *you* enough for him? What do you offer in exchange for all that you gain?"

Jillian wished she could banish this endless inquisition as Lewis had done, but she had no authority to make such demands as the supposed interloper. There was nothing for it but to answer as honestly and as patiently as possible. What *did* she offer for the gift that was Lewis? The answer, truly, was a simple one.

"Exactly what he offers me: a devoted heart." She was rather proud of how calmly she had spoken. Surely, a mother would wish mutual affection for her son?

"And that is all?"

Jillian could stand it no longer. She waved her arm about in frustration. "That is *everything*! In fact, Lewis knows that to offer me more would only make me uncomfortable. I have not known a lavish life and do not wish for one now. Your fears are quite unfounded."

"There is little comfort in what you say," Lady Bradford answered grimly. "For, if you do not wish for the life of a baroness, you cannot be what Lewis needs. He may not have expected the role that has been thrust upon him, but he must bear it with fortitude. And his wife must support him. She cannot be living in a cottage and baking little homely pies like some woodcutter's wife in a fairy tale. He is the heir to aristocracy. You will only shame him with your naïve desire for skipping in fields. Surely, you must see that?"

Jillian gritted her teeth. "I can manage myself well enough in the public eye, as the need arises. And if, as you say, I wish to skip naively in my own time, why should it trouble anyone? Why is it nobler to embroider or play the pianoforte?"

"Because," said Lady Bradford with an undisguised effort at patience, "these activities display skill and years of dedication to their craft. They speak of a mind that is disciplined and a body that is under its owner's control. And you lack these essential qualities entirely."

"Lewis doesn't seem to care," Jillian said stubbornly.

Lady Bradford closed her eyes and took a testy breath. "That is because he believes he is rebelling against us. You are but a means to secure animosity between us—a punishment because he did not benefit from being the first born. I am disappointed at his churlishness, but I am convinced he will sober with age. And when we are gone, the responsibility of his father's name and ancestral home will suddenly feel heavy and real. Then he will wish he had chosen differently. And the childlike feelings you now share will dissolve into resentment and frustration. For he *will* rise to his position. It is just a matter of time."

Lady Bradford sighed heavily. "I say this as much to protect you as I do to protect Lewis from himself. You cannot understand the world you are entering. You think you can skirt around its edges. But it will envelop you, overwhelm and consume you, for you are not educated to manage it. Lewis is cruel to lie to you as much as he lies to himself."

For the first time, a crack appeared in Jillian's armor. A sliver of doubt had pierced it and might, at any second, drive deeper and breech her heart. Lady Bradford must have sensed it, because she smiled sympathetically and said, "It is hard to hear the truth. I understand. And you now grasp why I have stood between you. Let me soften the blow. I can give you a goodly sum to spend as you wish. Perhaps you might even buy a pony upon which to lavish your affection while your hopes for a life with Lewis fade in time. Or you might consider some furniture to make your parents more comfortable. Is that something you would like?"

Lady Bradford sounded so sincere, Jillian believed she truly meant it all with the best of intentions. But she had underestimated how determined Jilly was to marry her son.

"I thought by now, you would know that money means nothing to me, Lady Bradford. It could never replace the love I feel for Lewis."

"Tch, what does a woman scarcely of age know about love?" her ladyship bit back irritably. "It is a word too easily thrown about. Love is more than kisses and a racing pulse."

Jillian's walls came up once more. How could such a cold woman understand the depths of love? She bristled silently.

Lady Bradford stopped and gathered herself. "Of course, if that is what matters, I could assist you in finding a different, but equally promising match. There are several handsome footmen who might set your heart going, and a tidy sum as dowry could set you up very comfortably. A man like that would not need you to be something you are not. There can be as much *skipping* as you desire."

"I think..." said Jilly, trying her very best to remain civil, "I think it is best if you go now. You have had your say, and not for the first time. I am convinced you think you act in your son's best interests, but I am equally certain you have no idea what they are. I will not give him up. Nor should I have to. I have accepted that I will not be beloved in your eyes. But I remain hopeful that time will soften the enmity between us. Perhaps, when you gauge how truly happy Lewis is…"

"Oh, he is happy," her ladyship said bitterly. "He is absolutely delighted that he has found a way to torment us. The question is rather what *you* will do when he has had his fill of throwing tantrums and takes on the role of gentleman more fully. It will be no comfort for me to say I told you so. Just remember, Miss Kinsey, marriage vows are forever. Take care that you have not imprisoned yourself with them."

And, with that, Lady Bradford stood quite suddenly and walked straight past Jillian as if she no longer existed. The sound of brushing silk receded rapidly. The front door opened and closed. Less than a minute later, carriage wheels crunched on the gravel of the drive until this sound, too, vanished into silence.

Jilly balled her fists. Trust Lewis's mother to spoil a day that should have been filled with excitement and joyful apprehension at seeing her own family again. If only Lady Bradford were more like them. She would not, then, be shunning her son's wedding or trying to bribe his betrothed to break it off with him.

Thank goodness she and Lewis would be staying in the summer cottage once they were wed! Jilly did not relish the thought of Sunday dinners with the Bradfords, but at least their interactions would be limited to a few hours a week. She was certain Lady Bradford shared this sentiment.

"Is everything all right?" came the worried voice of Ellena from the doorway of the drawing room. "I saw the carriage and thought perhaps Lewis had managed to swing by after all. But your face tells a different story. Has something happened?" Ellena stepped closer and seated herself carefully next to Jillian, her subtle perfume touching the air as Jillian breathed it in. "Do you want to talk about it?"

Did she? Jillian considered the question. Ellena shared many of the same concerns as Lady Bradford, although she remained loyal despite her misgivings. Even if Ellena said nothing, her reservations would be displayed unambiguously across her facial features. And Jillian was in no mood for it.

"It was Lady Bradford."

Ellena's body stiffened. "She was not unkind to you, I hope. It would be a tremendous impudence to come to our home with the purpose of insulting you even further."

"She seemed worried about me." Jilly shrugged. "The insult simply followed naturally."

Ellena considered this in silence. "Will she interfere with the wedding?" she asked with some concern.

"Not after today. We may never be friends, but I *shall* be her daughter-in-law. She has a week to accept the idea. Or she can choose to reject it for all time. But she will not stand in the way of our happiness."

"Jilly…" Ellena laid a cautious hand upon her friend's. "You *will* try to make peace with her, won't you? Lewis might bluster about how little he cares for their opinions, but they are still his family. If there is a chance for these high emotions to subside, you will encourage it, won't you?"

"Of course," said Jillian a little irritably, "though I could take umbrage at such a question. You know me better than to ask such a thing. It is not *I* who keeps bringing up reasons for future unhappiness. If I knew how to please her—other than abandoning Lewis—I would do it."

Ellena lowered her gaze. "I'm sorry to have asked it. And I'm sorrier still not to attend your wedding. You know I cannot yet travel with little Christopher, and I am not ready to be without him. But I understand that you are eager to wed. Else I would have asked you to be patient. It is a great pity that you could be at my wedding, but I cannot do the same for you."

Jillian fell back at once to her old habit of soothing her once-lonely friend. "Ah, now, you look about as miserable as you did the day you left Trenton Grange to be married. All worry and misery. And look how well it all turned out in the end! By contrast, I have every reason to be happy on the day. My parents have let me choose my own groom. And I have most of the village and my three brothers to cheer me on. Goodness knows which of those two parties will be the rowdiest in their support!"

She squeezed Ellena's hand. "I will miss you, but I know you will be with me in spirit. Besides, I shall be back in Munro within the month. You shall hear all my news from the source." Her face creased with a broad grin. "We might even invite ourselves over for Twelfth Night celebrations if Lord and Lady Bradford have not forgiven us just yet. Better to be in the company of friends if his family is still sulking."

"You will be more than welcome," Ellena assured her, "though I hope it does not come to that. With your own family such a distance away, it would be a blessing to have the comfort of a new one in Munro. Even if they are a little stuffy."

Jillian shot her friend a determined look. "If anyone can rid them of said stuffiness, I feel amply qualified. If it were up to me, I would have them all dancing a reel around the Christmas tree." She clapped her hands. "They will have one, don't you think? I hear several of the noble families have taken on this German tradition. I have never seen one, but they sound beautiful! Maybe even your parents will decorate one at Trenton Grange. They certainly have enough trees to choose from on their estate."

"My father would never dream of it!" Ellena exclaimed. "You know how tight-fisted he is. For all his wealth, he will never spend a single coin without considering if it can be spared. Mother and I even had to share a lady's maid. I'm amazed you have forgotten."

Jilly shook her head. "I never understood the fuss about a lady's maid until I came to Munro. I simply brushed my hair and dressed myself. There seemed little else to it. But a lady of the *ton*'s style of hair and garment is so much more complex. So many laces and ribbons in out-of-reach places! I hope Lewis knows how to undress me on our wedding night!"

"Jilly, you are incorrigible!" Ellena laughed. "Your husband will certainly have his hands full with you!"

"I should hope so! And I don't think he would mind that at all! I am grateful that we shall have the seclusion of the cottage, that he may chase me about the house and I may let him catch me…"

Ellena pretended to be shocked at such forward speech, but Jilly knew she understood these natural feelings. She therefore felt no need to force a blush upon her cheeks. Instead, she continued with her scandalous honesty. "Our servants will have many an afternoon off to allow such chases to occur in private. They shall like very much to be employed by us."

"Stop!" Ellena was still laughing, but she was making every effort to bring herself under control, her eyes wide with alarm. "My own servants are everywhere. They would love nothing better than to share such morsels of salacious gossip with each other."

"Oh, I have probably said as much to their faces." Jillian shrugged.

"You haven't!" Ellena's eyes grew large with horror, her mouth stalled in a half-open pose.

"You know very well I am cut more from their cloth than yours. This is how we simple folk talk."

Ellena's expression was serious now, all trace of laughter gone from her voice. "Promise me you will not continue this habit in your new home. Lady Bradford will not have the same ease with her staff as we have with ours. You will lose their respect if you are too familiar with them. And once lost, it will be impossible to win back. Worse yet, they might feel inclined to report your conversations and actions to her ladyship. She might even make it worth their while, if you catch my meaning. By all means, be yourself in private. But do not consider a room containing a servant to be private at all."

"Well, that's put a damper on things." Jillian pouted. But only for a moment. Then her eyes lit up and she cried, "Do you remember when I ran beside your carriage as you left Trenton Grange for the last time as an unmarried woman? Wouldn't it be funny if you did the same for me—skirts hitched up, hair fighting their pins to stay put, Lord Howell hollering at us to behave in front of the staff... Oh, I wish you would say you were going to do it just to see him do *that thing*... you know, when he wants to correct us but also wants to be kind about it. And his face does that sort of rippling as he struggles for the right expression that balances tact with order. He is such a darling. Oh, do say you'll do it."

"I most certainly will not! The poor dear already has his hands full with the two of us. And he has been respectfully silent on the whole topic of your betrothal, even though you know his concerns. We shan't torment him."

Jilly grew still. "You are right. That was thoughtless of me. I take it back at once. I appreciate that he has not made the same sort of fuss that the Bradfords have."

Ellena looked at Jilly without mirth. "He does not have as much to lose," she said softly.

"I still don't understand why I should be such a threat to them."

Ellena opened her mouth to explain, but Jilly spoke quickly. "No, no, don't tell me. I've heard enough on that subject this morning. Now I want to talk about weddings. And wedding nights..." Her eyes twinkled with mischief.

"I think we will need some tea to wash down such heated conversation," said Ellena, rising to pull the bell ribbon.

"Oh, and a biscuit or two with which to fortify ourselves," added Jilly.

"And we will have them sent to my room, where we may continue without the risk of an audience," insisted Ellena.

"Race you up the stairs!" Jilly leaped from her chair toward the door.

"You're cheating!" complained Ellena, giving the bellpull a hefty tug. "I still have to give the servants our instructions!"

"We can send for them upstairs. Come on!" And, for the last time, Jillian Kinsey allowed herself to race up the majestic staircase of Munro House, with the viscountess puffing with breathless laughter as she stumbled to keep up.

CHAPTER TEN

Oakwoods, late October 1815

L EWIS HAD JUST settled himself in the carriage when a squawk of alarm sounded outside. The footman lurched from the rearward-facing seat and ran in an odd, clenched sort of way toward the privy near the kitchen garden.

Poor fellow, thought Lewis. It was just as well the man tended to such unfortunate business before they left on their lengthy journey to Ermenbrough.

If they ever left.

The morning had suffered one delay after the other. If Lewis didn't know better, he would have wondered if his parents had taken steps to undermine his plans. First, Lewis's valet had discovered that his master's trunk had been tampered with and found one of Miss Bradford's dresses tucked inside it. No one could explain how it had ended up there and an hour had been lost interrogating the maidservants.

Then the footman who'd been assigned to the carriage had had his luggage vanish completely. It had only been a valise and probably contained little more than the young lad's change of uniform and toiletries, but without it, he would not be able to join the traveling party. The bag had reappeared just as mysteriously more than an hour later. Packing had resumed, and Miss Bradford had given the rattled footman a stiff drink to aid his relief.

By now, the entire household was distressed and Lady Bradford started making comments about the wedding upsetting their family even before it had begun. Lewis had decided to wait in the safety of the carriage so that he did not have to witness another outburst. Instead, he saw the footman seeking the urgent relief of the privy and knew that another delay was inevitable.

Sure enough, a kitchen maid soon emerged from that general direction and announced that the footman needed his valise for a change of trousers. The driver handed the bag down to her. Lewis closed his eyes and tried to shrink the distance between himself and Jillian with his mind. Time ticked by.

At last, Lewis felt the dip of the carriage suspension as the footman climbed back up to his seat, followed by a light thump as the man deposited his valise on the roof. The coachman clicked his tongue, and the horses tugged at the weighty resistance of the vehicle. The wheels turned slowly at first, then gathered momentum until the horses were trotting and the carriage sailed along easily.

Lewis sat alone with his thoughts. He had specifically rejected the notion of taking his valet with him. Taking the footman was more than enough. In Ermenbrough, he wanted to draw as little attention as possible to the difference in status between his family and the Kinseys. He would take a room at the posting inn, eat simple meals, walk wherever he could. He wanted no focus drawn to his wealth and rank. He was there as Jillian's betrothed, not her superior.

He had given his man two weeks' leave, starting the moment the carriage left the drive. A long-overdue trip to the country to visit his family was well-deserved. It made Lewis happy to think that his joy at marrying Jillian could be extended to such a fine fellow.

Besides, he would far rather his bride undress him on their honeymoon…

His mouth twitched as he remembered the sweet taste of Jillian's skin. Thus far, he had savored her lips, her eyelids, her neck, the tender skin inside her forearm. But there was much of her he had not yet sampled. He would have his fill. Time together in the carriage would simply fly by, the bumpy road barely noticed as they were lost in each other's arms.

For now, though, time could not pass fast enough. It felt an eternity rather than the two hours before they eventually reached the halfway point and changed horses. The footman seemed to have recovered sufficiently from his previous ailment, for he jumped briskly from his seat to open the door and lower the steps. He bowed rather deeper than usual and did not straighten until Lewis had passed, at which point Lewis could have sworn the fellow had shrunk several inches. He wrote his odd observations off to fatigue, shrugged them off mentally, and set off on a quick leg-stretch around the premises.

Within twenty minutes, they were ready to depart once more. Lewis was now so excited to be on the last leg of the journey that he could not care less if the footman danced a jig. He did, for a moment, take pity on the fellow, for he remembered his own distaste for the barrister's wig and did not envy the footman for having to wear a similar wig all day. The things itched something awful and needed constant care. Perhaps replacing his time at court with a position in the House of Commons would not be so bad if the wig could be got rid of. Lewis had to admit: being an heir to the aristocracy had its benefits.

Despite his enthusiasm at seeing Jilly and knowing less than a day stood between them and their nuptials, Lewis dozed off. The carriage swayed and the suspension dulled much of the road's assault upon the carriage wheels. Lewis slept deep and long, waking quite suddenly as the sounds of busy village life broached his ears.

The next onslaught upon his senses was the smell of pigs. He opened his eyes and drew his kerchief to his nose in haste. Mercifully, the carriage proceeded onward and away from the porcine odor, though the vehicle's course had slowed, its path being shared by folk going about their business and mothers chasing children who were not looking where they were going.

Lewis tugged the curtain string, and the dropped weight of the heavy velvet drapery shut both the view and the light out with immediate effect. The pungency of Ermenbrough also lessened, allowing Lewis to draw a deeper breath and gather himself.

So, this was the place his darling Jillian called home. Though their family cottage was on the grounds of Trenton Grange, *this* was the heartbeat of the community. These were her people. This was where she felt most comfortable. Lewis cautiously lifted the curtain again. He needed to learn. He needed to know what it was that made her happy.

A clod of mud splattered against the side of the coach. Lewis withdrew his head like a tortoise into the safety of the coach cubicle.

"Charlie Smith!" screeched a woman's voice, or at least what Lewis assumed was a woman. It was hard to tell, for the sound was rough and the person coughed spasmodically between phrases of chastisement. "If I've told you once..." *cough, cough...* "I've told you a thousand times..." *cough, a-sound-Lewis-thought-likely-to-be-a-projectile-of-spit, cough...*

And then he heard nothing more as the coach drew him farther up the main street.

Now the road widened as they approached the upper end of town. More glass made up the shopfronts and the signs were not hanging off their hinges. Lewis breathed out his relief. *This* was the part of Ermenbrough that Jilly would have spent time in. Here people walked more sedately, their attire more well-kept, their faces clean. Children held their mother's hands or, if they were older, carried her basket for her while she haggled with a merchant. Although there were no gentlemen with top hats and coattails, there were good, honest working men in wool jackets and caps, and young ladies whose happy faces suggested they had no idea their fashions were outdated or their dresses very plain. They looked like the sort of couples where the fellow might grab his partner by the waist and twirl with her because their hearts were fit to bursting with love for one another. There were women who patted their swollen bellies with shy pride. Children played with sticks or marbles instead of sitting on a pony while a footman might lead them up and down a lawn behind the stables. Lewis liked what he saw very much.

The carriage pulled to a halt outside the inn, a wholesome building of stone probably as old as the Oakwoods manor but without any of the same pomp. It stood with homely dignity, welcoming the traveler to a simple roof, a hot meal, and a comfortable bed of straw for his horse.

The footman was about to open the door when Lewis slid the windowpane down to give the lad instructions for their stay. The startled lad locked eyes with him before dipping his head away. But it was too late. Lewis knew what he had seen.

"Penelope?"

"The 'footman' looked up guiltily. With her identity discovered, the disguise appeared to poor effect. Lewis could not understand how he had not noticed before. She stood wrong for a footman. She was too short. Her uniform was too tight across the chest. And once you saw her dark-blue eyes, there was no mistaking the fierce stubbornness that was iconically Bradford.

"Get in here immediately!" he hissed.

"Are you inviting a footman into your carriage?" His sister sucked in her lips to hide her smile. "Whatever will the people say?"

"What are you doing here?" demanded Lewis. "And if you say, 'Opening your carriage door,' I shall pull your hair as the imp you are deserves."

She shrugged. "Isn't it obvious? I wanted to come to the wedding."

Lewis gaped at her. "I'm already at loggerheads with our parents because of my choices. Now you would add kidnapping to my charges."

"But I came willingly," protested Penelope. "It took a great deal of planning, you know. Women can't just up and ride off on a whim as men can. Besides, I left a letter. By now, they are bewailing ever having had such a daughter and probably hoping I never come home, which suits me perfectly. I like Ermenbrough." She looked down the cobbled street. "It's quaint. It seems a pleasant place to become a spinster."

"Don't you dare!" Lewis nearly choked at the thought. "I will hire a companion and send you straight home. Mother will not be holding *your* actions against me as well."

Penelope folded her arms and opened her mouth to argue, but Lewis cut her off. "Footmen don't sulk at their masters."

Penelope dropped her arms to her sides and glared at her brother.

He wasn't having it. "What do you think will happen to the poor servant whose place you took? He will no doubt be given the sack."

"Oh, no," Pen said rather proudly. "I thought it all through very carefully. First, I stole his bag and did a few minimal adjustments to his spare uniform. Footmen are monstrously tall, you know. I had to take in almost a third of the trouser legs! Then I gave him a dose of Father's gout medicine in a drink. It's always been a thorough purgative. When he made for the privy, I tied a string around the latch so that he couldn't get out again. I sent a maid for his valise, saying his motions had gotten the better of him and he needed to change his clothes. Instead, I changed into them and put my own dress and shoes in his bag. I had a much prettier gown in mind, but your valet was far too vigilant, and I had to make do with what I could. So, you see, our parents will have the letter which explains everything, and the footman will be cleared of all wrongdoing. Am I not the cleverest of sisters?"

Lewis had to admit, it was a well-hatched plan. But he was never going to give her the satisfaction of saying it out loud.

"Thanks to you, I have no actual footman with me," he complained. "And how am I to explain your sudden appearance in your lady's attire?"

Penelope had an easy answer for that, too. "I will request two rooms for the Bradford party and say that the lady—that is to say, me—has traveled with you—which is true—and that I, the footman, am taking your luggage up. Although," she said, tilting her head, "come to think of it, I may need help with that. The trunk looks heavy." Her brief frown evaporated, and she struck a very un-footmanlike pose. "It won't be long before Miss Penelope Bradford emerges triumphant in her glory from the room. And if the naughty footman has then run off to be with a village girl, we can but ask if there is a willing lad a trifle shorter than the usual fare who wishes to earn a few coins for the duration of our stay."

"First of all," said Lewis, "you might want to tuck your hips and straighten up. I have never seen such a deplorable attempt at faking a footman. Secondly, if I let you stay for the wedding, this is to be the end of your mischief. You will act like a lady and arrange no more schemes behind my back. Are we clear?"

"Ugh, you sound just like Philip."

The words were out before she could stop them, but the way she froze told Lewis she had regretted saying them immediately.

"I didn't mean…"

"Leave it." Lewis looked away. "Just make the arrangements for the rooms. I am tired."

"Lewis." Penelope put her hands on the edge of the window frame. "I'm sorry."

"I know."

"I won't be a bother. I just wanted to share your special day."

"I know."

"Will we take the carriage up to Trenton Grange later? Once we've hired a temporary footman?"

Lewis turned toward her and found the hope in her eyes that he knew would be there. He cheered up in spite of himself. He, too, had been looking forward to meeting the Kinseys. It would be all the more special for having his incorrigible sister with him.

"I think we will walk," he said. "I do not want our presence to cause a fuss. But right now, I want to rest. I want to be my best when we meet the rest of Jillian's family."

"They're going to love you," Penelope said softly.

"Shoo now," said Lewis, but a tiny smile had returned. "You are a very precocious footman."

IT WAS MID-AFTERNOON when Lewis and Penelope arrived at Trenton Grange, having followed a pretty path through the very meadow Jillian had referred to countless times. Though Lewis was not the skipping type, he could easily see Jilly being her nymphlike self in these surroundings. Even in late October, the grass was still a lush green, and the trees, though some had begun to change color, were heavy with foliage. Lewis imagined that there were many months when the ground was carpeted with wildflowers, including the daisies that Jilly loved to weave into a crown.

The transition to the formal grounds of Trenton Grange was equally stirring. The landscape was alive with color and fragrance, despite the lateness of the season. The delicate, tendrilled petals of the Guernsey lily, the mustard shades of chrysanthemum, pale-pink clusters of yarrow, the musky scent of roses, and a profusion of sweet peas pervaded the senses from flowerbeds and wall trellises alike.

Lewis couldn't help but notice the stark contrast to Oakwoods, which slept moodily through the colder months, doing nothing to draw the eye from the gray tones of the stone-clad house. But here Mr. Kinsey and his helpers had worked a special kind of magic. It certainly put one in the state of mind for a wedding.

After admiring the garden and the groundskeeper's handiwork, Lewis and his sister inquired as to where they might find the home of the Kinseys. It was not far from the main house and belonged to a cluster of cottages at the edge of the formal grounds. A low wall led up to the nearest one. As the pair approached, two heads popped up from behind the wall.

"Who are you?" asked the head that seemed to belong to a taller body.

"Do you like hazelnuts?" asked the shorter head. Its owner clambered up onto the wall, perched cross-legged on its broad surface, and held out a rather grubby hand filled with the nuts in question.

"Er, no thank you," said Lewis. "Is Miss Kinsey home?"

"Who's asking?" demanded the first head before the lad it belonged to vaulted over the wall and planted himself in the path before them. "Did the Bradfords send you? She's getting married tomorrow and no one is going to spoil it for her, so you can just clear off." The threat was made so quietly and matter-of-factly that Lewis did not for a moment doubt the lad's intention to carry it through.

Penelope, on the other hand, apparently found it adorable. "Oh, Lewis, what a charming little bodyguard!" she cried, her fingers resting on her bosom. "So, this is where the real gentlemen have been hiding. No wonder I could not find a worthy husband in Munro. They have been in Ermenbrough all along."

"Oy," said the lad, taking a step back. "I'm only nine! I ain't ready to be nobody's husband."

Penelope looked about ready to pinch the boy's cheeks, and he hastily backed away a few more steps.

Lewis extended a hand. "You must be Jack. Jilly has told me all about you. I am Lewis Bradford, soon to be your brother-in-law. And this is Miss Penelope Bradford, my sister, and yours, too, from tomorrow."

"Cor!" said the smaller boy through a mouthful of hazelnuts. "Our new sister is ever so pretty!" With that, he jumped down from the wall and came to slip his sticky, little hand into Penelope's. "I'm Timothy," he said. "But you can call me 'Timmy' because we're going to be family."

Penelope didn't seem to mind the gooey fingers wrapped

around hers in the least. "Then you shall call me 'Pen,' as Lewis does when he is fond of me." She winked at both boys. "I hope *you* shall be fond of me."

For Timmy, this seemed to be a *fait accompli*. But Jack was decidedly less sure. He shook Penelope's hand suspiciously. If it were going anywhere near his cheeks, he was clearly ready to run. He reclaimed his hand and stepped back to a safer position. "Follow me. I'll take you to Jilly. She's helping our mum in the kitchen. Sam is with Da', but they'll be home soon for some grub."

The little assembly trooped after Jack as he pushed open the door to the cottage. They wiped their feet carefully with some straw placed outside for this very purpose to avoid traipsing mud onto the meticulously clean floor.

The room they entered was a good size, but it needed to be, as it served as sitting room, dining room, and kitchen combined. Jilly, her hair tucked under a cap, was just turning in their direction and straightening up with a hot bread tin in her dishcloth-protected hands. Her face, already pink with the heat of the oven, brightened even further at the sight of them.

"Oh!" she cried. "You're here!" A quick dance followed as she wrapped the hot tin in the rag and placed it upon the table before trying to maneuver her mother away from the stove. "Leave the soup, Mum. You can spare a minute without it burning. Lewis is here! *And* Miss Bradford!"

Mrs. Kinsey spun 'round, soup ladle raised and dripping, her face creasing into a smile remarkably like Jillian's. Her daughter retrieved the ladle from her and dropped it back into the saucepan while Mrs. Kinsey wiped her hands upon her apron. They both stepped around the table, the mother bobbing a shy and unnecessary curtsey while Jilly flung herself into Lewis's arms.

"I've missed you terribly!"

"And I you," he murmured into her cap.

She leaned away from him a little to see Penelope. "I'm so glad you have come. I felt simply awful that Lewis would have no family here." A thought struck her. "Would you like to see my dress?"

"I would love to," answered Penelope, "but I must grant my brother a longer stay in your company, for he has sorely missed you. We shall talk of dresses when he has sated himself with your presence."

"That will never happen," Lewis declared, smitten fellow that he was.

Jack pulled a face. He sidestepped the small crowd and made his way with quiet determination to the steaming, fresh bread. He was stealthily unwrapping it when Timmy pointed a finger and announced, "Jack is at the bread again," before beaming proudly up at Penelope for his traitor's reward.

"Jack! That is our dinner!" his mother scolded before turning back to her guests. "He's a growing boy, but I can't keep up with his stomach. Soon, I will have to bake a second loaf just for him."

"I will be tall and strong like Da'," Jack retorted, his currently scrawny chest puffed out.

"I've no doubt you will," his mother said, but a small pleat had formed upon her brow. "Though how I am to keep up with feeding ye when Jilly is not here to help me, I do not know."

"Could you supplement your own cooking with the baker's help?" asked Lewis.

Jilly gave him a little shake of her head and indicated with a surreptitiously empty-cupped hand the lack of funds for such a solution.

Lewis was not discouraged. "It would be only fair if I provided a stipend toward this purpose since I am stealing your helper away, ma'am. I shall make arrangements in town before we return to Munro. Would two loaves a day be sufficient? And maybe the odd meat pie to build up Jack's strength? He can repay me by chopping wood and carrying buckets of water for his dear mother, who cares for him so well."

"I do all that already," grumbled Jack ungratefully.

"That is good to hear," Lewis acknowledged with a nod.

"Then I feel the stipend will be well spent. It will greatly reduce my guilt that your sister will not be here to see you grow into the excellent young man you will no doubt become."

"What about me?" Timmy wanted to know. "Will there be meat pies for everyone? I like kidney pie best, but Sam likes pork and Mum always makes what he likes because he is the eldest."

The sting of these words momentarily put Lewis off his stride. But Mrs. Kinsey quickly corrected her youngest.

"Sam gets to choose because he works all day with your father and therefore deserves a treat. You are at home, sampling the biscuits I make while he sweats in the sun. Now, let's hear no more about favorites. For you know full well I don't have any." She grabbed both boys by the arm and pulled them close to her. "If I squish you all together *like this*, I have room in my arms for all of ye." And she proceeded to do just that, with Jilly joining in and the boys squirming and complaining that they weren't babies anymore.

All at once, the room fell into shadow as a large figure filled the doorway.

"Da's home!" Timmy wriggled out of his mother's arms to climb into his father's.

Mr. Kinsey scooped him up and tucked him under one muscular arm like a piglet. "It seems I've caught my dinner." Grinning, he ruffled Timmy's hair before setting him back on his feet again.

"What fine guests we have," commented Mr. Kinsey. He winked at Jilly before adding, "If only your husband-to-be was as smart a fellow as this, you would have done well, indeed, Jilly girl."

Jilly stepped forward and took Lewis's hand. "This is Lewis, Da'. But of course you knew that. And here is his sister, Miss Penelope Bradford, come to watch us be married."

Lewis extended a hand to Mr. Kinsey, who took it firmly. "I am grateful for your blessing, sir, though I wish I could have asked for it in person."

"No harm done, lad. You just be good to our daughter and we'll never have a cross word between us." There was a slight increase in pressure in the handshake. Lewis could feel it wasn't a patch on the sheer force the powerful man could exert. But it was enough. A not-so-subtle warning from a protective father who loved his daughter. As friendly as the man appeared, Lewis would not want to be on his wrong side. Fortunately, he could imagine no scenario in which he would be.

A tall, lanky lad stepped around Mr. Kinsey. He could have been Jack's twin, except he was several inches taller, and his hands, though free of dirt, were rough and stained from the juices of many plants—unlike his father who probably wore working gloves.

Lewis reached out to shake his hand, but the youngster self-consciously tucked his own into his pockets and dipped his head to acknowledge the greeting instead. Then he ignored Lewis and called to his mother. "Is dinner ready, Mum? I'm starving."

"Just about," she answered and turned back to the saucepan to give the soup a quick stir. "Jilly, set the table, will you?" she said. "And remember to add bowls for our guests."

Pen nudged Lewis. "We should go," she whispered.

"I've hardly got here," he muttered back.

"Do you mean to take food from their mouths?" she replied with a note of dismay.

Lewis had not considered this. He was ashamed that he had given it no thought at all. He was just so happy to be with Jillian again. And the interactions of the family drew him like a magnet. He was loath to leave, but it was the right thing to do.

"Thank you, Mrs. Kinsey," he said, "but we have made arrangements to dine at the inn. Besides, I probably shouldn't really see my bride before the wedding. I did very much want to meet you all, but I suppose the rest must wait until tomorrow. We will see you at church and after, when we sample your delicious cake." He paused and shifted his weight from one foot to the other. "I would like to contribute toward the celebrations, but

Jillian has assured me in her correspondence that the ladies of the neighborhood have everything in hand. I confess this degree of unhelpfulness makes me very uncomfortable. Is there nothing at all I can do?"

"Look yer best for the ceremony," said Mrs. Kinsey, "and be good to our Jilly, and you've got it all covered, I'd say."

"A crate of drink wouldn't go amiss with the village lads," added Mr. Kinsey, patting Lewis on the shoulder with his broad hand.

"An excellent thought, sir," Lewis answered gratefully. He didn't doubt for a minute that ample drink had been arranged. Mr. Kinsey was taking pity on him, as one provider to another. The task, small as it was, gave Lewis a satisfying sense of purpose. He felt better about leaving now when he knew he would not be returning empty-handed.

"Enjoy your dinner, everyone," he said. "Make sure Jilly isn't late for church." He drew her hand to his lips. "Until tomorrow, my love."

Jilly did not release his hand at once, even though he had begun to draw his fingers back. The parting was necessary, but bitter so soon after their reunion. In the morning, they would be wed. He had to remind himself of this when his hand slipped free and Jilly's went to her heart—a goodbye like that of two lovers who were to suffer a severance of great distance and time, not one night and only a few miles.

The boys and their father had already seated themselves at the table, eager for their simple repast. Mrs. Kinsey stood with saucepan and ladle in hand, waiting to dish up.

"Jilly, love, come on. We're waiting for those bowls," she said. "Mr. Kinsey, you cut the bread in the meantime, please." She threw a quick glance at their guests. "You have a safe walk back to the village, Mr. Bradford, Miss Bradford. Enjoy your dinner."

"Thank you, ma'am," Penelope replied, stepping out into the soft light of the fading day. "Lewis, we need to go. We have but an hour before the sun begins to set."

Lewis withdrew from the house with great reluctance. The walk back, though equally beautiful, lacked the novelty of its first discovery and the anticipation of its outcome. At the inn, they ate a meal of more substance than that shared by the Kinseys, though Lewis couldn't but think their togetherness would have made it more enjoyable.

First thing tomorrow, he would take Penelope to obtain a dress in the village for her to wear to the wedding, as the one she had used today was marred by dust and sweat from their outing. It was a nuisance, but—he had to admit—worth the joy of having her with him for his special day.

Come the night, he found he wasn't tired at all, the afternoon rest having been sufficient, and the prospect of making Jillian his wife thrilling him into a state of eager restlessness.

He crept quietly down the passage and knocked on his sister's door.

"Pen, are you asleep?"

"No, I'm too excited."

"Me too. Are you presentable? May I come in?"

"I'll just throw a blanket over my shoulders. Give me a second."

Her bare feet pattered across the floor, and she drew the bolt that protected her from strangers.

Lewis stepped inside and pulled up a chair next to the bed so that Penelope could get back under her warm covers while they talked.

"Are you nervous?" she asked when she had settled with her back against the headboard.

Lewis leaned forward. "Not at all. I thought I would be. But it just feels right, you know? Like slipping your hand into a perfectly fitting glove." He splayed his fingers away from him, as if he could see the glove resting upon his skin.

Penelope hugged a pillow happily. "I like her very much," she declared. "She is good for you. May tomorrow be the beginning of a smooth-flowing future."

Lewis nodded. "I will make sure of it."

"As far as you are *able*, dear brother," Pen corrected him. "There is a reason why the wedding vows cover sickness and poverty, to name but two of the troubles that life may throw at the best of couples. You cannot control every situation. But you may weather it together."

Lewis cocked his head to the side. "Why do I think that neither of these troubles is what truly concerns you?"

"Indeed, you understand me well enough." His sister placed her hand upon her heart. "I, for one, pledge my support to you both. Sadly, there are many who will not. You will soon know who your truest friends are. Your world will shrink awhile. It is unavoidable. But you will thrive. As long as you remember what it is you love about each other and celebrate it every day."

"Wise words, Pen. But too soon. I would prefer, at least for the next few days, to live in a state of oblivion. This is not naïveté or willful blindness, but a decision. There will be plenty of time for the rudeness of others. And I know it will come. You may think me a fool, but Jillian is worth every minute of it. Such antagonists will be like dung on my shoe, to be scraped off and discarded, forgotten about. But Jilly is my north star, a constant bright presence. And I am the luckiest of men."

"Ah," sighed Penelope, "if I could find someone who loved me as you do Miss Kinsey, I, too, might tie the knot."

"I am glad you will not settle for less."

"What a pair we are: two hopeless romantics."

There was silence for a while as they pondered this.

"I am glad you are here, Pen."

"I wouldn't miss it for the world."

Another pause.

"Mother is going to have our guts for garters when we get home."

They stared wide-eyed at each other. Then a contagious smile from Penelope caused one to form on the face of Lewis. Soon, they were chuckling together like two naughty children.

"Poor Mother," said Pen, wiping tears of laughter from her eyes. "She really hasn't had much luck with her offspring."

The smile dropped from Lewis's face. "She brought much of it upon herself."

"Be that as it may," replied Pen sagely, "we, at least, have had satisfaction—I, in my freedom from marriage and you in your attainment of it. Our parents have not been as fortunate with their goals. Now that you are claiming your bride, perhaps a little kindness toward them and the dreams they have lost might be in order. Whatever bitterness there has been in the past, this would be a good time to pave the way toward a better connection between you. Let them see the positive effect Jillian has on you."

"What do you suggest?"

"Maybe a little less talk of rejecting all of society and running barefoot across the estate. Instead, bring some of the Kinsey warmth into our family. Goodness knows we could use it."

"I won't have Jilly stick her neck out, only to have her efforts slapped away," said Lewis fiercely.

"Just don't hide her away. Her natural goodness will shine if you would let our parents see it."

Lewis hesitated.

"I suppose," he admitted grudgingly.

"You know I'm right."

"Hmph, you certainly like to think you are."

"Have I ever led you astray?"

"Yes! I have lost count of all your wayward escapades."

"But they've always left you smiling."

"Ye-es. That is true."

"Then take the advice from your loyal footman." Penelope grinned.

"You're silly." Lewis smiled. "I'm going to bed before some form of giddy inspiration hits you." He stood and leaned over to kiss her on her forehead.

Penelope gazed at him earnestly. "I promised to behave myself in Ermenbrough, and I shall. But you must think on my words, Lewis."

"I will. Now, go to sleep. Tomorrow is a busy day of shopping, marrying, and celebrating. And you have tired me out. I think I shall rest easily now."

"Happy to be of service," Penelope answered.

"Come and bolt the door."

"I shall once you are gone."

"Good night, Pen."

"Good night, Lew."

Lewis waited in the corridor until he heard the bolt slide into place. Then he padded back to his own room. Changing into his nightshirt took a little longer without his valet. But it was only a bother for one night. Tomorrow, his bride would help him undress.

He ran his fingers down his torso, imagining they were Jillian's. Her hands slipping his shirt from his shoulders. Her body pressed against his, skin to skin.

A rush of current surged within.

Lewis strode quickly to the basin on the stand beside his bed and splashed his face with cold water. He must set aside these thoughts, else he would never sleep. Tomorrow night, though... Ah, yes, he would be well tired then. They would fall asleep in each other's arms, her hair spread like strands of gold upon the pillow, her scent upon his body. Just one more night...

The sheets were cold and rough. Lewis tucked his feet into the fold of the blanket to warm them. As he drifted off, he smiled dreamily. Tomorrow night, he would not be cold at all.

CHAPTER ELEVEN

JILLIAN DID NOT feel like a princess on her wedding day. She couldn't imagine anything more awful. A princess would have been weighed down by jewels, a train, and a hundred unnecessary traditions.

Instead, she felt like her best self.

Her dress was not her finest. At least, not by fashionable standards. It lacked excessive frills and lace and ribbon. Instead, it was a low-waisted, deep-blue velvet with a matching short pelerine that covered her shoulders and upper arms. The long sleeves of her dress ended in boldly embroidered cuffs. Her bonnet was enveloped in flowers of all shapes, sizes, and colors, reminiscent of the meadow of her childhood from which they were sourced.

She had, for the briefest of moments, considered going barefoot. But common sense quickly overcame her more individual tastes. It was too cold, for one. She didn't think the vicar would approve, for another. But, most importantly, she thought the day warranted a degree of formality.

Her visits with Ellena, in an environment where she had felt welcome and accepted despite it being of the highest caliber while she was not, had taught her that there was a time and a place for everything. If you played by the rules in public, you could still be yourself in private.

At first, it had seemed a very counterfeit way to live, and she had kicked against it when she'd been in Munro. But the sheer force of society had quickly taught her to behave. It was just too exhausting to swim constantly against the tide. She had learned the most critical elements of etiquette—there were simply far too many to master them all—and gotten by with the minimum of odd glances being cast her way. To be honest, she was usually too busy having fun to even notice the more subtle forms of criticism.

Today was nothing like that. If she *had* kicked off her shoes, most people would simply have laughed and said it was so like her. The rest did not know her well enough for their disapproval to matter.

But Jilly, excited as she was, also sensed the gravity of the occasion. She was making a pledge, before God and a multitude of witnesses, that she would stand by Lewis for the rest of their lives. The promise itself was easy to make. She loved him so very, very much. However, uttering the words aloud lent them greater weight, and she would not have her attire—or lack thereof—detract from it.

So, she entered the church with her good boots on. Her bouquet, unlike her gay and profusive bonnet, was a small posy of Mrs. Trenton's best roses, for which Jillian's father had asked special permission. Their scent was the only perfume she needed. It drifted about her in a fragrant cloud as she walked down the aisle, her father's strong arm supporting her and also restraining her from rushing forward to her darling Lewis.

Jillian *felt* rather than saw the happy faces turning up as she passed, for her eyes were upon Lewis, looking very dapper in his wedding suit. He was all in black, except for his white, linen shirt and silk cravat and a colorful embroidered waistcoat that rivaled the display on her bonnet.

Her heart sang at the sight of him. She must have quickened her step, for she felt her father gently increase the firmness of his hold on her. Jilly relented. There would be plenty of time for wild abandon later.

When Jillian was in reach of her betrothed, her father released her. She was thinking only of the nearness of Lewis and their imminent vows, but Lewis looked over her shoulder and bowed his head to her father. She twisted around and saw her father bow back more fully, his towering frame folding forward before straightening again. He looked both sad and pleased at the same time. Her mother, too, smiled while dabbing a tear from her eye.

Uncomfortable in their Sunday best, Timmy, Jack, and Sam perched next to their parents on the hard pew. Timmy appeared to be chewing something, possibly a toffee handed to him by their mum to keep him quiet.

Across the aisle, Penelope Bradford sat alone. She had taken care not to dress ostentatiously, having chosen an apricot satin gown in a simple design with an inch-wide cream, satin ribbon beneath her bosom. Her bonnet was in a plain, cream satin with a matching apricot ribbon, a perfect complement for her dress. Jillian had seen the uncomplicated ensemble in the window of the dressmaker. It was strange that Miss Bradford should have acquired it. Perhaps she had felt her own attire was too much for a village wedding that lacked the presence of other fine folk. Bless her heart for choosing elegant simplicity over a need for display! She was so much like her brother. This part of the family, at least, would be easy to love.

Now Lewis took her hand and tucked it into his arm. The vicar began his sermon. Jillian tried to drink in every word. This was *their* sermon, the only one they would hear on their wedding day. Every utterance meant more than the usual Sunday service. At the same time, she was deeply conscious of Lewis beside her, their shoulders touching, their gloved hands warmed further by proximity to each other.

As much as she wanted to take in every moment to savor at leisure, the ceremony seemed to pass in the blink of an eye. In a remarkably short time, they had said their vows, sung the benediction, and signed the register. They were married. Husband and wife. Mr. and Mrs. Bradford. What had taken weeks to fight for was theirs now, suddenly and completely.

They emerged from the church into the bright noonday sun to be showered with flower petals and a multitude of well-wishing. The crowd surged around them like a tide, then ebbed away from the church to pour down the street and swirl outside the doors of the local inn instead. The innkeeper waited until the happy couple had joined everyone before throwing open the doors and announcing the festivities well and truly begun.

⊱⊱⊰⊰

"COME AND CUT the cake!" called Timmy, who already had something else in his mouth. Blackberries, if the juices on his chin were any indication. He tugged Jillian by the hand. Lewis, who held the other, was obliged to follow. The tables were replete with said blackberries, devilled eggs, currant loaves, baked apples and custard, and tea for the ladies. On the counter separating the dining area from the kitchen, the innkeeper had started placing jugs of ale for the general male populace, who did not hesitate, but began to knock their tankards together and toast the couple.

A hearty and melodious *Oh, save thee, fair barley, so good ale may flow! We raise up our tankards and down it will go!* followed Lewis and Jillian as they made their way to the table that had the honor of displaying the dense, rich cake her mother had made. Its honeyed glaze shone. The generous helping of various nuts that had gone into the mixture protruded at various angles from its sweet surface.

Mrs. Kinsey handed her daughter a long knife with a bow tied to the handle. Jillian angled it down at the center of the confection.

"Speech!" someone cried. The call was immediately taken up by another voice, then several more, accompanied by the hammering of tankards upon tables until the room thrummed with the sound.

Jilly paused and looked at Lewis.

He cleared his throat.

"Thank you all for being here..." he began, but he was drowned out by continued calls for the speech he was trying to make.

A piercing, two-fingered whistle from Jack silenced everyone. Lewis cleared his throat and tried again.

"My wife and I..."

A new chant of "Hurrah!" and a renewed refrain of *Ooooooooooooh, save thee, fair barley* drowned him out once more.

Lewis looked with helpless frustration at his bride. Jillian was laughing and completely unbothered by the constant interruptions.

"Do they want me to make a speech or not?" he asked her.

"They certainly want you to try!" she said. "Just keep talking. They'll settle down soon."

Lewis attempted another sentence or two. One of the lads began a rather ribald drinking song, which was picked up by his friends. They sang one verse, only to resume their calls of "Speech! Speech!"

To Lewis's abject horror, a multitude of hands took hold of him and lifted him to the nearest table. "Let's have it, then!" they called. "Have yer say!"

In all the consideration Lewis had given to his marriage to Jillian, he had only ever thought about how *he* would protect *her* from embarrassing scenarios. He had never dreamed that the tables could be turned. Yet here he was, standing on the rough, wooden counter of a village inn, surrounded almost entirely by strangers—as well as his bride waving a knife with a bow on it—trying unsuccessfully to maintain the semblance of dignity.

Pen whispered something in Jillian's ear and took the knife from her. The next moment, Jilly was clambering up next to him and nudging him playfully.

"Come on," she said, "let them hear the fine words of a barrister. They've never heard the like before except when they've been caught poaching and are at the wrong end of the magistrate's court. Show them how a finely educated man compliments his wife." She nudged him again. "Go on. They'll not stay quiet long."

Her faith in him gave Lewis renewed courage. He turned to the assembled throng and coughed into his fist.

"Ladies and gentlemen," he began, only to be met with uproarious laughter and teasing comments.

"You hear that, lads? We're rubbin' shoulders with the best of 'em!"

"Where are the ladies at, then?"

"Let me get me top hat out me trousers!"

A loud bang reverberated through the noise, bringing it to an abrupt stop. A serious young man turned from the door on which he had just hammered. His tanned face and muscular frame were suggestive of a laborer, though his neat tweed jacket and voice of authority said clearly he was not.

"Now then, lads," he chastised them. "We are putting Ermenbrough to shame. Mr. Bradford has been stood for all to see by your very selves, yet you offer him no respect. Let the man talk. I'm sure we all want to hear how our Miss Kinsey—beg pardon, *Mrs. Bradford*—is admired by her husband. They say the city folk have a better way with words. Let's find out. If the groom does well, we'll drink to their health."

A cheer rose up and died down just as quickly amid mildly drunken shushes.

Despite finally having the floor, Lewis was strangely tongue-tied. He had never felt this nervous before a judge. In front of these rapidly inebriating townsfolk, however, he sensed an expectation for something grand.

He turned to Jillian for inspiration. And found it.

"Here is my wife," he stated simply. "You have known her a lifetime and been blessed for it. She is a beauty, it is true, but that is not why you have loved her. It is her openness of spirit, her abundance of natural joy, her ferocious loyalty that has won your hearts. And now I count myself among you lucky few who have known and adored her. I await the privilege of knowing that blessing for a lifetime too."

"Now *that's* a speech!" cried a lone voice, followed by cheering and shouts of "to their health!" before Lewis stepped cautiously down from the table and lifted Jilly down by her waist.

Penelope came up to them, as did the stranger who had spoken up earlier.

"Well said!" They spoke in unison, turning with mouths open and eyes dancing to face each other.

"I yield the floor," said the stranger, eyeing the long, ribboned knife still in Penelope's hand. "At least while you are armed." He smiled. There was no mischief in it, only a lightness of spirit that sat slightly awkwardly upon his otherwise-solemn face.

Penelope blushed and tucked the knife behind her back. "I did not mean to appear so war-like," she said with uncharacteristic shyness.

Jillian made quick introductions.

"Miss Bradford, this is Mr. Simon Boyd. I have known him since we were children. Of late, he has been the land steward on the estate adjacent to Trenton Grange. Simon, this is Miss Penelope Bradford, my wonderful new sister. And of course, Mr. Lewis Bradford, my very own husband and speechmaker of note."

Mr. Boyd nodded at them both but did not extend a hand to either. "My work early this morning involved a rather more down-to-earth approach, if you take my meaning," he explained. "I have not been able to scrub my fingers as clean as I'd like for me to shake the hands of fine folk such as yourselves. However, I am very pleased to make your acquaintance."

"I wish we had a steward with your industrious qualities on our estate," said Lewis. "Our Mr. Cooper seems content to only do the minimum. I would be grateful if you could share your expertise with me before we return to Munro. I want very much to improve the way we manage our affairs. Would you have time to meet with me and walk me through your approach?"

"If you are willing to talk as we go, certainly," answered Mr. Boyd. "I have little time for conversation unless it occurs in the course of my duties."

"I can respect that. Perhaps the day after tomorrow?"

"I am usually done with the morning rounds and bookkeeping around two o'clock, if you would like to meet me at the main house. Then we can do the afternoon rounds before dinner and you can ask me what you will."

"That is more than generous. I appreciate your willingness to accommodate me, Mr. Boyd."

"Enough talk of business," Jillian complained. "It is time to cut the cake. My first task as a wife shall be to feed my husband."

Penelope handed the knife back to Jillian, who strode forward with it like a spear maiden to battle. Now that the speech and playful taunting was done, she had no further interruptions, quickly removing a slice and placing it on her palm.

"It seems you already have me eating out of your hand." Lewis smiled and took a bite as Jillian lifted the cake to his lips.

It was decadent in a wholesome, earthy sort of way, its nut-rich sweetness coming from honey rather than the usual sugary layers of icing.

Jillian took a bite next and returned her syrupy fingers to Lewis to have another. The last morsel was hers, and she began to lick the stickiness from her hand. Lewis reached out and claimed her wrist, drawing her fingertips to his mouth and slipping them inside. He slid his tongue across her sweet skin, savoring the flavor of his beloved bathed in honey.

Her cuff had slid back, the fine hairs on her forearm standing up as his touch thrilled through her, the pink of her cheeks deepening as blood rushed to the surface.

Lewis held her eyes with his own, letting her know he felt it too. That he wanted more. That he wanted *her*.

"Our guests…" she murmured.

"They hardly know we exist."

"The cake…" she reminded him. But her heart was not in it.

Lewis took the knife gently from her other hand and passed it to Pen. "Cut the rest for us, will you? We wish to retire."

"It's the middle of the day, Lew," his sister commented.

"It's my wedding day," he answered softly, lest the raw desire be heard in his voice.

Penelope hesitated a second, then nodded. "I'll see you in the morning."

Lewis took his wife's hand and led her through the crowd, who made pockets of room for them as they proceeded toward the staircase. They raced up the stairs before anyone might see them escape, arriving at the door of their room, breathless and laughing silently.

Jillian leaned against the door. "Aren't you going to carry me over the threshold?" she asked, her hands gripping his lapels and tugging Lewis closer.

Without another word, Lewis fumbled for the handle behind her and swung the door open. Twisting down, he scooped his wife into his arms and stepped into the room.

Jilly slipped slowly to the floor again but did not step away. Instead, she tilted her head back, exposing the soft flesh of her neck. The last semblance of his resistance crumbled. Lewis splayed his fingers through her hair, cupping her head as his tongue found the hollow between her clavicles and followed the upward curve of her throat.

His heel pushed back. The door closed with a soft click. The bolt was drawn. They were alone at last.

CHAPTER TWELVE

THE BRIDE AND groom had planned to honeymoon for a week before returning to Munro. But, after his third night at the inn, even with Jilly's presence to distract him, Lewis was finding he missed the comforts of home. The bed here was small and lumpy. His clothing was not laid out for him in the morning. He missed the smooth shave his valet gave from years of knowing the contours of his master's face.

The inn's meals, though filling, were rough fare. And time spent with the Kinseys, while pleasant, was limited, for they had chores to do. Jillian fitted right in, helping her mother in the kitchen. But Lewis was hardly able to assist her father. Other than the few hours he had spent with Simon Boyd to learn more about the sound management of an estate, and the nights he enjoyed with his wife, Lewis was growing bored.

And then there was Penelope to consider. She was possibly having the most fun of them all. She craved time in the meadow, especially since she had no horse to ride. But she also wanted to walk up and down the main road and look into all the charming little shops where the owners knew everyone by name. For the first time in years, she was enjoying the company of others, laughing, talking freely. Pen had no need to avoid her parents or servants or society at large where they frowned upon her choice not to marry. She was, it would seem, growing more like Jillian each day: not only free in thought, but in action as well. No longer confined to the estate like a bird in a gilded cage, Penelope bloomed.

But she was a lady. She needed a chaperone. And the newly-wed couple did not want to accompany her in her endless explorations. As her new brother, Timmy would have gladly volunteered, but he was too little to understand it was a role he could not play. Besides, as far as Lewis could tell, if rules were going to be broken, his sister would prefer to do so on the arm of Mr. Boyd.

In the end, it was this observation that persuaded Lewis it was time to return to Munro. He had nothing against the honest fellow, but if Penelope came home engaged to a land steward, his parents might very well disown them both.

Fortunately, Jillian, ever the enthusiast, was keen to see their new home by the lake at Oakwoods and did not mind returning to the city. Perhaps she hoped, now that they were officially and irrevocably married, his parents would make peace with it all. If not, the summer cottage was isolated enough from the main house to keep any simmering animosity from their doorstep.

And so, their bags were packed, goodbyes were said, and the temporary footman paid for his brief service. Penelope, dressed more according to her station, took her place inside the carriage rather than on the perch she had occupied on their journey from Munro.

Glad as he had been of Pen's presence at the wedding, Lewis now rather resented her company on the half-day journey in the coach. He and his bride were to have no privacy and all the sensual scenes he had imagined on his journey to Ermenbrough were never to occur. He had a good mind to sulk all the way home.

The ladies, oblivious of his lost hopes, did not share his disappointment, but chattered away cheerfully. It was only when Penelope snuck in a question about Simon Boyd that Lewis rapidly changed the subject to one of his own choosing.

Despite his inner grumbling, Lewis had to admit time passed pleasantly enough, and the new sisters bonded well and truly, which made his heart glad. Meanwhile, the surroundings grew steadily more familiar as they neared Munro. Lewis, who had been staring out the window, instantly recognized the lane that led past their estate.

As they turned into the drive to Oakwoods, he rapped on the roof of the carriage and called, "To the cottage, if you please." The driver obeyed and steered the horses along the secondary drive that led to the home of the bride and groom.

"Are you not coming with me to greet our parents?" Penelope asked.

"Sorry, Pen," said Lewis, "but you're on your own with this one. We are still officially on our honeymoon. You will have to brave the consequences of your escapades alone. I have no desire to see our parents until they have expended the worst of their energies on you."

"I suppose that is fair," Pen answered grimly. "I shall have to remind myself how much I enjoyed the wedding, and Ermenbrough as a whole, while they have their say. Let us hope Mother wears herself out quickly." She lifted her chin at a happier thought. "You will at least come for dinner on Sunday, won't you?"

Lewis nodded. "With any luck, it will be a civilized meal. Afterward, you can show Jilly your rose garden while Father and I talk about matters of business." He looked warmly upon Jillian. "Until then, we plan to keep to ourselves."

By now, the cottage footman had, with the usual stiff formality, readied the steps so that the new master and mistress could descend.

The housekeeper was far less composed. Lewis would not be surprised if she had instantly sprung a few new gray hairs, for she patted her head as if to acknowledge them.

"Mr. Bradford!" she exclaimed as they entered the foyer. "We weren't expecting you for some days yet! We have nothing ready for you—no linen, no meals…"

Lewis lifted a hand in appeasement. "That's all right, Mrs. Johnson, you are not at fault. We changed our plans rather suddenly. If you would be so kind as to arrange hot water for a bath and prepare our room with fresh bedding and a fire, that is all we need for now. Later, we may call for some sandwiches and tea. Meanwhile, we will take a walk about the grounds so that Mrs. Bradford may admire her new home from all angles."

"Oh, yes!" cried Jillian. "I would love that! And a chance to move about a little after being seated for such a long time."

Mrs. Johnson nodded and rushed off to tend to her duties. Lewis took Jillian's arm and led her outside once more.

"I will only give you a short tour today. I would not want to tire you out. Not yet…"

Jillian leaned her head against his shoulder. Whether it was as a show of agreement or an attempt to seek connection, Lewis could not say. He only knew that the touch made him feel strangely safe. As if nothing bad in the world could touch him. Perhaps that did not sound very manly to his own mind. He only knew it to be true. With Jillian, he felt a security he had not known before. A real sense of belonging.

"Show me the lake," said his wife.

"Are you hoping it will be a reminder of the river that runs adjacent to Trenton Grange?"

She hugged his arm. "You understand me so well."

"It will not have the lively motion of a river, but we can row on it if you like, come summer."

"And fish?"

"You want to go fishing?"

"Why not?"

Lewis hesitated. The Bradfords had only ever had a very passive relationship with their land. The tenants worked the soil and paid rent. The groundskeeper oversaw the landscaping. But his family merely floated upon its surface. For the centuries that the estate had been in their care, the Bradfords, it now seemed to

Lewis, had never put down real roots. They were possessive in their ownership but had no relationship with what they owned.

"We shall go fishing," he agreed. "And Cook shall make a dinner of our catch. And I will teach you to ride so that we may explore every inch of Oakwoods."

"And I can have a garden, like Penelope does?" Jillian's eyes were now sparkling with anticipation.

"I don't see why not. We shall begin here, at the cottage. When Father sees what excellent taste you have, and what extensive knowledge you have gained from your own dear father, he will be begging you to do the same at the main house."

Jillian huffed a wry laugh. "I can't imagine Lord Bradford begging anyone to do anything. But if he is willing to consider it, I would be most grateful."

By now, they had reached a hedge. The path ran through an opening in the shrubbery. A few steps more and the shimmering waters were before them.

"Oh!" Jilly marveled. "It's so close to our home! I didn't realize."

"On a quiet day, you can hear the ducks. And on a quiet night, when the ducks are asleep, we hear frogs."

"I wish the water made a sound. The river at Trenton Grange is always rushing and gurgling and tumbling."

"We could have a fountain installed," suggested Lewis.

"No," Jilly answered sadly. "It's not the same. It would be just another manmade structure added to a manmade lake."

"Do you have another suggestion?"

"Well, it would be better if we could at least see the lake and its little visitors. Why has the hedge been placed to block it?"

"Who knows? Everything at Oakwoods has been the same for as long as I can remember. I will ask our groundskeeper. If there is no practical reason, it is yet another project we may suggest for improvement."

"I think," said Jilly, "we should not offer them up all at once. I do not want your parents thinking I have no respect for the way they have done things."

"The suggestions will come from me," Lewis answered. "And if they like the idea," he added with a smile, "I shall say it was yours."

Jillian slipped her hands around her husband's waist and lay herself full-bodied against him.

"Thank you," she said, her cheek to his chest. "I already begin to feel at home."

"Ah, my love," Lewis crooned as he stroked her long locks, her warmth blending with his own. "I will do everything and anything to make you happy."

Jilly lifted her head to look upon his face. "I believe you. And I would like to do the same. But I cannot offer gardens or lakes or anything half as grand."

Lewis shook his head. "These are only things, whether they be grand or not." He cupped his hand to her cheek. "You have trusted me with your heart. What greater gift is there?"

His thumb ran down the length of her neck. When his hand reached her delicate collarbone, it tugged at her sleeve, revealing the softness of her shoulder. Lewis nipped at the skin, just enough to be playful and to let her know he desired her.

Jillian tilted her chin and caught his earlobe gently between her teeth. His skin prickled into goose-flesh, a shivering pulse running through his entire body.

"I think," said Lewis, his voice raspy and low, "I know why the hedge is here."

And he pulled Jillian down with him onto the lush lawn behind the cover of the thick shrubs.

Somewhere in the cottage, their bath grew cold. But here, by the quiet of the lake, it was very warm, indeed.

CHAPTER THIRTEEN

J ILLIAN HAD BEEN practicing the names and order of use of the multitude of dinner knives and forks with Lewis. She had promised to be a lady when necessary, and Sunday family dinner was definitely going to be one of those occasions.

Lord and Lady Bradford must have been practicing too, of a kind—whether it was as a result of Penelope's urging, or because, as with their allowance of Pen's eccentricities, they had made peace with their remaining son's odd choices. They were definitely more subdued and civil. And conversation was able to proceed rather more pleasantly than it had at the last meal they had shared.

"My mother sends her best wishes," Jillian told Lady Bradford as they waited for the soup to be served.

"That is very kind," said her ladyship before nodding to the butler.

"And she sent a jar of her special ointment for your gout, sir," said Jilly to Lewis's father. "It works wonders. She could sell it and make a pretty penny, but most folks back home just repay her kindness with some eggs or whatever they grow in their little piece of garden."

Lady Bradford sucked in her breath and exhaled it again in a controlled manner.

"Jillian, dear," she said as calmly as possible, "we do not mention people's personal health at the table. Nor do we discuss money unless it is in reference to the greater economic situation of our country."

"Oh," said Jilly. "Oh, sorry. I shall try to remember that."

"Please do," her ladyship replied firmly. Then her face softened a little and she added, "Although it was kind of you to think of Lord Bradford's well-being." She ignored the *hmph* that marked his lordship's opinion on the matter.

"Of course. I would not want him to suffer needlessly." Jillian shot a quick smile at her father-in-law before returning her attention to Lady Bradford. "Er, what would you recommend as appropriate subject matter instead?"

"Well, the men—if we let them—will spend most of their time discussing politics, as many of them attend Parliament and carry the cares of our great nation upon their shoulders."

Jillian tried not to pull a face. "And if we don't? Let them, I mean." She caught sight of Lewis hiding a grin behind his wineglass before he took a sip.

"Then one might have the opportunity to speak of the theater, or the latest betrothal among families with whom we are acquainted. Anything civilized, really."

"She means 'boring,'" Penelope remarked. She may have said a lot more, but her father cleared his throat loudly and Penelope subsided into silence once more.

Jillian agreed wholeheartedly with the comment. She had the distinct impression that she and Lady Bradford also did not share the same concept of what was civilized. Nor did she think her mother-in-law had considered their own betrothal to be suitable for dinner conversation.

She sipped a spoonful of her soup. It was very fine soup. This seemed to be a safe and civilized topic.

"This is very fine soup," said Jilly to the table at large.

"I am glad you like it," answered Lady Bradford. "Our cook has been with us many years. I do not doubt there are other households who have tried to steal her from us, but she is deeply loyal, for which we are, of course, thankful."

Jillian paused her spoon mid-sip. "People try to steal each other's staff?"

"Oh, yes! It is a compliment, really. It means they do their job better than most. Of course, if they actually leave your service when another offer is made, it reflects very poorly on how you have treated them."

Jilly couldn't help thinking she might have fared better at Oakwoods as a servant rather than the supposed interloper. Then again, none of the staff had tried to marry the Bradfords' son.

"Do you think Mrs. Johnson would teach me how she manages a gentleman's home?" Jillian asked, keen to find common ground. "Or is she not as excellent as your own housekeeper?"

Lady Bradford spluttered as her spoonful of soup went down the wrong way. A little of it dribbled onto her chin and she hastily wiped it off with her serviette.

"Are you all right, my dear?" her husband inquired with a frown.

Lady Bradford waved her hand as she attempted to regain her dignity. Two delicate coughs later, her serviette was back upon her lap and she turned to Jillian, her eyes closed as if she were seeking inner peace.

When she opened them again, they focused on Jilly with what seemed to be a very tenuous grip on patience.

"Mrs. Johnson," she said slowly, as though to an errant child, "may be newly in our employ, but her qualifications are not lacking in any way. *However...*" And now Lady Bradford's tone became quite stern. "We do *not*, under any circumstances, allow the staff"—here, she visibly shuddered at the thought—"to teach us *anything*. You need know nothing of managing a house of any proportion. You simply say what it is you want, and it is their task to see it done. For example, you select a menu for dinner, and the housekeeper instructs the staff accordingly. *You* may entertain, or embroider, or take the air. Perhaps you might learn the piano or paint. We also have a large collection of books in the library. I assume you can read."

"Mother!" Lewis cut in.

"What?" Lady Bradford replied. "How am I to know what your wife can do when so much of her education has been neglected? I cannot know if I do not ask."

"I can read," Jillian said calmly. "But I prefer to be doing something useful. I would just as soon be cooking as reading about cooking, or tending to a garden rather than painting a pretty landscape."

Lady Bradford considered Jilly's words with gravity. "I take it you think a lady's life is rather a passive one, and not equal to your cause?"

"To be honest, yes."

Lady Bradford lifted an arm bent at the elbow and wrist as if she were about to deliver a line of poetry. She waved it in small circles as she spoke, the gentle rhythm of the gesture matching the measured tone of her speech.

"Just because a lady does not need to perform the menial tasks of a working-class woman does not mean she has no purpose. It is her duty to bring beauty and elegance to her husband's home." The hand now waved more broadly to encompass the room and, by implication, the whole house.

"Guests must know what quality of person they have be-friended. Everything—from the upkeep of the house to proper dinner conversation to the fine presentation of self—is our domain. We might not labor physically, but our responsibilities touch upon all aspects of life. We are what lifts our husband's reputation from the superficialness of the bachelor to the substantial prestige of the established man. Do you understand?"

Jilly did not. Frankly, it sounded ridiculous. If a woman's only purpose was to make her husband appear remarkable, it didn't say very much for the husband. Should he not be maintaining his own reputation? Lewis certainly did not need her help in this. He had made a name for himself, both as a barrister and a gentleman. Surely, she should bring something more—something new and fresh—to the union?

Jillian would love to have spoken freely, to have her new family see what greater worth she might have by adding her own strengths rather than being yet another pretty prop in the theater of their lives. But she must not rush in where fragile peace existed. Her answer could not be too honest, lest it stir up displeasure. Lady Bradford had managed to refrain from insulting her—at least, not intentionally. She must show similar restraint.

"I confess, what you describe is an alien concept to me," she said. "But I have never needed to understand it before. Just as you cannot fathom a role in which the appearance of things would be unimportant, I struggle to fathom a role in which it is so central." Jillian lowered her gaze, a promise that her intention was not to offend. Then she added the only words that could match that promise. "I shall, however, pay attention to your example and learn what I can from it."

"I suppose that is a start," conceded Lady Bradford.

Peace had been established. Dinner could resume without incident.

Penelope piped up. "I have an idea."

Her parents looked at each other and placed their spoons within their bowls as if readying themselves for whatever might follow. No doubt Pen's ideas had caused much consternation in the past. Running off as a footman to attend her brother's wedding was only the most recent example.

"If we are going to show Jillian what the mistress of a fine home can *do*," Pen said, "we should host a ball! What better way to show her all the aspects of planning and entertaining?"

"Absolutely not!" came the sharp retort from her father. "Have you lost all your bearings, Daughter? Philip has not been gone even a two-month and yet you would have us dancing and feasting? I know you like to test the boundaries of what might be expected from a lady, but you will certainly not shame the memory of your brother by pretending he did not exist!"

Penelope's bright smile fell at once. "I did not mean... Oh, dear… I was not thinking. I am very sorry. Of course, the time is not right for receiving guests *en masse*."

Lord Bradford glared at her. "Nor was it right for a wedding, or running off to attend the same. But my children seem to lack all sense of duty."

The convivial atmosphere that had reigned over the soup collapsed into a stony silence all through the next course. Jillian was of the opinion that fish was a most unfortunate dish on the Bradford menu.

This time, however, there was no devastating visit from a constable, and they were able to proceed to the main course. Jillian watched the smooth transition of plates and cutlery, observed the butler cut the roast ham. She had experienced such procedure in the home of the viscount and viscountess but had never paid it much attention. At Munro House, there was always lively conversation, which made the subtler details of the dinner almost invisible. Now, however, Jillian noted the pristine gloves of the footman, the buttons of his uniform polished to perfection. All his movements were practiced and smooth. The china patterns of the service set were skillfully painted, the dishes upon them made by experienced hands. Every element of the meal involved attention to detail.

And yet she would far rather eat from a wooden bowl, tasting the love with which her mother made their simple meals, surrounded by people who laughed and teased, where the only decorum was to wash one's hands before sitting down.

Ermenbrough had given her this. But it was very far away right now, in every sense of the word. *This* was home now. This place where rules and refinement were more important than people and connection.

The room grew close. The walls seemed to rush at her. Her chest pushed against her bodice, which felt tighter with each breath.

"Jilly? What's the matter?" Lewis asked, his brow furrowed, his shoulders leaning forward.

"I think… think I need some air," she murmured.

Lewis stood at once.

"There is no need for everyone to abandon the dinner, Lewis," Lord Bradford said gruffly. He beckoned to the nearest footman. "Fetch a maidservant to attend to Mrs. Bradford."

"Father," Lewis urged, "I really think I should…"

But Lord Bradford ignored him, addressing Jillian instead. "You may be excused until you are recovered. The drawing room is close by and comfortable. Settle yourself there and a servant will see to your needs."

Jillian stood slowly, her heart beating with great force. She could see Lewis hovering at his seat, his father staring him down until he was sitting again. She sucked in a lungful of air, but it only made her feel dizzy.

The footman reappeared, a maidservant at his elbow. He stepped forward briskly and offered an arm held some distance from his body. It was not the sort of motion Lewis would have made. He would have buoyed her, drawing her close to offer not only his body, but his heart for support.

Still, she managed well enough on the bough-like arm that extended from the footman. The trio made their way from the room solemnly. Her husband's eyes followed her every step, but Lord Bradford gazed straight ahead and continued to cut the roast on his plate.

As they progressed down the corridor, Jillian heard Lady Bradford say, "Is she with child, Lewis? It is not even ten days since the wedding. She should not yet be so far along as to be as out of sorts as this. Unless… Is this why you married her?"

Jillian could picture Lewis bristling at the comment.

"Honestly, Mother!" His exasperation rang clear down the hallway. "It's bad enough you believe me capable of seducing a young woman, but to think that Jillian would accommodate such advances!"

"Why, Lewis, I hardly know her or the effect she might have had upon you. She is hardly the sort of quality lady…"

Her words fell behind as Jillian, the footman, and the maid passed beyond reach of hearing them. Neither of the servants said a word of their own, nor would they, but Jilly burned with embarrassment.

The footman stood by as Jillian settled into a very expensive-looking upholstered chair. Of course, it would be. Everything at Oakwoods revolved around the outward show of things.

"Janet will see to you now, ma'am," said the young man, his eyes soft, a small frown not quite hidden. "I must return to my duties."

"Thank you," Jillian answered before leaning back and catching her breath. She was starting to feel better here, away from the constant reminder that everything about herself was wrong—certainly in Lord and Lady Bradford's eyes, anyway.

Janet stood quietly and waited. Her light-brown fringe was tucked neatly under her cap, but a few wisps had escaped in the nape of her neck. She had intelligent, brown eyes, which were only noticeable because Jillian caught her staring. She was probably wondering if there was any truth to her mistress's suspicions.

Jillian hated that such implied indiscretion should hang over her head.

"I'm not… with child," she told the maid. "Not yet, anyway."

"It's none of my business, ma'am," answered Janet with the words she was no doubt expected to say. And then, perhaps because she felt Jilly needed some support, she added, "And even if you were, you wouldn't be the first lady to marry so."

"But I'm not a lady, am I, Janet?" Jillian sighed.

Janet sniffed. "Hasn't stopped them sorts of folks from getting in the family way ahead of themselves, ma'am."

Jillian smiled in spite of herself. "Why, Janet, you have opinions! How absolutely wonderful!"

Janet quickly looked over her shoulder, then leaned in toward Jillian a little. "Opinions ain't popular when you're a servant. But we have them all the same."

Jilly pulled a face. "I don't think they're particularly popular when you're a lady, either. It seems only the master and mistress of the house may utter their thoughts aloud. Poor Lewis! This is all he's ever known."

Jillian's forthright manner must have let the little maid's guard down, for Janet rapidly shared a host of her previously private thoughts. "Our Mr. Bradford's not as bold as Miss Bradford," she declared. "She's a feisty one, that. He's always been the quieter type. Bit odd for a barrister, I often thought. They talk in court all the time, don't they? But here at Oakwoods, he was ever in Master Philip's shadow."

Jillian was silent for a while, mulling over the truth of these words.

"Janet…"

"Yes, ma'am?"

"Do you think I have made things worse for him?"

"Oh, *no*, ma'am!" Janet's eyes widened and her hand stretched out as if to stop the very thought in its tracks. "Ever since you came into his life a year ago, he's been positively bloomin'! Everyone's noticed."

"But he is constantly sparring with his parents because of me," Jilly said miserably.

"That ain't *your* fault. Their lordship and ladyship have always wanted things *just so*. It didn't matter if it made their children unhappy. They got lucky with Master Philip. He lapped it all up 'cos he was the heir, see? The only reason why Mr. Bradford hadn't much argued with his parents before now is 'cos he didn't care enough to make the effort. But you matter to him. It's quite romantic, actually."

"It doesn't *feel* very romantic, I must say. All I can do is hope that the worst of it settles over time."

"Don't take it too much to heart, ma'am. They can't help how they are any more than you can. It's not personal."

"It feels jolly personal to *me*," huffed Jilly.

Janet must have had no answer to that because she lapsed

into silence.

Jillian, too, had nothing more to say, but she was in no hurry to leave the sanctuary of the drawing room. Still, there was no need to have Janet stand beside her like a sentry.

"I'm keeping you from your duties," she told the little maid. "You can leave me. I am perfectly well now. I just don't wish to return to dinner quite yet."

"My duties are whatever they tell me." Janet indicated with her chin toward the dining room. "I can stay as long as you like."

Jillian tilted her head at an angle and looked at the young maid with new eyes.

"Tell me, Janet, what makes you loyal to the Bradfords when they are so exacting?"

"Oh, that ain't no reason to quit," Janet answered. "All the great houses have similar demands. If you're a servant, you know to work hard and follow orders. But the Bradfords have a large enough staff that no one is run completely ragged. Our quarters are clean, our wages on time. We are not punished unduly. Our wages are not garnished for petty reasons. It is honest work, and fair. Believe me, there are masters enough of whom the same cannot be said."

"But it can still be a challenge, is that not true? My own family has managed to fare well enough since my father has a senior position, but many servants I know have struggled to get by on what they earn. What do the staff of Oakwoods wish for?"

"Oh, no, ma'am, I cannot say! It would be impertinent of me to complain, and to the master's family, no less!"

"You have my word. It will go no further than this room."

Janet considered these words for several moments. "Well, I suppose it would help if we got the occasional food basket when times are hard, like in winter, or after a bad harvest, or if someone is sick. The Bradfords are very generous at the holidays, especially Boxing Day, but they seem unaware of what befalls us throughout the year."

"Does your housekeeper not know when her staff is suffering? Surely, she could suggest to Lady Bradford when further assistance might be welcome?"

Janet lifted her shoulders in a shrug. "She will know if one of us is too ill to work. As for the rest, I do not think it falls under her responsibilities."

"Well," said Jillian, sitting up straight, "I have just made the responsibility mine. Thank you, Janet, for giving me something to *do*. I think I can face the others at dinner now. Whenever Lord or Lady Bradford make me feel less than enough, I shall stop listening and picture myself delivering baskets instead. It will be a treat to become acquainted with the tenants, too. They will be so much easier to talk to. And I will be better able to assist Mr. Bradford when he must take the reins from his father if I understand the needs and workings of the estate."

She slapped her hands upon her knees and stood. "Do you know, I feel quite splendid! I think I shall enjoy my ham now, if it has not grown cold." Jillian began to walk toward the doorway, stopped, turned, and added, "Oh, Janet, when next you have a day off, come and take tea with me at the cottage. We have much to discuss."

"Oh, ma'am, I couldn't possibly come as your guest! It's not proper for…"

Jillian waved an impatient hand. "Shu-shu-shush, I won't hear of it. At the cottage, I make my own rules."

She sighed a happy sigh of satisfaction, set her shoulders squarely, and marched off to the dining room. Whatever had transpired in her absence would not affect her now. She had a plan. And no one would thwart it. She might not know how to set a fine table, but she knew about kindness.

Oakwoods was about to become a very well-loved place, indeed.

CHAPTER FOURTEEN

Oakwoods, November 1815

ON THURSDAY, THERE was a rather timid knock at the kitchen door of the cottage. Lewis—who was once again trying to explain to Jillian that she should *not* have been helping Cook, and that any questions she had should be directed to the housekeeper—looked up briefly to see Mrs. Johnson ushering in one of his mother's housemaids.

The poor girl looked absolutely terrified to see him, but Jillian rushed toward her with a broad smile as if she were expected.

"Janet! You have come! Excellent!"

Little Janet bobbed a curtsey, but her frightened eyes remained on Lewis.

"Is it all right that I have come now, ma'am? I did not want to disturb you, so I waited until after Lady Bradford usually has her breakfast, hoping that would be when you had yours too."

"Well, it's a little early for tea, but we shall make do."

By now, the curious kitchen staff had slowed in their tasks to take in the spectacle of a servant come to call on their mistress. Lewis could feel the curiosity prickle throughout the room, including in his own mind.

Janet, whose cheeks burned with embarrassment, answered, "I don't need tea. Honest, Mrs. Bradford, I don't. I could just as easily tell you what you want to know in the master's study, if he will allow it." Her eyes circled back to Lewis, filled with a pleading that she not be punished for his wife's schemes.

His own gaze pivoted to Jillian. "What is this all about?" he asked, barely restraining his irritation. Jillian's enthusiasm for spending time with the servants had already crossed the line multiple times in his opinion. He was all for her being her usual friendly, delightful self, but she also had to learn the extent to which she could do so. So far, his tutelage had fallen on very stubborn ears.

"Oh," Jilly replied, "Janet and I are going to have a little chat about how I can best make use of my time here at Oakwoods."

"I'm sorry, what?" Lewis could have sworn his wife had just made a housemaid her advisor. "Why would you..." He felt the stares of the staff and reined in his chastisement of his wife, storing it up for a later, more private moment. "If you had wanted advice, all you had to do..." No, no, still too abrasive. He pushed his churning frustration down and out of the way, seeking a more civilized starting point for the interrogation. "When, exactly, was this arrangement made?"

"On Sunday, during dinner. You remember when I wasn't feeling well and Janet watched over me? Well, we had a wonderful conversation"—Lewis could just imagine—"and I realized that it's people like Janet who will give me the insight I really want. Everyone else is either too formal with me or tells me what they think I *should* hear instead of what I *need* to hear. So, I invited her to tea on her day off so we could chat."

Jillian had uttered every single word as if it were the most natural thing in the world. Janet, meanwhile, was trying very hard, it seemed, to sink into her shoes, and the kitchen staff had now frozen in place, only their eyes moving, reaching for each other as if to say, *"Are you hearing what I'm hearing?"*

"I see." Lewis saw all too clearly. He had known that life at Oakwoods would be an adjustment for Jilly, but he had trusted that she would at least make an attempt toward achieving said adjustment. Was it too much to ask that she not turn everything on its head? He had pictured her the charming mistress, beloved by all staff for her warm-hearted character. Never in a month of Sundays had he imagined her seeking them out as if she were one of them.

"I think," he said slowly, weighing every thought that shot toward his mouth before carefully putting it aside, "we should make our way to the garden."

"But it's freezing, Lewis! And Janet does not have a good coat."

The redness in Janet's face deepened a shade at the mention of her inadequate attire. Lewis pitied her, but there was no helping it.

"We shan't be long. *Now*, if you please." And he marched out the back door toward the kitchen garden, which still boasted a multitude of vegetables in the rich, moist soil, despite it being November.

Janet had followed all too willingly, probably very happy to escape the discomfort of the scene in the house. Jillian joined them, but her folded arms, hunched shoulders, and obvious scowl suggested she was both cold and displeased.

"Janet," said Lewis, "Do you have a good coat you could borrow?"

"No, Mr. Bradford," she said, hanging her head. "Those as has one will be using it on a day like this."

"Then may I suggest you postpone your meeting to a sunnier day, when you can walk and talk. Perhaps in May?"

"But that's in six months!" cried Jillian.

"That's all right, Mrs. Bradford," Janet answered, perking up. "I don't mind waiting." She settled into a more familiar servile stance and asked Lewis, "May I be excused now, sir?" When he nodded, she bobbed a quick curtsey and all but ran back to the main house, where the maids' rooms were.

Jillian stared at the departing figure, then whipped around to Lewis. "Why did you do that? Why did you send her away? She was my guest!"

"She is a servant, Jillian. She can never be your guest."

"Says who? Your parents? Society?"

"Yes, and yes. But common sense says so also. Have you considered her feelings in the matter?"

"What do you mean? How can inviting her to tea hurt her feelings?"

"Not hurt, Jilly. Confuse. Embarrass. She has a position in the household that fits within a known structure. You might not agree with it, but you cannot undo it with a single invitation. Nor should you undo it at all," he added hastily.

"And why not? Why can I not do things my way in my own home?"

Lewis sighed. This was taking a lot more patience than he had expected.

"Because your household also runs on the same principles. The staff *want* the separation from the family."

"I don't believe that!"

"They work long hours, Jilly. If you are going to try to befriend them, they will have to give of their work time to accommodate you."

"I asked Janet to come on her day off."

"And did you not think she might have other things planned for her free time?"

"She could just have told me."

"No, she couldn't. Because you are her superior. She has been taught that your needs are her duties."

Jillian paused before declaring, "I hate that."

She began to rub her arms as the chill in the air settled upon her.

Lewis drew his wife to him, wrapping his own arms around hers. "I know, my love. You want the whole world to be friends, and to enjoy the sunshine and pick daisies. But it cannot be. Someone must wash. Someone must dig. It does not have to mean they are unhappy. And your kindness can make their burden lighter, knowing they work for a fair mistress. But you must leave them to their tasks that they may work among their peers, where they are relaxed and comfortable, with people whom they don't have to please."

Jilly's frame still shivered within his embrace. "Can we talk more in the house?" she asked, her teeth beginning to chatter.

"Is there more to say? I do not want to have the servants listening in on our private debate."

"I am too cold to argue with you."

"But you want to."

Jillian began to stomp back to the house. Lewis could not tell if it was out of frustration or to combat the cold.

"Why can Penelope do whatever she wants?" Her voice trailed back toward him.

"She most certainly cannot," he countered, throwing his words toward her as he hastened to catch up. "While she may have more freedom than many young ladies, it is not without limitation. Even the Prince Regent, to whom every knee bends, is not without restriction. That is just the way it is."

Jillian stopped her furious march and faced Lewis squarely.

"You said I could be myself. You said you would not expect me to change."

Her words irked him. He did not deserve the implied accusation. "You're being unreasonable," he told her. "How have I asked you to be someone you are not? I have only asked you to express your nature and carry yourself within the bounds of propriety. That was what we agreed. You would maintain the necessary decorum that your position demands. It is you who have broken the contract."

"Oh!" The outrage burst forth in a plosive breath. Jilly seemed to be struggling for a suitable response, her fingers splayed, her arms stiff, her mouth gaping and wordless, while her eyes flashed an angry retort. "*Oh!!*" she said again, her own frustration doubling down on the singular word.

She began to shiver again, no doubt as much in fury as with cold. When neither heat nor a suitable response was forthcoming, she whirled around and resumed her trudge back to the kitchen.

Lewis could only imagine the scene as she entered. The maids would stare while trying not to. Cook would roll her eyes at another disruption. But all would return to normal in the softening ripples of Jillian's wake once she had swept through the kitchen and into that part of the house where they felt she belonged.

Lewis stuck his fingers into his pockets. Despite his informal banyan which kept out some of the chill, he was cold. But entering the house meant another possible confrontation with Jilly, who may well have gathered her thoughts in the interim. Nor was he in the mood to see the expressions on the faces of the kitchen staff.

To solve these difficulties, Lewis strode around to the front of the house and let himself in. His outdoor coat and hat hung on the stand near the door and he claimed them. He hailed their passing footman. "Fetch my country boots," he instructed, "and bring them to my study."

Lewis walked to the room in question and sat down in the nearest chair. Kicking off his house shoes, he tucked them under the seat and waited for the footman to return with his boots and help him put them on.

Properly attired for the weather, Lewis quietly left the house and headed across the lawn to the woods that gave the estate its name. Mist hung between the trees and the ground was damp underfoot, for all the world like a scene from a Gothic romance. Something fluttered among the branches. A twig crunched beneath his boot. The small sounds were amplified by the dense silence that pervaded the woods. The mist limited his vision to the closest trees and the well-trodden path ahead. The silence grew intact once again. Lewis was alone, with only his thoughts for company.

This would not do. Although he was avoiding Jilly, she was still with him, her words circling his peace of mind.

She was in the wrong. He felt no guilt in thinking that. He loved her. He desired her happiness. He supported her finding her place at Oakwoods. But she was going about it in entirely the wrong way. He had thought she would trust him to let her know where the line was and would harken to him showing her when she had crossed it.

But she did not.

Lewis did not know how to proceed without putting out the light that was at the very heart of her. How could he guide her to blend into his life without making her feel she was giving up hers? If Philip had still been alive, none of this would have mattered. They would have lived in their own home, away from Oakwoods, with a few servants whom Jillian could have treated like family if she wanted to. It wouldn't have mattered if she broke a few rules.

And yet…

Even then, he would have put his foot down when it came to inviting a maidservant to tea. Really, what had Jillian been thinking?! Surely, she must understand that she could not act on every impulse?

His mother had warned him. Lord Howell had warned him. But Lewis had been convinced he'd known better. Was he wrong? Surely, it was just a matter of finding balance. They had enough love to conquer anything.

Didn't they?

Perhaps this walk in the woods was not such a good idea, after all. His thoughts, far from distracted, were able to focus entirely on Jilly and their quarrel. He had no solution for their disagreement, nor did he want to dwell on it.

With this in mind, Lewis took the first fork in the path, leading out of the woods and along the fence that separated the farmland from the estate proper. The path widened into a cart track and then still further to form the main avenue—if such a grand word could be used—between the tenant cottages. Lewis could see the single-roomed buildings emerging from the mist, one by one, as he passed their humble doorways.

He was very surprised, indeed when, as the shifting pocket of visibility revealed the next dwelling, he saw his father and Mr. Cooper, the land steward, at the stone step of the small home's only entrance. The sound of Lewis's boots was muffled in the cloying damp, yet both men looked up as he approached.

"This is well met indeed, Lewis," his father said. "We were just discussing necessary repairs to the roof. It would do you good to see how these things are managed."

"As I was saying to his lordship," said Mr. Cooper, "we would need to remove all the broken tiles first before replacing them. Once we know how many are required, we can order them and assign the necessary labor to complete the task. It could take a few days or weeks, depending on the availability of stock."

"Where do we order them from?" asked Lewis.

"Houghton and Co."

"And where will we house the tenants until their home is habitable again?"

The steward seemed to have trouble processing the question. He turned to Lord Bradford for assistance, but none was forthcoming. "Er…" he said before falling silent once more.

Lewis did not like what the lack of answer implied.

"We do house them elsewhere, do we not?" The question was for his father, since Cooper clearly took his cue from his employer.

"Don't be naïve, Lewis," his father answered stiffly. "They pay rent for this cottage, so this is where they stay."

"But there's a hole in their roof!"

"And we are repairing it. At no cost to them, I may add."

"I should think not." Lewis scoffed. "These buildings are our property and therefore our responsibility."

Lord Bradford lowered his chin and looked at his son as if over the rim of a pair of spectacles. "Even a baron's money must be carefully managed," he said. "And the rent we receive barely covers the upkeep of the structures. It is not so mercenary an enterprise as you seem to suggest."

"But it's November," persisted Lewis. "The heat from their

fire will be lost to the sky. They can barely afford to keep their fire going as it is."

His father sighed. "I see you've been getting to know our tenants. A commendable use of your time. I only wish you would show an equal interest in our bookkeeping. It might give you a more balanced outlook."

"I would learn everything you wish to teach me, Father. But it can mean little if you will not hear my concerns."

"What would you have me do?"

"What about a temporary solution? Perhaps a sheet of canvas held down with stones. Anything to help keep the heat in and the elements out."

Lord Bradford tilted his head toward his steward. "Might that be easily managed?"

"I believe so, your lordship. We could use one of the covers for the hay bales. There should be one or two folded in storage, as some of the hay has already been used. I could see to it today."

"Well, we appear to have a solution that satisfies everyone. A rarity, I would say. You will have to acquaint yourself with disappointment, Lewis," his father said. "Not everything can be argued away as if in a courtroom."

"That may be so," Lewis countered, "but it would be remiss of me not to at least try."

His father nodded.

Lewis felt ridiculously pleased with himself. He had helped a tenant, shown his father he could be trusted with affairs of the estate, and received a nod of approval. An actual nod!

He couldn't wait to go home to Jillian and share his small triumph. She would be especially pleased that he had persevered in seeking a solution for the poor inhabitants of the stricken cottage.

He excused himself with a promise to come up to the main house and educate himself about the nuances of running such a large and complex property. His father, in turn, offered to send for him the next time he did his rounds with their steward.

Lewis practically floated back to their own cottage—though he now considered the use of the term "cottage" a trifle embarrassing. *Their* home had several bedrooms, a study, a drawing room, a dining room, and three rooms for the servants. Not to mention its own stables, a veranda, and a greenhouse. It was a far cry from the laborer cottage, where an entire family cooked, ate, washed, and slept within the confines of one room.

It was a sobering reminder that there were many who could use his help. Loving Jillian had meant opening his eyes to the world of the less fortunate. It had made him a better man. And he loved her all the more for it.

After some searching, he found Jilly in the greenhouse, her gloved hands wrist-deep in potting soil. She was hollowing out a space to transplant a thriving hibiscus into a larger pot. A smudge on her cheek told him she had tried to sweep hair from her face.

Lewis snuck up to her shoulder and tucked the errant strands behind her ear. "I see you've been busy," he said.

"I don't like to sit around," she answered.

"I know. I'm glad you have a warm spot to potter about in." He grinned at the intended pun.

Jillian did not acknowledge the humor. "There is little enough I'm allowed to do," she said, making no attempt to hide the bitterness that underscored her words.

Lewis was momentarily put off his stride. Her comment reflected the mood in which he had left her. But he would soon cheer her up, just as he had been gladdened by his interaction with his father.

"I took a walk past the tenant cottages," he began.

Jillian's fingers worked nimbly with the roots of the hibiscus.

"My father and his steward, Mr. Cooper, were there."

Jillian took hold of the watering can she had readied beside her and poured the liquid into the hole she had prepared.

"They were discussing repairs to the roof of one of the cottages," Lewis continued.

Holding the plant upright with one hand, Jilly began to scoop soil into the cavity that now housed the roots.

"I was concerned that it might take several days, even a week or two to complete repairs, leaving the tenants without proper shelter." Lewis waited for a response. He was disappointed.

Jillian began prodding the soil around the roots with her fingers. Rather more assertively than necessary, Lewis thought.

"I suggested that they provide a temporary solution."

More water. More prodding.

"They are going to use one of the covers for the hay bales to seal the hole in the roof and offer some protection against the elements."

Jillian peeled off her gloves and discarded them upon the shelf. Then, and only then, did she look at Lewis. "That will not keep the heat in as well as tiles would," she said. "And you know how cold it is today."

"What would you have us do?" Lewis replied. Despite the fact that she was bringing up the same concerns he had shared with his father, he took umbrage at her words. He had cared. He had come up with a solution. The situation was temporary. Why was she not pleased with him?

"Provide them with alternate housing," she said flatly.

Although Lewis had wanted the exact same arrangement, his father's response had made him understand that this was not a reasonable request. And so, to his ears, Jilly now sounded unreasonable.

"Is that what they did at Trenton Grange?" he asked.

"No, but…"

"And did Mr. Trenton's tenants expect that from him?"

Jilly's hands went to her hips. "Mr. Trenton is notoriously close-fisted. I did not think you wished to be compared to him. Besides, I had no say in the running of that estate. At Oakwoods, I hoped I might speak my mind."

Lewis lifted his palms and shook them at her. "Where should we house them? All the cottages are filled to capacity. I suppose you would prefer that they stayed with us while their roof is repaired!"

"I should not mind that at all," Jillian retorted. "We have room enough."

"You can't be serious!"

"Why not? Because that is not how things are done?"

"Yes! No! Argh! Why do you insist on making things difficult?! There is much we can do to run the estate fairly and treat those who depend on us with empathy. But you cannot break every single rule that you don't like. They are there for a reason."

Jillian's lips grew tight. "You said you liked that I did not follow rules blindly."

"But you are breaking them blindly, too! The staff have already been complaining that you make them uncomfortable. You linger in the kitchen, converse with them while they're trying to work, even offering to help! You may want to treat them like friends, but they are not ready to receive such friendship. You cannot be their peer as you were with the servants at Trenton Grange. Here you are wife to the heir of Oakwoods. You *must* learn to engage within those parameters."

Jillian's arms fell to her sides, defeated. "So, I am to read and embroider and learn the piano," she said numbly.

A pang of pity shot through Lewis's heart. He softened his tone and took his wife's hand. "You could take the carriage and your new lady's maid and visit Ellena. You have not seen her since the wedding. She will no doubt be keen to hear all about it."

Jilly shook her head, her eyes to the floor. "I cannot visit her every day. And I have no other friends in Munro."

"What about Pen? You two enjoy each other's company. You could visit a museum together." He tapped her playfully on the arm. "It would be *your* turn to be the chaperone."

"We have done," Jillian replied. "But even Munro does not have an endless supply of curiosities that interest me. And Penelope is often out riding. I cannot tag along, as I have no skill on a horse. Besides, I think she prefers her own company. So you see, I must have something meaningful with which to occupy myself."

"Come spring, I shall value your advice on how to beautify the gardens," suggested Lewis, quite proud that he had thought of this. "And we shall make friends in time. Munro is not completely devoid of decent folk. Just be patient. It will work itself out."

Jillian had perked up at the mention of the garden, her eyes brightening, her body leaning toward him. "And I could join you when you meet with the steward or the groundskeeper," she said eagerly. "I have lots of ideas that they might not have considered."

"And you shall share them with me," countered Lewis. "But you cannot attend the meetings, dearest. That is not seemly."

At once, Jilly's sparkle vanished. "What is unseemly about it? Why must I be kept hidden like some decoration on the mantelpiece? I want to be *doing* things!"

Lewis had come to the end of his tether. His wife, it seemed, was wholly unable to see reason. As yet, she had shown no willingness to understand her new position or adjust to its expectations. There was no compromise, only frustration.

"Jillian," he said firmly, his patience at an end. "You are not married to a farmer. If that was what you wanted, you have chosen poorly indeed."

"It seems I have."

The air twanged between them.

Jillian turned back to the innocent hibiscus. Picking up the pruning shears, she began to snip away at the branchlings that were growing at cross-purposes to the rest of the shrub.

In his mind, Lewis knew her words had been spoken in a sulky fit of pique. But in his heart, they had cut deep.

How had it come to this? Lewis was at a loss. His joyful expectation was now thoroughly quashed, and Jillian was making it clear she was no longer participating in any reconciliatory efforts.

So be it. He would not beg.

He took a step away from his wife, turned on his heel, and strode from the greenhouse into the chilly air. By now, the mist was thinning and he could see the hedge that blocked the view of the lake. He remembered the day they had arrived at the cottage and spent a passionate hour behind those shrubs.

Not long ago, they had been not only of one body, but of one mind. Today, that connection had buckled under the weight of their different upbringings. If they were not careful, it would plummet into the depths of anger and bitterness. They must find a way to strengthen the bond between them. But if Jillian would not meet him halfway, he could not manage it all on his own.

Outdoors, the day was warming, the sky clearing. But in Lewis's heart, the cold and dark remained. Only Jilly could bring back the light.

But Jilly was silent.

CHAPTER FIFTEEN

Oakwoods, January 1816

THEY HAD CALLED a truce that night. In each other's arms, the conflict of that day in November had dissolved. Jillian had promised herself she would never again punish Lewis for the frustration she felt. She knew he was doing everything within his power to make her happy.

The problem was that he seemed to have very little power at all.

The couple had celebrated Christmas and Twelfth Night with the family at the main house. The decorations had been tasteful, the food excellent, as usual. Jillian had been delighted to discover that Lewis had arranged for a real tree to be placed in the foyer. He had even consulted with her as to what decorations she'd wanted to add to it. All had proceeded pleasantly and civilly.

And then, with the celebrations behind them, he had brought her news that had taken the wind out of her bellows.

The first Sunday family dinner of 1816 had occurred the afternoon after Twelfth Night. It was a simpler affair than that which Jillian had grown accustomed to, mainly involving soup and bread and cold meat leftovers. Everyone was a little subdued after the festivities of the night before. It wasn't long before the ladies retired to the drawing room to engage in what Jilly called "the tedium of the *ton*." Lady Bradford read. Penelope played piano. Jillian tried to stay awake.

Lewis and his father, meanwhile, had their weekly meeting in the study. It seemed to Jillian to go on longer than usual. The minutes ticked by in the drawing room. Even Penelope began to tire and exchanged her seat at the piano for a more comfortable one with a book.

Conversation had already been depleted at the dinner table, and little remained for idle discourse in the drawing room. Jillian found herself roaming the room and browsing the paintings and knickknacks that constituted its decoration.

They did not appeal to her. The paintings were large oils of people in various solo and family poses—no doubt the Bradford ancestors. None of them looked particularly happy. Their wealth, however, was unmistakable. The ladies wore furs and jewels and the gentlemen assumed proud postures with hunting dogs or a sword or on horseback. And every single one carried an expression of privileged boredom.

The vases and statuettes offered little more by way of artistry. For one thing, all the vases were empty. Their gold-painted rims and floral designs did not, in Jillian's opinion, make up for the absence of real flowers. The statuettes were, once again, depictions of people, or the heads of people. Why someone's head should be worth displaying was a mystery to Jillian.

The more time she spent with the Bradfords, the less she understood them. They exuded tremendous pride in their heritage and a furious zeal to maintain it all for the future. But their day-to-day lives lacked any of the same vigor. From what she could gather, an inordinate amount of time was spent changing clothes, eating elaborate meals, and learning skills that had no real use. At least Ellena and her husband kept such lavishness to a minimum.

Why did it not drive the ladies of the house to madness? Were they really fulfilled by promenading, dining, painting and the like?

There did seem to be some hope for Penelope, who had insisted on taking charge of the kitchen garden, where vegetables, herbs, roses and lavender were grown to be used in meals and scented water. She had regularly invited Jilly to join her, which made a pleasant break from the loneliness of the cottage. Mostly, however, Pen was out riding for ages at a time—with a groom or stablehand in tow, just in case of an accident.

It made Jillian think back to her walks with Lewis at Munro House, where Ingsley had been assigned to keep an eye on them. It seemed such a long time ago. Something of the innocence of those days had since been lost.

Still, she had what she wanted, didn't she? Lewis was hers. Forever. Hers to hold. Hers to love and to cherish. For better or for worse.

Not for a minute had Jillian guessed that "for better" would be the problem. The more privilege she was given, the more she felt denied. The life she'd thought she had agreed to could no longer exist. Not now that Lewis was the heir.

It was not his fault. It was no one's fault. But she wanted someone to blame. Someone whom she could berate for her unexpected misery. She wanted to be angry with his parents for needing him to take on new responsibilities. And yet she knew it could not be helped. She wanted to reject society for creating this strange hierarchy of people based on not very much sense at all. But society, it was obvious, cared nothing for her opinion.

She needed to blame *someone*. And so, when Lewis finally reappeared in her company, his face flushed, his manner flustered, she was not in a forgiving mood.

At Lewis's urging, they said their goodbyes immediately and made their way to the waiting carriage. Although the distance to the cottage was only half a mile, it was windy and freezing out and Lewis had thought it risky—they could easily catch cold or slip on the smooth, almost-invisible patches of ice.

It was but a few minutes' drive, yet Jillian was perched and ready to exit the cubicle into their home, knowing the unfortunate groom had to sit atop the carriage in the very weather she and Lewis had sought to avoid.

Lewis, however, stayed his hand upon the door.

"Hold a moment," he said. "There is something I must tell you and I do not wish to have this discussion where the staff can listen."

His words boded ill. If he wanted privacy, it could not be good news.

"What is it?" she asked, though she wished desperately he would not tell her.

"As you know, Philip sat in the House of Commons."

"Did I? I suppose I did, but I have not given it much thought."

"And I spoke of relinquishing my services as a barrister to take up a position in Parliament."

"You may have mentioned it, but I do not recall a great discussion on the topic."

"My father has reminded me that Parliament will reopen soon. If I am to take my brother's seat, I will need to run in a by-election within the week and, if successful, be sworn in at the opening of Parliament."

Jillian had never shown much interest in matters of finance or politics. Everything Lewis was saying sounded vaguely familiar in a background sort of way but meant little to her in a personal capacity.

"I see," she answered, for lack of anything else to say.

"Do you?" Lewis leaned toward her, his brow deeply creased. He started to chew his bottom lip.

"I don't know," replied Jilly, not sure of herself at all now. "What am I supposed to see?"

"Parliament is in London."

Jillian hesitated. "Would you be gone long?"

"The season this year is expected to run from February to July."

"You mean dances and debutantes and making friends?" asked Jilly, perking up.

"Well, yes, that happens concurrently with Parliament. For which I would need to be in London."

The penny finally dropped.

"You need to be in London for *half the year*?! What is to become of *me*?"

"I want you with me, of course. Daily sessions only begin in the late afternoon. We will have all day together. We could walk through the impressive parks, of which there are several. Here we only have Munro Park. In London, you will be spoiled for choice."

"If the sessions only begin in the afternoon, when do they finish?" Jillian wanted to know.

Lewis fidgeted. No doubt he had been dreading questions like these. "Er, they can continue into the early hours of the morning."

"I see." Now she really did see all too clearly. "Then you will not be sharing my bed." The weight of her words sank between them.

"Parliament does not meet on weekends," Lewis deflected hastily. "We can attend balls and sleep in until noon if we wish. There will be so many people for you to meet, not just the Munro crowd. You are bound to discover new acquaintances you like."

"Only to be parted from them when the season ends," muttered Jilly.

"We would see them every year for months at a time when Parliament is in session, and you could write each other to sustain the friendship when you are apart."

"Six months a year in London…" Jilly considered this. So far, Munro had not offered her as much as she had hoped. Could London do any better? A sudden thought brightened her mood.

"We would be out from under your parents at last," she said, excitement building. "It would be as we first imagined—just the two of us making our own decisions…"

"Er…"

It was not even a whole word, but it was enough to stop Jilly dead in mid-sentence.

"What? What haven't you told me?"

"Well, er, the thing is… London is very expensive. And, you see, my parents already own a townhouse in one of the more fashionable areas."

Jilly tried not to think of oil paintings of ancestors and bronze busts of people whom she did not recognize. At least she would be able to fill the vases with flowers. "I suppose I could live with their particular taste in furnishings."

"I am glad to hear it," said Lewis. "Er…"

"What? *What*? Why do you draw it out so? What else must I know that I obviously will not like?"

"The thing is," said Lewis wretchedly, "my father serves in the House of Lords. When his six months of mourning are over in April, he and Mother will join us in the townhouse."

Jilly felt her body stiffen. This was so much worse. Under the same roof! Every action, every utterance to be judged. Months of it, every hour of every day.

"We will occupy separate floors," added Lewis. "Our interactions will be limited." His eyes pleaded with her to find such arrangements tolerable. "We can go out as often as you want. If you wish, we can stick to our Sunday family dinner and nothing more."

"And you think your parents will respect our wishes to be left alone? The temptation to ascend or descend a flight of stairs to poke about in our lives will be hard to resist. And what of the many evenings when you are away? Will I be able to attend a dinner without you if I do make friends? Or will I be at the mercy of either your parents or solitude?"

"Pen will be coming too. If you like, we can ask her to come with us now in January and introduce you to some of the more likeable folk she knows."

"You said February before," Jillian reminded him sharply.

"Well, yes. Parliament opens on the first of February. But we must allow several days to travel and settle into our new accommodations."

"I've heard enough," said Jillian abruptly. "I see you have planned everything neatly with your father. In a matter of weeks, we are to upend our already strained existence here and be transplanted to the largest city in the world, where I know no one but you and possibly your sister. I am to be abandoned at night and cautioned in my behavior by your parents for months on end. I will have nowhere to escape to—no woods, no lake, no greenhouse, not even Ellena to comfort me. And you would have me find merit in this. I do not see it."

With that, Jillian threw open the carriage door, almost hitting the poor footman on the nose. Remembering that he had stood in the brutal cold while they had their infuriating conversation only made her more agitated. Her instinct was to invite both him and the groom inside for a cup of hot chocolate and a warm seat in the kitchen. But she would not make that mistake again.

No, indeed, she was learning that she must hide her true self deep down, where it could not shame her husband—the one who had once loved her for her fearlessness.

Where was that love now?

It was there, she conceded, but shackled by expectations. Shackles that she must now help him carry. The more pretense at power he was given, the more it bound and restricted him, squeezing ever tighter until no real autonomy existed at all.

Her heart ached for her beloved. It bled for the both of them. But the constriction about the throat of her freedom also made her angry. And resentful. She would cast it off forcefully if she could. But it would mean throwing off her bond with Lewis. Though she clawed at the circumstances that oppressed her, she would not desert him.

For better or worse.

If only this would finally be the worst of it.

CHAPTER SIXTEEN

London, May 1816

PENELOPE HAD BEEN more than willing to join them at the start of the London season. The freedom of being able to roam the large Bradford estate was as nothing compared to the relief of being out from under their parents. In this regard, as with many things, she and Jillian were of one mind.

Their sharing of the same spaces also meant that Jillian's loneliness was held at bay. Though Lewis had kept his word and spent all his free time with her, showing her the sights, introducing her to what he hoped would be good friends in time, even spending some mornings just lying in with his wife, she still missed him terribly when he was occupied with his new position in Parliament. None of the people he had introduced her to had shared any of her interests. They were polite enough, and certainly less blunt in their disapproval of her than many of the folk she had encountered in Munro, but Jilly could not relax in their company. She had fallen back into the habit of hiding her awkwardness with excessive speech, plowing through her discomfort with a barrage of chatty sentences. If anything, this had only made her feel more ill at ease. And the looks shared between the other guests told her they thought her too odd for future acquaintance.

Penelope, like Jillian, grew easily bored in such environs, and thought up the sort of distractions that Lewis would not have considered. He certainly would not have guessed that grown women might enjoy playing hide-and seek in the spacious triple-storeyed townhouse. Nor would he *ever* have suggested they disguise themselves as delivery boys and see if Cook would let them in the back door without recognizing them.

Penelope's high spirits became especially valuable to Jillian once Lord and Lady Bradford arrived in April and the space the younger trio had occupied in the townhouse grew instantly close and cheerless. Whereas Lewis almost immediately fell in step with his parents, Penelope continued to encourage Jillian to be herself.

Jillian was no longer as hurt when Lewis could not be what she needed, since she had a dear friend in her sister-in-law, who would lighten her mood. Thus it was, on the first of May—Lewis having come home almost at dawn and desperately needing sleep—Jillian shrugged off her disappointment and the two women disappeared to the Spring Fair together.

They took the curricle with Penelope at the reins and a tiger to hold said reins while the ladies were wandering from stall to stall. Jillian had been quite shocked when Penelope had mentioned they would be taking such a fearsome creature along. She had no idea that "tiger" was merely an informal term for a small groom. When no animal had been forthcoming, and they had left the house without a well-trained, orange panther tagging along, Jillian had made polite enquiry and caused Pen to laugh out loud.

"You *are* funny!" Pen had said, wiping tears of mirth from her eyes. "Perhaps we can ask the lad to growl every so often, since you are clearly disappointed that he is a mere human."

The "tiger" had not obliged, however, much to Jilly's relief. She had not wished her ignorance to cause him embarrassment. She had been guilty of that too often already.

The day began sunny without being too hot, though it was still morning and would likely grow much warmer as the hours passed. The women were both dressed in light muslin and straw bonnet, with a fan each to ward off the heat if it should oppress them in the afternoon.

As they turned the corner to the commons where the event was being held, they could hear the bustle of activity—the music from various sources playing at cross-purposes to each other, the multitude of tones and pitches of hundreds of voices forming a strange music of its own, the cry of "Pies! Get them while they're hot!"

The smells of pies and people and animals and scented garlands wafted toward them as Penelope slowed the curricle and the tiger hopped down to receive the reins. The two women stepped down quickly and were soon in the thick of it all, the sounds and sights and smells pressing upon their senses in a wonderful deluge.

It was one of the happiest days Jillian had experienced since coming to London. The fair had the feel of a village festival to it. Despite the number of sophisticated ladies promenading on their husbands' arms, the atmosphere was light and playful, and Jillian felt the weight of the past months begin to lift from her heart.

The sound of jingling bells drew their attention at once to the Morris dancers, their bright-green waistcoats and hats decked with flowers serving as reminders that all was newly in bloom. However, the two women did not linger to watch them.

Instead, they hurried to a tree-shaded hedge in the hopes of finding some of the morning dew that had not been claimed by the crowd. Several other ladies, their parasols hiding their actions, were wiping their hands across the top of the hedge and rubbing the collected dew delicately across their faces.

When Penelope and Jillian arrived, there was no moisture left to be gathered.

"Ah, they needed it more than you," soothed Pen at Jillian's disappointed pout. "You have a natural beauty and do not need to rely on cosmetics or the mythical properties of first May dew to enhance your looks. You look as fresh as this untrampled grass." She indicated a patch of ground that circled the base of the nearest tree.

"Pen, you're brilliant!" Jilly cried. "The grass will have dew! These ladies will not have stooped so low to retrieve it. But I have no such qualms." She reached down and drew her palm across the moist grass blades, lifting her hand to her cheeks and rubbing the cool droplets into them.

"Well, you certainly have a rosier glow, but that may just be the vigor with which you applied the magical dew." Penelope laughed before herself doing much the same. "See? Am I not now an apple-cheeked maiden?"

"You certainly are! But I would take care if I were you," warned Jillian. "If you wish to stay unmarried, you should avoid adding anything to your existing loveliness. It is unfair toward the hapless young men who think you brighten your looks for them."

"It serves them right if they believe I do this for their benefit," Pen retorted. Her gaze rose over Jillian's shoulder. "Come on. The women are lining up for a footrace. We can add even more color to our complexions." She giggled. "Perhaps if we are as red as beetroot, no men shall look at us!"

The assembled group was a mishmash of fine ladies with feathered bonnets, working-class women who had the day off from thoughtful masters, and those like Jillian and Penelope who wore white muslin in celebration of the fresh beginnings of spring.

The footwear, too, varied a great deal in style and material. The two sisters-in-law had agreed to throw propriety out of the window and come to the fair barelegged so that they could now slip off their light pumps and partake in the race without the hindrance of shoes.

They arrived behind the starting line just as the referee lowered the flag. One or two of the ladies grabbed their skirts and pulled them up an inch to avoid tripping over their hems. But Jillian, Pen, and all the women of the lower classes hitched their hems up to their knees, bolting forward.

The distance of the race was not great, but the finer ladies were soon left far behind while the rest fought to cross the ribbon first. Pen nearly took the win, but an elbow-pumping maid shot past her and claimed the victory.

Jillian puffed across the finish with the remaining bundle of runners. "I have become unfit since my stay in London," she complained, breathing hard, her hands on her knees. "There is nowhere to run wild as I once did." She straightened and allowed herself to catch her breath. "At least Oakwoods offered me a little of that when the weather wasn't too bad. Here, I have spent too much time sitting or merely walking. I have missed a good gallop in my bare feet."

"You really should let me teach you to ride," said Pen. "You can canter in Hyde Park once you have enough skill and confidence. Such exercise would provide some of that exhilaration you seek. It does wonders for my mood when I feel hemmed in."

"I suppose it will have to be sidesaddle," grumbled Jillian.

"Yes, in public at least. But you will soon get the hang of it. You are not timid. I think a horse would enjoy your spirit. It is rather like theirs. Once you find your connection with the animal, you will progress quickly."

"Even in such an uncomfortable position?"

"Even then."

Someone—or something—jostled Jilly from behind. "Beg pardon," muttered what appeared for all the world to be a walking shrub.

"Jack o' the Green!" cried Jilly, "I shan't give you a coin if you knock it out of my hand!" She laughed as she reached inside her hidden pocket to fetch a sixpence.

"Don't mind him, mistress," said a milkmaid, wearing a flower garland and dancing around the leafy framework that hid all of "Jack" except for his face. "He may already have had a pint or two. It's hot in that there bower he wears. Just toss the coin in the sweep's bowl. Thank 'ee mightily."

The chimney sweep, who must have been similarly warm dancing in his sooty clothes, was equally unsure on his feet but held out the bowl firmly in one hand, tipping his hat with the other. A fiddler completed the ensemble.

Nearby, a group of bystanders parted and a long line of more milkmaids and sweeps caught up with the four leading the troupe. They made their way to the maypole, where they each took hold of a ribbon until every such band was seized, whereupon they continued their dance, weaving in and out, plaiting and unplaiting the ribbons as they circled 'round.

Then came the children, their parents coaxing and clapping, the little girls in shiny, patent leather shoes, the boys with broad buckles on the toes of theirs. In and out they wove, a little less confidently than the adults who had come before them, their shy smiles lifted to their proud mamas and papas.

"One day, that will be you," whispered Penelope, nodding her head at a mother calling words of encouragement to a particularly small child who stood and sucked its thumb and would not move into the circle with the others.

"Ah, you assume I shall have the offspring who will not do as asked," teased Jillian. "Which, then, will be yours? Perhaps that boy who prances like a horse?"

Penelope shook her head. "I am content to be an aunt. It is too much bother to find a husband."

The two women meandered through the fair, watching the jugglers and calling out with the crowd during a pantomime of Robin Hood and Maid Marian. Someone recited a scene from Shakespeare, but this did not hold their attention and they drifted along the tide of people to watch a pie-eating contest instead.

The day was now beginning to grow hot. Even their bonnets and fans and light dresses could not stop the film of sweat that began to form upon their brows.

"Let's go in here," suggested Jillian, ducking into the shade of a traveler's tent. A sign outside announced: *Madame Zahara. Fortunes told.* The heavy fabric of the structure kept the direct sun from burning their skin, but a musty warmth was trapped inside the enclosure. The sounds outside grew muted, quiet enough that they could hear the crackling voice of the crone sitting at the small table.

"G'day, dearies." She grinned, an action that revealed surprisingly healthy teeth amidst a sea of wrinkles. "Come to have your fortune read? Cross my palm with silver and I shall tell you what your future holds."

Penelope sat herself down at once and placed a coin in the old woman's hand—though "woman" was a stretch of the imagination. Her features, crisscrossed with lines and painted in a deep tan, were big-boned and looked to have been recently shaved. She was also unusually cheery for a woman in her profession, as they tended to carry an air of dark mystery about them. At least, the ones who used to pass through her village had.

"Let's have a little look, shall we?" said the woman, laying down her own rather large hand for Penelope to place hers in.

"Ooo! What have we here?" The palmist leaned in closer, her head shawl draping over the table. "A changeling! Brought by the fairies and raised by human folk. Have you ever had an itch between your shoulders where your wings should have been?"

Penelope's gaze rose toward the palmist's face, possibly seeking to know if she was having a laugh at her expense.

A movement at the entrance to the tent made all three of them look up to see another woman with shawls and bangles stop in her tracks and open her mouth to cry, "Kaven! You useless son of a dog! What have I told you about messing with my business? Get out! Get out right now before I put a curse on 'ee!"

The first palmist, chortling and ducking as the newcomer planted a heavy hand on "her" back, darted past the furious creature to escape the tent, but not before "her" head shawl was unceremoniously yanked off to reveal the short hair of a man.

"And don't come back until you've earned your supper with some real work!" shouted Madame Zahara before turning to her wide-eyed customers. "'Usbands," she muttered. "What use are they?"

She sat down slowly, her bangles jingling on her wrists as she flicked the fringes of her shawl from her face. "What's it to be?" she asked, getting straight to business. "Crystal, cards, or palm? I don't 'old with no tea leaves. Messy and wasteful, they are."

"Oh," said Penelope, somewhat rattled, "I've already had my reading."

"Wha'? From Kaven? That weren't no readin'. He's just a foolish old goat who likes to have fun with my customers." Her eyes darkened. "*I'll* tell you the truth. You'd best be sure you want to 'ear it."

"Er, no thank you," Penelope answered, standing up quite suddenly. "Perhaps Jillian would like to have a go."

Madame Zahara eyed Jillian in a manner that was most unsettling. It was completely opposite to the mischief of Kaven. Her eyes bored into Jilly's, seeking. "Yes," she said slowly, "you have an open soul. You will be easy to read."

As if in a trance, Jilly sat down and laid her hand upon the table like an offering.

"Silver first," said the old woman.

For a moment, the trance was broken. Jilly fished inside her pocket for the necessary coin while her mind raced. *Is this wise? Do I want the hear the truth?*

The answer came back with surprising speed. *Yes.* Yes, she did want the truth. Whatever it was, it was better to know it. Perhaps it would show her the way through the difficulties that besieged her marriage.

She planted her hand down firmly, the coin resting in her palm. "I am ready."

The coin disappeared inside the multitude of shawls. Madame Zahara bent over Jillian's hand, scrutinizing it. She nodded as she did so, as if agreeing with a voice only she could hear. "You have choices. That is good. Here are the signs." She closed her eyes, as if reading something written in her mind. "The new will feel old. The old will feel new. Now heed my warning: love will grow cold until you embrace new beginnings."

Madame Zahara sat back abruptly. "That is all." She waved a

hand toward the open flap that served as a doorway. "Go now. I wish to eat my lunch." Without further ado, she reached under the table and drew out a basket from which she claimed a sandwich. As if her customers were no longer there, she sank her teeth into the bread. "Go on," she said, munching as she spoke, "Off with 'ee."

Slightly stunned, Jillian rose and made to leave. Pen slipped her arm through Jilly's and led her from the dark interior of the tent. "Come on. Let's find some ices. We can forget about that old woman. She makes her money scaring gullible people. We will not be her fools."

"I'm not so sure, Pen," said Jillian. "There *is* some truth to what she said."

"Oh, poppycock. She was especially vague. You could apply what she said to anyone. That is her tactic. Don't be misled by her clever act."

"I don't know. Things between me and Lewis have been strained for some time. Our life together was a new beginning, and I have not embraced it."

"Anyone who has been placed in an unfamiliar environment will struggle," answered Penelope. "As for love growing cold, anyone can see how much you and my brother adore each other. You've both had adjustments to make. Give it time. You'll figure it out together."

Jilly wanted to agree. She nodded as if she did. But the old woman's words kept milling about in her thoughts. What was the new that felt old? Was it the excitement of their love that was waning? What old thing would feel new? The Bradford way of life?

No, Penelope was right. The prediction was purposefully vague to make her believe whatever thoughts fitted the open-ended words.

As she stood, deep in thought, another body bumped into hers. This time, it spun away before being tackled by a man in a white apron. The body was small and bedraggled and belonged to a dirty urchin who cradled an apple to his chest while the stall owner lifted him to his feet by the scruff.

"Got you, you little thief! It's off to the Old Bailey with you. I've had enough of you lot pilfering my goods."

The boy squirmed and wriggled in an attempt to get free, which only earned him a cuff about the ears.

"What's he done?" Jillian asked, although the answer was as clear as daylight.

"He stole an apple from my stall, the little beggar," answered the man.

"An apple? He stole one apple? And for that, you would have him up before the judge? Where is your mercy, sir? Can you not see he is hungry?"

"Let his parents feed him, then!" said the man.

"Ain't got no parents," the boy told him, though it was doubtful this would make a difference to his accuser.

"Should be in the workhouse, earning your bread," was the harsh reply.

"Excuse me," Jillian interrupted. "How much for the apple?"

"They're four for a penny."

"Is that all?" Jilly dug her hand into her pocket. "Here. That will cover the cost of the apple and a few more besides. He probably knows at least three other hungry children."

The man looked at the penny and shook his head. "Don't bother. He'll only be back to his thieving again tomorrow."

"No doubt you are correct, if no one will help him. One apple is hardly going to keep him from starving."

"They'll feed him in prison," was the man's indifferent answer. He renewed his grip on the boy's arm.

Jillian knelt on her haunches before the boy. "Do you have nowhere to go where you can be cared for?"

"I ran away. Got tired of being beaten," said the boy blandly, his eyes revealing a soul that was already old and cynical.

Jillian cast her gaze helplessly at Penelope. "What can we do for him?"

Penelope touched her shoulder gently. "Come, Jilly, we have no authority in this matter. If this man will not retract his accusation, the law demands the boy be taken into custody."

"Can we not take him with us?" Jillian pleaded, the weight of helplessness pushing on her chest.

Pen bent down and took Jilly's arm. "Come away, sister. What you are asking is impossible."

Tears shot hotly into Jillian's eyes. She looked once more at the boy. "I'm sorry. I'm so very sorry."

The boy stared back at her as Penelope pulled her away. He appeared to have accepted his fate. It even seemed he felt a measure of pity for her, someone for whom such hardship and callousness was unfamiliar.

For Jillian, the outing was ruined. She had no further interest in the fair or the joys of spring. Penelope, who had tried to distract her with sights they had not yet explored, eventually gave up and agreed to return to the curricle.

They rode in silence, the figure of the tiger—his hands and face spotless, his smart livery an indication that he had a home and food enough—served as a stark contrast to the boy at the fair, reminding Jillian of her heartbreak at leaving the poor lad to his fate.

Back at the townhouse, Lewis was now well-rested. He smiled broadly as they entered the drawing room. "So, did you have fun?" he asked, stepping forward to kiss Jilly's cheek. "Tell us all about it!"

Us.

Jillian turned to the right and found Lord and Lady Bradford seated on the settee. They looked up expectantly. Perhaps they were truly interested in her news. Perhaps they awaited the courtesy of a greeting.

Jillian felt too wretched to provide either.

"What's wrong?" asked Lewis, stepping back and seeing no smile, his own now falling from his face.

"It's probably best spoken of in private," said Penelope hurriedly, her eyes flicking to her parents.

But Jillian was in no mood to hold back for their sakes.

"They arrested a boy. For taking an apple." The disgust was evident in her voice. She imagined it was visible in her face, too.

"Where? At the fair?" asked Lewis.

"The fruit seller hauled him off. The poor lad is probably sitting in some damp, crowded cell right now with ten other boys just like him. He couldn't have been more than twelve years old."

"Then he is old enough to know better," declared Lord Bradford.

Jillian ignored him.

"You're a barrister," she told Lewis. "Can't you speak on his behalf?" She grabbed her husband's hand and squeezed it.

Lewis laid his other hand over hers. "If he is guilty, there is nothing I can do for him. The law is the law." He said this with little conviction, and Jillian could see that he, too, was troubled by the incident.

"Then the law must change!" she said firmly. "If you cannot help as a barrister, you can help as a member of Parliament. We should be taking better care of the poor and the helpless. Children like him have nowhere to turn to where they won't be abused."

"Nonsense!" scoffed Lord Bradford. "There are orphanages and workhouses, where they are clothed, housed, and fed. He probably ran away because he was lazy. So many of them are."

Jillian whirled around before Lewis could stop her.

"And what would you know of this? Have you ever visited these places you recommend so highly? Have you spoken to these children? Have you seen the gruel they are fed, the bruises on their bodies?"

The baron was unmoved. "What would you have us do? Hand over money that belongs to our children to these strays instead?"

"Yes! It's not as though *you* have worked any harder for it than you expect *them* to! And you have so much, why can you not spare some to see that innocents do not suffer?"

"My dear child," said Lord Bradford with condescending calm. "Would you not rather teach them to live honest lives? Why should we loosen our purse strings for these people when they will use it to drink and gamble?"

Lady Bradford nodded in agreement. "We know you are… passionate about such things. But I do not think you have quite thought this through. To be honest, I do not believe I have ever heard you speak on these children's behalf until today. Tomorrow, something else will hold your attention instead."

"You do not hear me speak about these matters," Jillian said with barely contained irritation, "because I know you have little interest in them. Lewis and I discuss such concerns all the time. And the incident with this poor boy has only fed my desire to delay action no longer."

Jilly turned back to Lewis. "If I cannot change the laws or give them money, I would at least want to see to it that the places where they are housed are truly safe environments with enough food and no ill treatment. Since London is so big, there must be a children's home where I could volunteer my time. I could cook, teach, anything to make their lives a little better."

"My love, such activity is not…"

Jillian balled her fists at her side. "Lewis Bradford, if you are going to tell me that it is 'not appropriate' again, I think I shall scream! When will you allow me to do something meaningful with my time, something that really matters to me? Am I forever to be taking baskets to struggling tenants, and nothing more?"

Lewis glanced from his wife to his parents and back. He looked as if he were caught between Scylla and Charybdis.

"Perhaps a less hands-on role might be a worthy compromise?" he suggested cautiously. "You could hold fundraising teas and use the monies you collect to purchase food or clothing for these orphans."

Jillian stared at her husband. Tea? He wanted her to arrange tea parties? "I feel…" she said slowly, trying to hold back what she really wanted to blurt out, "that is not the best use of my time.

Besides, how would I know if these supplies were given to the neediest or whether the children received kindness in addition to these items of charity? I want to stop the cruelty, not just the hunger, Lewis. Don't you understand how important this is to me?"

The scathing tones of Lady Bradford cut off any response from Lewis. "Our son understands that your involvement in such low work would dishonor the Bradford name. Are you so intent on making a fool of us and your husband? You cannot simply run off like a…"

"Groundskeeper's daughter?" finished Jilly. "Because that's what I am. And I have never been ashamed of it. Being part of the so-called upper class, however, has brought me nothing but frustration and disappointment. All this strutting and posing and sticking to arbitrary rules just so that you can appear more important while forgetting what it is to be human. I don't want it. I never did."

She turned mournful eyes upon Lewis. He opened his mouth to say something, then decided against it. So, he was choosing their side once again.

Jillian stared at the family. Even Penelope, her fellow free spirit, was silent. At least she had the good grace to look at the floor with some embarrassment.

Jillian wanted to flee the room, the house, the whole of London. She wanted to run until she could run no more. Then walk until her knees buckled. Crawl and drag herself if she must, anything to reach Ermenbrough again—the place where she was understood and valued as she was.

She loved Lewis. But it was not enough. He had accepted his role as Philip's replacement, dragged them both into a life they had not agreed upon. Where were the barefoot picnics? Where were the chickens? The laughter? It had all disappeared into a distant mist of forgotten promises.

Compromise? It was a word he liked to throw about. But what was *he* giving up? The compromise seemed always to be hers.

"Jillian," he said at last, "I'm sure we can find a way…"

"For me to compromise? No, thank you. Not this time. You ask too much of me, Lewis. Too much."

And with a parting glance of antipathy toward his parents, she rushed from the room. Cry. Scream. Burst into song. She could do none of these without a similar look of disapproval from them.

To prove her point, she heard Lady Bradford say with what Jilly imagined were pursed lips and rolling eyes, "Do you see, my son? This is what we tried to warn you about."

Jillian did not wait to hear Lewis's reply. She did not want to know how he would explain away her actions. More and more, she had become a nuisance. More and more, he had become like his parents.

What was here for her now? She did not mean London. She meant this marriage. It was no longer a source of happiness. She was losing herself to it.

Jilly halted in her headlong rush to get away. After all, where would she go? She must take a stand, here and now. Fight for herself. Claim the right to *be* herself. What did she have to lose? They didn't approve of her even when she played by *their* rules.

It was time, Jilly decided, to live by her own.

CHAPTER SEVENTEEN

London, late May 1816

LEWIS COULD SENSE his wife pulling away from him. She no longer waited up in the hopes of seeing him before she fell asleep. He would kiss her when he crept quietly into the bed beside her, and she would turn and curl into his embrace. But she did not open sleepy eyes and ask if the session had gone well. Nor did she lie in with him in the morning until he awoke so that they might plan their day together.

More often than not, she was already out on some errand by the time he'd started breakfast. She did not share what her errands were. She neither asked him to join her nor reported on what she had accomplished. It felt to Lewis as if they had started to live separate lives.

Jillian would no longer attend dinners that were not intimate, which to her meant more than eight people. Apparently, this was a reasonably-sized group in which to have real conversation and actually get to know people. According to her, anything larger served no purpose other than to bring together important influential people for discussing business or whatever was currently being debated in Parliament. Since Lewis was one of these people, he was invited out often. However, he had stopped trying to persuade Jillian to join him. It was embarrassing to turn up alone, but she had grown stubborn. And he had learned to choose his arguments with her carefully. For argue, they would.

To Lewis, it seemed as if Jilly were finding fault with everything under the sun. She, who had been so agreeable and full of life, had grown blunt of speech when they conversed and tight-lipped when she refused further discussion.

He understood that the change of circumstance had been challenging. It felt to him, however, that she simply refused to adjust. He had tried to shield her from the worst of it, which meant spending time alone with her on almost all free days, since she did not enjoy the company of his parents or peers. Of course, he loved being with her. But he was beginning to feel isolated from society.

He would never tell her that. Besides, she would probably answer by saying she felt the same. But that was her *choice*, wasn't it? She could be happier if she let herself ease into the world in which they had found themselves.

Within him, a measure of resentment was building up. Jillian blamed him because the dreams they had shared remained unfulfilled. Well, she hadn't actually said as much. But he was sure she thought it. And it wasn't fair. She must have known how the guilt ate at him. Couldn't she be a little more reasonable? Why must she pick at everything?

A small voice—in fact, a *very* small voice, if truth be told—whispered to his conscience. *What happened to the chickens?* He tried to ignore it, but it grew a little bolder. *You shared her rebellious attitude. The rules only mattered when you were in court. That was the life you promised her. You should keep your promises.*

But it wasn't *his* fault that Philip had died! Hadn't he married her anyway? Hadn't he gone against his parents, against the norms of mourning, to keep that promise?

What were you going to do instead? Suddenly denounce her as unsuitable? Break the engagement, as if she had somehow failed you and should be discarded? You assured her nothing had changed. And nothing had *changed between you. And yet, somehow, it has.*

Lewis tried to block out the voice. He had been doing so with increasing success over the past eight months. What else was he supposed to do? Ignore all his responsibilities? If he could step up, why couldn't she? Didn't she love him enough?

The growing distance between them was the reason he had asked his mother to arrange tonight's dinner instead of his wife. Jillian had made it clear she wanted nothing to do with superfluity. And twenty guests, she had said, were excessive. Most of them, she had commented, were the sort with whom they would never have mingled in Munro, so why was he inviting them into his home in London?

His mother had said nothing when he had asked her to play the hostess. There was nothing new to be said. Jilly's inability or point-blank refusal to take on the role of future baroness was now so frequently the topic of the day that it was pointless to bring it up again.

Lewis had half-expected his wife to declare that she would not be attending the dinner, despite its being held in their home. In some ways, it would have been better if she did not. But this morning, she had returned from her errand with a happy spring in her step and asked her lady's maid to air her cardinal red dress for the dinner. The one her mother-in-law had gifted her.

Perhaps this should have given Lewis pause. Jillian hated that gown. She had said it made her look like a flaming beacon. What was more, the bodice had been stitched with intricate patterns of gold brocade. Jillian always insisted it had been designed for someone who liked to be noticed. She preferred more subtle shades of lilac, rose pink, or cloudy blue by day and the deep tones of forest green, rusted orange, or dark blue at night. These were the colors of nature. When she wore them, she was the nymph of the meadow. And the colors wore well beneath her golden mane. Tonight, however—Lewis had heard her tell her maid earlier—her hair would be up in complicated braids so they had best allow enough time.

He had been so grateful for her apparent enthusiasm that he had not questioned the suddenness of it or the fact that she was dressing in a manner that contradicted her personality.

It was only when he and his mother were in the dining room discussing a seating adjustment due to a last-minute apology, and a kitchen maid came hurtling into the room to bounce a breathless curtsey, that he discovered his willful wife had been making plans of her own.

"Cook says to come to kitchen at once…if you please, Lady Bradford, Mr. Bradford." The deference was almost an after-thought. If the handwringing and shifting from one foot to the other was any indication, the maid was far more worried about getting them to the kitchen than appeasing their need for a show of respect.

Lewis and his mother did not hesitate. With a dinner party mere hours away, this was not the time for anything to go wrong. They rushed with as much decorum as they could, the little maid racing ahead to let the cook know they were on their way.

It was obvious from the moment they stepped into what should have been an area bustling with activity that something was terribly wrong. The kitchen servants were frozen in horrified suspension, their eyes trained upon the back door, where Cook and Jillian were occupied in a heated conversation while several apron-wearing men stood with their arms full of what appeared to be parcels of food.

Upon their arrival, Cook turned with obvious relief to her mistress and exclaimed, "Oh, Lady Bradford, thank goodness you are here! I've been trying to explain to Mrs. Bradford that these items were set aside to be part of this evening's dinner. Perhaps you can help her understand."

"I understand perfectly," said Jilly with a calm that Lewis had not expected. "We are not feeding an army who have marched on empty stomachs and need such an abundance of victuals to sustain them. Three courses are required and three courses they shall have. But they do not have to consist of quite such a vast array of dishes. It is excessive and there is bound to be wastage. I merely wish to intercept the wastefulness before it occurs."

Lewis was almost too afraid to ask. But his mother was not.

"What do you mean by 'intercept'? And who are these men?"

"They work at St. Giles Asylum for Orphans," explained Jillian. "These supplies will make it possible to make a hearty soup or stew for the children who live off bread and porridge most days."

Cook waved a hand at the parcels in the men's arms. "They've taken all five of the beef shanks, and a whole churn of milk that was set aside for the blancmange."

"Will there not be enough desserts without that insipid wobbly thing to spoil our appetites?" Jillian scoffed. "Imagine instead the nourishment of a warm glass of milk for these children, especially if it softens the stale loaves they are forced to ingest."

Cook continued her complaint. "And a whole bushel of apples that were meant to be stewed for pie."

"I noticed an abundance of plums you could use," Jillian pointed out. "I am rather partial to a plum cake myself."

"The menu's already been decided!" wailed Cook. "I don't have time to rethink all the recipes that have to be managed by this evening."

Jillian shrugged. "Then simply leave out the ones you can no longer make."

"Jillian," Lady Bradford said sternly, "you cannot simply give away half the storeroom from our house…"

"If it is, in fact, *our* house," Jilly interrupted, "that makes half the storeroom mine to distribute as I see fit. Not that I have come even close to such an extravagant amount."

"Your ignorance has betrayed you yet again," said the baroness. "This home, and everything in it, is the property of his lordship. You are guests here at his lordship's leisure. Even tonight's dinner was cleared with him first."

Jillian was unmoved. "And yet his lordship leaves his daily menu up to you. Did you not think to discuss *my* husband's dinner menu with *me*, so that I may be apprised of what was essential and what was free to distribute elsewhere?"

A stony silence followed. The kitchen maids, who had been

watching the entire scene unfolding before them, turned hastily back to their tasks.

"You have never shown interest in arranging such dinners before," Lady Bradford reminded Jillian.

"You are correct. I consider such large gatherings to be nothing more than the usual display of wealth and self-importance."

"This dinner is important to *me*, Jillian," Lewis interjected.

"Why?" his wife asked, turning to him with upturned palms. "Help me to understand what is gained from bringing together so large a group that they cannot possibly all interact with you or each other, eating dish after dish as if they have been starving for a week."

"It is a matter of influence," Lewis explained. "Such social events help to build alliances so that meaningful laws can be passed."

Jillian folded her arms across her chest. "Such as?"

"Well, repealing the Corn Laws, for a start."

"And did the members who wrote the Corn Laws also have such dinners to gather their forces and gain the necessary support to push it through?"

"I suppose they would have, but that's not…"

"Seems a waste of a lot of good food if people are going to throw parties just to contradict each other as they do on the House floor," said Jilly.

"It's a lot more complex than that," said Lewis, feeling his ire rise once more. What was it about Jillian that provoked such a heated response in him? She had been so amenable to his ideas before they'd been married. Why could she not fall in with them as she had once been inclined to do?

"I suggest we shelve further discourse until we are in a more private space," warned Lady Bradford. "Meanwhile, you gentlemen can put those items down and return to your other duties, whatever they may be."

"No." Jillian planted her feet firmly on the ground.

"'No'?" The look of utter disbelief on his mother's face made

Lewis fear for what might follow. If Jillian did not back down now, months of relative peace would be undone.

"No," repeated Jillian. "I have already shown how the subtraction of a few unnecessary dishes would in no way harm the dinner or the outcome Lewis hopes for. I do not believe the absence of an apple pie or blancmange will in any way hinder the success of the evening. And I have promised these supplies to these gentlemen to be used for the children, to whom even simple foods will make a very big difference, indeed."

"Lewis!" Lady Bradford cried, a fingertip to her forehead as if staving off a headache. "Do speak to your wife. This cannot be allowed."

Before Lewis could even open his mouth—not that he had the foggiest idea what he might say under the circumstances—Jillian turned to the men waiting at the door and said with a voice of authority that matched his mother's, "Take these and go. Now. You have heard my instruction."

The men shuffled off in a great hurry, not least of all, Lewis imagined, to escape the furor that might very well erupt any second.

Jillian stood tall and proud and unflinching. "You have wanted me to act more like a future baroness. Well, here I am. Making demands. Ordering the staff about. Being unreasonable because I have the power to do so. I have made my will known and I expect it to be carried out. The menu will be adjusted. The dinner will continue. In future, plans involving my husband's parties will be cleared through me. That is all."

And she swept from the room—a sight that was as disturbing to Lewis as it was perplexing. The coldness. The disdain. These were not the hallmarks of his Jilly. They were the distinctive traits of his mother.

He had wanted her to fit in with his family, to be less herself. This was the example she had chosen to follow.

Lewis was under no illusion. She had done this on purpose, to teach him a lesson, to show him what she thought of the role of baroness. It was pure rebellion and crossed so many lines that he lost count.

His sweet Jillian—the one he had fallen in love with—would never have behaved this way... Or would she? Lewis remembered her goading him on to run from their chaperoning footman. It was Jilly who had snuck an urgent letter in the post to tell him she was being exiled to Trenton Grange, and if he wanted her, he must claim her. Perhaps, then, the question he should have been asking instead was why it had taken her this long to rebel.

In the midst of these illuminating thoughts, he heard his mother say to the staff, "Mrs. Bradford is not herself. We may have to send for the doctor. If she gives any instruction that seems out of bounds, let me know at once. Lewis, I think everyone would understand if she did not attend this evening's dinner."

A fist of ice squeezed his heart. His mother had come within a hair's breadth of calling his wife mad.

Jillian did not deserve such an accusation. It was the beginning of a very dangerous, very slippery slope. If word got out—and all it would take was idle gossip among servants—Jillian's reputation would be in tatters.

Was she frustrated? Yes. *Oh*, yes. Had she taken his mother on in her own home? Absolutely. A fierce, desperate move, indeed. But that was just it. It was Jilly's way of trying to make sense of her surroundings. If she could not bring her own touch to the world she found herself in, she would meet it head on, show up its flaws.

The poor, brave thing! It was not madness. It was a final battle cry.

He should have been paying closer attention. She had told him, over and over, what she needed. To his shame, he knew they were the things he had promised her from the start. And then he had fallen in step with his parents and left her to flounder. Worse still, he had accused her of not making an effort. But what, exactly, had he expected her to do? Each of her missteps had been reflections of her warm and open heart. And he had demanded that she shut it down. Demanded that, if she truly loved him, she would love less.

It was time to put her first. He must protect her from his mother, from the narrow-mindedness of the elite, from Jillian's desire to help being turned against her. If she stayed in London, he was certain disaster was but two steps away.

There was little over a month left of the parliamentary season. He would stay and complete his duties here. And then, together, they would rethink their future. The shape of it. How to do his duties while giving Jillian room to spread her wings a little. His angel. His nymph. His love.

But she would not stay here with him to see the season through. He would write to Lady Howell and ask if the two friends might visit together as they once had. The viscountess would bring Jillian out of her shell again, restore some of her liveliness. With the entire estate of Munro House once again at her disposal, Jilly would be able to run and pick flowers and draw from nature to replenish her depleted joy.

Lewis did agree with his mother about one thing: there was no need for Jilly to endure tonight's dinner. Instead, she should enjoy a long, hot bath. He would personally tuck her into bed, cover her in kisses, and make her understand she was still exactly the woman of his dreams.

Feeling rather pleased with himself, Lewis left the kitchen to find his wife. Everything was going to be better now. He would see to it. And Jilly would love him all the more for it. The future was suddenly much brighter. He only regretted it had taken him this long to make it happen.

He found Jillian in the bedroom, staring out through the window at the busy street below. Lewis slipped his arms around her waist and whispered, "I think it's time we changed that view."

CHAPTER EIGHTEEN

Ellena had not only been happy to receive Jillian as her guest once more, she had invited her to travel with her to their erstwhile home at Trenton Grange. Little Christopher was now almost ten months old and had not yet been introduced to Ellena's parents. She was ready at last to make the long journey to Ermenbrough with him since he was old enough to sit on his nurse's lap instead of being held in her arms for the duration of the trip.

Jillian, who had not seen her own parents for almost as long, nearly wept with relief at the suggestion.

After such a long time without the gentler, simpler ways of her family and the village folk, she had nearly forgotten what it was to be able to be herself and be loved for it.

Sorry as she was to be parted from Lewis for the next six weeks, the time apart would be good for them. Here, in the carriage with Ellena, Christopher, and his nurse—the footman and the lady's maids riding outside—Jillian felt she could breathe again. Even Penelope and her escapades could not help Jilly feel as safe as this. She no longer had to watch everything she said and did. She could laugh freely, talk of silly childhood things, even engage with the nurse without Ellena responding with anything beyond a knowing smile.

The only complication that lay ahead was the matter of

where she would stay. As wife of the Bradford heir, she could not stay in the crowded Kinsey cottage, much as she wanted to. Instead, she would be a guest at Trenton Grange itself, the home of the very people who had considered her a bad influence on Ellena.

It was still better than being under the same roof as the Bradfords, for the Trentons had known her all her life. They had disapproved of her, to be sure, but only in so far as she had scampered off to the meadow with their daughter when they'd been trying to raise a future nobleman's wife. Now that she herself was one of them, they could hardly complain. And if she chose to revert to her meadow-scampering ways, she would not involve Ellena… unless Ellena wanted to, that is.

Despite Jillian's devil-may-care attitude, her being shown into the guest room in the home of her father's employer was nothing less than surreal. Mrs. Trenton, distracted as she was by the sight of her only grandchild, paid Jillian little mind. However, the footman who brought her belongings to her room was an old friend, and soon the façade of noblewoman-to-be melted clean away.

"How is the family, Tommy?" she asked as he straightened from depositing the luggage on the floor of her room.

"I go by 'Thomas' now, ma'am. A bit more formal to match the uniform, like," he explained.

"I'll happily call you 'Thomas,' especially since you're no longer in boy's britches, but you are certainly not going to call me 'ma'am.' I've known you since you were knee-high to a bumblebee!"

"That may be true an' all, but you weren't Mrs. Bradford then. I have to keep up with what's expected of me."

"Well, I expect you to call me 'Jilly,' as you always have done."

"Sorry, ma'am, can't do that," Thomas insisted. "I am employed by Mr. Trenton. It's his word is law."

This sounded all too familiar to Jillian. Ellena's father was many things, but a reasonable man, he was not. If something could make him money, he would consider its merits. Everything else was just in his way. This was the reason poor Mrs. Trenton had not met her grandson until today. Her husband would not spare her to visit Munro House. She kept all distraction from him, whether it be the simple running of the household, or the more complex circumstances that required a human touch. Small wonder Ellena's upbringing had been so cold. Her mother had bowed to her husband's instruction, and his idea of parenting had been to raise his daughter for a profitable marriage. If it hadn't been for Jillian and the escape she'd provided, Ellena would probably have ended up a sad, mousy sort of thing.

Instead, here Ellena was, Viscountess Howell, with a loving husband and an heir secured. And, thanks to Ellena and the sort of friends she and her husband surrounded themselves with, Jillian was married to the heir to the Bradford barony.

This meant that Mr. Trenton—though a gentleman and a man of great wealth—was completely outranked by both his daughter and their guest—a fact that Jilly gleefully imagined he found disconcerting. He not only had the groundskeeper's daughter as his guest, but he was bound to show her the utmost respect, both for the sake of his daughter and the title of baroness that Jillian would one day inherit.

She could therefore easily have insisted that Thomas call her "Jilly" and watch Mr. Trenton quietly implode with rage, powerless to counter her wishes. But she would not do that to an old friend. Thomas had solid employment in which he seemed to take great pride. Despite what the Bradfords thought, she had enough presence of mind not to cause trouble where it wasn't warranted.

"All right, Thomas," she conceded, "I shan't insist. I will play the role of a fancy guest. Here, then, is a coin for carrying my luggage. And another if you will explain to the rest of the staff that I still love them as the friends we always were and will treat them as such if we cross paths outside of this house."

She placed the coins—rather larger than she knew he would expect—into his palm and watched his smile grow wide toward his ears.

"Thank you, ma'am," he answered with a little bow. He retreated to the door, hesitated, turned to her with his hand wrapped around the door's edge, and said in a low voice meant only for her hearing, "There's to be a bit of a shindy at the neighbor's on Saturday. It's a roof-wetting for the new barn and their master is giving all his staff and laborers the day off. Just thought it might be a good place to see old friends, like."

The thought of an evening of country dancing with honest country folk, many of whom she had known since she'd been a mere babe, was exactly the sort of balm her wounded spirit needed.

"Oh, you can count me in," she replied with a grin. "Wild horses could not keep me away!"

"Glad to hear it... ma'am." Thomas threw a little wink her way, then stepped out and pulled the door closed behind him.

The new barn. That would be a good excuse for her first walk. She would go and admire its construction and compliment the workmanship. Ladies were allowed to do that, weren't they? But first, a quick change of clothing...

Jillian collected one of her plainer dresses, of which she had brought several, even though Wallace had complained that people would judge her for letting her lady dress in so drab a fashion. Poor Wallace! Mrs. Jillian Bradford was not the sort of mistress a lady's maid hoped to serve. She would be mortified if she knew Jillian was dressing herself at this very moment.

As if to prove she was not "one of those ladies," Jilly began to skip down the stairs, only to be met with the narrowed eyes of Mr. Trenton come to see who was trip-trapping through his solemn home.

"Oh, it's you, Mrs. Bradford. I should have known." He looked about him with an air of one who could not find what he was seeking. "Have you seen my wife?"

Of course. He would want to know where his gatekeeper was, the designated shield that protected him from any and all disturbance.

"I suppose she is with your grandson," said Jillian with a mildly accusatory tone. After all, why was *he* not admiring sweet little Christopher also? Did he really have no warm blood in his veins?

"Fetch her for me, will you?"

Jillian's hackles rose. She was not his servant. She never had been. Nor was she bound to him with the loyalty of a wife. His own wife, as it happens, was meaningfully engaged elsewhere. Jillian was certainly not going to assist him in disrupting those precious moments.

"*Actually*," she replied, "I was about to stretch my legs after the long ride. I am sure it will be easier for you to locate Mrs. Trenton yourself, as you know her likely whereabouts in your home, the layout of which I am not familiar with, since I have never been permitted inside." She paused to let her words sink in, then added, "And may I say congratulations on your beautiful grandson? You *must* be so proud."

Without waiting for an answer, Jillian not-skipped from the room, offering this small courtesy to a man she otherwise could not stand.

Outside, the air smelled familiar and welcoming. She did a quick sweep of the garden but could not spy her father. She would look for him again later when she popped in at the cottage. Right now, what she really needed was a brisk walk and the oily aroma of sheep's wool as she ran her hands over their docile backs.

The late May sun was bright and warm, but not uncomfortably so. The crops displayed healthy growth, the wheat, barley, and oats a rich green, their heads fully formed but not yet ripe. Jillian tramped past them, heading toward the new stone structure that would be the center of attention on Saturday. Even from a distance, she could see that it was still empty, but a man with a notebook and pencil seemed to be scribbling something, perhaps taking stock of what would be stored there. He lifted his tweed cap and wiped his brow with the sleeve of his jacket, revealing a mop of blond hair that Jillian knew all too well.

"Mr. Boyd!" she called, waving her hand as she approached. "What a lovely surprise to run into you!"

"Mrs. Bradford." His blue eyes sparkled against his tanned skin. He tipped his cap to her before tucking his curls back under it. "I see you are back in Ermenbrough. Come to see your folks?"

"I have. And to escape the rigors of London. You do not know how lucky you are to spend your days here." She indicated with a sweep of her arm. "These fields. These people. This uncomplicated life. I am deeply envious of you."

"I imagine the memories of a young woman without too many cares are different to the realities of being a land steward," he corrected her plainly, yet without malice. "I would say the management of the estate and these lands is a complex set of tasks. Though I do agree, the surroundings are certainly pleasant. London would suffocate me. But then I suppose I am an ordinary man with simple desires."

"That's it, exactly!" *A kindred soul at last! Oh, it is good to be home among people like Simon Boyd!* "For all their dinners and dances and fine riding through Hyde Park, I do not think the wealthy really know how to *live*," she exclaimed.

"I shall have to take your word for it."

"I mean, what greater fun can be had than a roof-wetting? No need for fancy frocks or row upon row of dishes with unpronounceable French names needing twelve different forks. No nasty, backstabbing 'ladies' who smile at you while wishing you ill." Her voice dropped low as the memory weighed on her. "No one judging you because you don't paint or play piano. I'd rather be celebrating the new barn than attend a ball with the *ton* any day."

Mr. Boyd, who had been looking at the ground as a sign of respect, now tilted his head up at an angle and looked thoughtfully at Jillian. "It seems your time in London has caused you pain. I am sorry for it. You do not deserve such treatment. No one does."

His words startled Jillian. It had been months since someone had told her, plainly and honestly, that her feelings of hurt were valid and the cause inexcusable. No justification. No demand that she fall in line with such mean thinking. Just pure kindness and heartfelt support.

It was in such stark contrast to how Lewis had handled her sense of isolation that a warmth rushed from her heart—nay, her whole being—toward Simon Boyd. She felt oddly safe with him. As she used to feel with Lewis. Before he'd abandoned her in a world that was utterly alien to her.

Yes, it appeared her husband had come to deeper insights now. He might even be ready to start again, to make the dreams they'd first shared new once more. But the months between had been long and hard and lonely.

Whereas Mr. Boyd had understood her straight away.

Jillian had the strangest desire to fling her arms about him and say, "Thank you." *Thank you for making it so easy. Thank you for not making me doubt myself.*

She rubbed her eyes. Was she really going to cry?

"Is everything all right?" he asked. The concern in his voice was sincere and only made Jillian want to blubber more.

Get a hold of yourself! What must he think of you? You haven't spoken in ages and now you want to cry on his shoulder? Don't be daft, Jillian! Even groundskeepers' daughters don't behave in such a ridiculous fashion!

"I'm fine." She took her handkerchief and blew her nose indelicately. "I've grown unused to the dust and pollen of farm life."

"I was under the impression that the baron's estate had its own farm. Are you not affected there?"

"Oh, er… no, I mainly walk in the woods or by the lake."

"It sounds as if one could be content in such a place, especially when you have found happiness in love. How is Mr. Bradford? We've been experimenting with new crop rotations this season to great effect. I thought he might be interested."

"He is still in London, busy with Parliament." *And dinner parties.* "He took pity on me and gave up the pleasure of my company so that I could spend time with my own family and friends." *I wonder if he misses me?* "I have come with Lady Howell, who brings her infant son to be cooed at by his grandmother." *And thoroughly ignored by his grandfather.* "If you like, you could show *me* what you've been doing. I would be happy to report back to Mr. Bradford. I could do with some useful way to occupy my time here. I don't think Lady Howell will allow me to work in the garden with my father. And, much as I would like to help my mother, I worry that I have lost the knack. The Bradford servants have ruined me with their attentiveness."

She laughed lightly, but there was no heart in it.

Mr. Boyd's eyes rested on her with disconcerting contemplation. What did he see? Could he detect her dissatisfaction with a life others might have greatly desired? Had he picked up on her feelings of isolation when she had only ever known community?

He seemed to have made up his mind, for he tilted a hand toward her as if offering her something and then spoke this offer into being. "You are welcome to accompany me on my rounds tomorrow, if you wish. That is, if you don't mind trudging along muddy paths and breathing in more dust and pollen?"

"I *love* trudging through mud!" Jilly exclaimed before she could stop herself. Her cheeks grew warm—a sign of embarrassment, she reminded herself, that she never used to feel.

Mr. Boyd formed a little smile of amusement on an otherwise-serious face. He was always thus, Jilly remembered. Which was probably why at such a young age—What was he now? Twenty-three? Twenty-four? She knew he was not much older than herself—he had secured such a responsible position.

"Well," he said, the smile diminishing but not fading completely, "that is all in order, then. Do you ride, Mrs. Bradford?"

Jilly's heart fell. "I do not."

"No matter," he said to her enormous relief. "I will do my patrol of the fencing on horseback and see to the duties farthest out on the estate while I am at it. I usually do these quite early, and I believe you would not mind a later start after your tiring journey. Shall we meet after breakfast, say ten o'clock? I will attend to the matters of farming with you. When you have had your fill, I will resume my other duties. Does this suit?"

"It's suits very well, indeed," said Jilly.

"I bid you a good day, then. There are still many tasks that require my attention this afternoon." He touched his cap to her, stuck his pencil halfway under it, and shoved the notebook into his pocket before heading off to see to his other duties.

Her excuse for visiting the neighbor now carried out, Jillian felt a little stranded, a single top spinning by itself while the rest of the world went about its business. And yet, as she started walking back to Trenton Grange, where her family would draw her into its welcoming cocoon, she sensed that some healing had already begun. Tomorrow, she would have dirt on her boots, the sun at her back, and the company of a kindhearted man who thought her perfectly fine as she was.

These were the hopes she'd had once had of Lewis. And he had recently pledged his promises to her anew. After the London season, they would try again, do better.

But he had let her down before.

Mr. Boyd had not.

And so it was, as she made her way across the boundary between the two properties, that Jillian was not thinking with excitement of seeing Lewis in July but instead relished the prospect of seeing Simon Boyd on the morrow.

She saw no harm in this. Why should she not choose the happier thoughts, the ones that assured her of pleasant hours? Contentment and bliss with Lewis seemed unattainable. There was always a price to pay. He would have to show her how he would manage things differently for her faith to be restored. And he could show her nothing for some weeks yet.

No, she saw no wrong in enjoying Mr. Boyd's company. His manner toward her was restorative after such a long period of emotional drought. It wasn't as though she were losing her heart to him. That would have been silly. She was a married woman.

Confident of her choices, Jillian climbed over the fence. It saved a long walk around. More importantly, she craved the freedom to clamber. It was exhilarating, shedding a layer of inhibition she had worn like an ill-fitting garment. Yes, she was definitely home again, more herself, settling back into her own truth.

What was Lewis doing now? Honestly, she was giving it very little thought. Following some societal norm, no doubt. It only mattered that *she* did not have to. For the next six weeks, she would remember what it was to spread her wings fully.

After that?

Her heart grew tight. No, no, she must not think of that now. She must fly, run, sing, laugh. Twirl barefoot among the grasses of the meadow. Get her face full of flour as she helped her mother bake bread. Hold Timmy's sticky hand.

Perhaps, when she had grown full and round with joy, she would have the strength for what must follow. Today, however, she would only think of her family's warm embrace and the pure delight of a home within which judgment had no place.

Before she knew it, her steps had grown lighter, bouncier, until she was skipping, her arms swinging, a tune upon her lips. She could see her brother Jack in the distance and waved to him, increasing her pace to a run, until she had the startled lad in her arms and swung him around while he squirmed and complained that he was nine and not a baby anymore.

Ah, yes, she was home at last.

CHAPTER NINETEEN

FOR THE FIRST time in a long while, Jillian woke up early and greeted the day with a smile. Without waiting for Wallace, Jillian dressed herself in another of her simpler garments, brushed and tied her hair back with a ribbon, and made her way down to breakfast.

Mr. and Mrs. Trenton were already seated, the master of the house behind a newspaper, and the lady busy pouring tea for him. As Jillian entered, Mr. Trenton stretched out his arm and collected the cup, bringing it to his lips without taking his eyes from his paper or acknowledging his wife's thoughtfulness.

"Would you like some tea, Mrs. Bradford?" asked the hostess.

"That would be lovely," replied Jillian, even though she had no real desire for any. She merely wanted to create an opportunity for Mrs. Trenton to be appreciated. "Mmm," she sounded, taking a sip. "Delicious. It is your own blend, if I am not mistaken."

Mrs. Trenton's eyebrows arched and her mouth opened in a half smile. "Why, Mrs. Bradford, you know your tea. Did Lady Bradford teach you?"

"Her daughter did." Jillian took another sip before placing the cup back onto the saucer, making a delicate clinking sound. "It was one of the less tedious things she taught me."

"I can imagine your experience at Oakwoods was quite a

shock at first," Mrs. Trenton said with no underlying condescension.

"Oh, yes," Jilly answered plainly, "and London even more so. I had hoped for a life that more closely resembled what I was used to. But circumstances dictated otherwise." The last sentence was uttered with some ill-concealed bitterness. Jilly gave the buttering of her toast her full attention to avoid saying anything more.

From behind the newspaper, Mr. Trenton's voice sounded out unsympathetically. "Lots of women would give their eyeteeth for the circumstances you lament."

Jilly paused the buttering process and stared at her toast, biting down on her tongue to keep herself from tossing back an equally uncalled-for remark. This time, it was Mrs. Trenton's turn to busy herself with her breakfast, her shame apparent in her flushed cheeks.

In the midst of the loaded silence, Ellena entered the breakfast room. A lifetime of experience and a sharp mind guided her to a quick assessment of the situation. "I knocked on your door," she told Jillian, "but I see you are quicker to dress than I. I trust you have found everything to your satisfaction?" She cast a grim glance at her father.

"The bed was most comfortable, thank you," answered her friend. "And your mother makes an excellent cup of tea. I am hoping she will show me how to make this particular blend. I believe Miss Bradford would find it to her taste also."

"And everyone treats you well?" asked Ellena pointedly, staring down at her father.

As if by some lever, his newspaper crushed down toward his lap, and the humorless face was revealed. "What are you on about?" he snapped. "Of course everyone treats her well. Our servants know their duty."

Ellena glided toward an empty chair, saying as she went, "So pleased to hear it. Lord Howell will be most grateful that our dear friend has been so well received."

At the mention of those two magical words—Lord Howell—

Mr. Trenton grew somewhat more amenable. "Well, of course, any friend of his lordship… A very fine gentleman, indeed… How is my son-in-law? Business good?"

"It is not something we frequently discuss," said Ellena, settling into the seat the footman held for her, "but I am sure I would have noticed if something were amiss. The answer to your question must therefore be 'Yes, Father, business is good.'"

Jillian, who had never enjoyed conversation about finance any more than she did matters of politics, quickly introduced what she considered a more pleasant topic. "Does young Christopher enjoy Trenton Grange?"

"Oh, yes!" Ellena turned bright eyes to her mother. "I was thinking of taking him for a stroll into the village. Shall we ladies make a day of it?"

"Viscountesses do not stroll along country roads, Daughter," came the rigid tones of Mr. Trenton. "You may take the carriage. I have no need of it today."

Ellena pressed her lips together in a tight line. "I think you will find, Father, that a viscountess may do almost anything she wants. But I will certainly take a footman to carry any parcels we acquire. And if we tire, I will send him home to fetch the carriage to collect us."

Both parents froze with shock at her outspokenness. Mrs. Trenton hastily brought her cup up to her mouth, but Jillian noticed she did not drink. Instead, she held the fine porcelain in front of her lips to hide a slowly spreading smile. The crinkle at the corners of her eyes were harder to disguise, but she was likely unaware that they had formed.

Mr. Trenton, on the other hand, was growing a fine shade of indignant red. He seemed to be fighting an internal battle with himself. His self-control must have won because he pulled his newspaper up and open with some ferocity and said, from the hidden recess of its pages, "Suit yourself."

Jillian did not want to undermine her friend's small triumph, but she had to respond to Ellena's suggestion. "I'm afraid you will have to go without me," she said. "I would usually like nothing more than an outing of this nature, but I have promised to meet with Mr. Boyd to learn what I can about his latest farming innovations so that I might share these insights with Mr. Bradford."

"I'm not sure it is proper for you to meet with the gentleman alone," said Mrs. Trenton.

"We will be out in the open for all to see," Jillian countered. "There will be at least twenty farmhands to chaperone us. Not that a *married lady* needs one."

"It's not a woman's place to learn about farm work," Mr. Trenton grumbled from behind his screen of words.

"I am sure you would agree," Jillian said, mustering as much patience for the man as she could, "that a woman's place is wherever her husband needs her. Since Mr. Bradford cannot meet with Mr. Boyd himself, I am a willing ambassador for him."

But Mr. Trenton was not deterred in his opinion. A portion of the newspaper came down once more, though his mood only warranted a folding of one corner so that he might see over it. "If Mr. Boyd has such meaningful advice to share, he could do so in a letter sent directly to Mr. Bradford. There is no need to have a lady"—Jillian was amazed he willingly counted her as such—"traipsing up and down the fields, making a mockery of her position."

Now it was Jillian's turn to glow with suppressed irritation. She had heard enough of this sort of chastisement from the Bradfords, and even Lewis himself. The only reason she did not speak up as she would have with them was for the sake of Mrs. Trenton, who was already shrinking into herself as the commanding tones of her husband had their effect.

"Father," Ellena interceded, "I am sure Mrs. Bradford values your wisdom in such matters and will take it into due consideration."

"What is there to consider?" he wanted to know.

"Could you pass me the strawberry preserves, Mother?"

asked Ellena, her father's question left hanging. "Shall we ask Cook to make us a picnic? Or shall we have a light luncheon at the inn?"

Mr. Trenton glared at her, waiting to be acknowledged. He waited in vain. Unused to such treatment, he focused his attention on Jillian, perhaps viewing her as a weaker target.

Jillian shoved the last piece of toast into her mouth, washed it down with the remainder of her tea, and pushed her chair back to stand. "If you will excuse me," she said to everyone and no one, for she did not dare to make eye contact, "I do not wish to be late for my meeting. Mr. Boyd shall not think that a member of the Bradford household has such poor manners."

Here at Trenton Grange, it was easier to escape from the master's attempts to prescribe to her. He was a lone tyrant and his status less commanding. Her experiences at Oakwoods and in London had been more restrictive. Today, at least, she could step from the house when she wished. On any day she liked, she could meet with Mr. Boyd, attend a country dance, walk to the village, delight in the meadow. Her steps felt light, in spite of the brief shadow cast by her surly host.

Simon Boyd was already waiting for her, even though she was a little early. Despite his dusty boots, the rest of him appeared clean and well-groomed, as was his habit. His notebook was tucked under one arm and he nodded when she waved her own notebook at him to show she was well prepared.

"Good morning, Mrs. Bradford," he said, "I see you are ready to take copious notes. That is commendable. However, we shall be walking and talking, so you may have to wait to jot down your thoughts when I am engaged with the various men who report to me."

"I shall do my best. I hope I shan't have to ask you to repeat yourself too often. I would like to think I am not an addle-brained sort of woman."

"That is not how I remember you," he said, offering reassurance with the sincerity of his tone rather than a smile.

Mr. Boyd proceeded to walk at a fairly brisk pace, which Jillian matched with reasonable ease, partly because he was not much taller than her. He pointed out the crops they were growing, some of which were new and some of which were planted on rotation every three years. He explained what was working well and which attempts had failed.

Jillian soon tired of all the facts and figures, struggling to hold them in her head until Mr. Boyd paused to speak to one of the laborers and she could scribble down the salient points. She became distracted by the smell of the fresh alfalfa, the bouncing lambs with their wriggly tails, the low call of a cow to her calf.

After an hour, she had managed to store several pages of information in her notebook and likely forgotten several pages more. But her soul was full and she felt worn out in a healthy, satisfied sort of way.

"You have done well, Mrs. Bradford," Mr. Boyd said. "Mr. Bradford cannot be anything but pleased with your kind interest on his behalf."

Jilly hugged her notebook to her chest like a trophy. "Thank you for allowing me to tag along. I have learned much, but I fear we have but scratched the surface of all there is to know."

Mr. Boyd allowed himself a sardonic smile. "I am relieved to hear it. If you had mastered all I could teach in one morning, my employer might think my position could be too easily filled."

"Oh, heavens, no! It is clear to me that you have your hands full from dusk until dawn. Everything that runs smoothly on the estate does so because you have your finger on the pulse of all activity."

"That is very kind of you to say. Speaking of which, I had better get back to it. The day is but half-done. There is still much that needs my attention."

Jillian was sorry for him to go. She had enjoyed his company, even if it had meant learning an exhaustive list of facts and theories. Here in the fields with Simon Boyd, she was not bound by a pointless array of rules for dining, sitting, speaking. No one would comment that her features looked common if they became tanned by the glorious sunshine. She could speak of animal husbandry without being thought of as crass. She could climb a fence and not be called unladylike.

And then there was the dance on Saturday.

"Will you be attending the roof-wetting celebration?" she asked Mr. Boyd.

He nodded. "I will." It was hard to tell from his solemn response whether or not he was looking forward to it.

"I shall be disappointed if I have no one to dance with, as Mr. Bradford is not able to attend, especially since the informal nature of the event allows me, as a married woman, to dance at all. It seems a sin for a woman as young as I to be denied such a jolly activity and I have been looking very much forward to this opportunity. Sadly, many of the staff have grown wary of me now, even though we were all quite comfortably acquainted before." She formed what she hoped was a pitiful expression and added, "Perhaps you will do me the kindness of partnering me in a reel or two."

"It would be my privilege. Though I am quite certain that, away from the strict rules of service, many of your friends will enjoy your company again. You will have no shortage of partners, if I am correct."

"Perhaps if you set an example with the first dance, others will follow."

"Then that is what we shall do."

Jilly lowered her lashes shyly. "Thank you for accommodating my doubts. I did not used to have so many."

"It is no great task. There is no need for thanks."

"Nevertheless, I appreciate it."

"I am happy to oblige."

"Until Saturday, then."

"Until Saturday."

It had been a simple exchange, but there had been such a shortage of these for so long, Jillian found herself deeply moved by the small kindness. She headed back to Trenton Grange with a happy heart, crossed the path that led to the village, and paused. With Christopher along, Ellena and her mother would not have gotten very far on their outing. There was still time to catch up. It would be the perfect way to shake her mind free of her intensive morning lesson on farming.

A quick shift in direction and she was on her way to join them, savoring the sweet scent of the imminent presence of summer. She bloomed as the flowers did, her face, like theirs, turned to the sun. The warmth of it matched the glow of satisfaction within.

She was truly home again.

CHAPTER TWENTY

THE NEXT MORNING, Jillian lay in bed and thought upon all she had learned the day before. She was gratified to discover that she remembered a good deal of what Mr. Boyd had told her. She reviewed their conversation in her mind, walking from field to field in her imagination, remembering the sights and sounds of farm life, but also the tutelage of her companion.

When her thoughts reached the memory of the fallow ground that had been plowed and left to rest, she pulled up short. What was the crop Mr. Boyd had recommended for the unused land? At the moment he had told her, she had become distracted by a little lamb in the grass beyond the fence who had spied his mother and dove in under her legs, tail waggling furiously, head bumping up against her belly to release the milk he eagerly sought. Jillian's concentration having been interrupted at that point in Mr. Boyd's deluge of information, the name of the suitable crop had been missed and not recorded in her notes.

No matter, she thought cheerfully as she bounded out of bed. She would walk across to the field and ask one of the laborers if they knew what crop it was. She could, of course, delay until Saturday and ask Mr. Boyd then. But why wait? If she filled in the gaps of her knowledge now, she could write a lovely long letter to Lewis and tell him all that she had learned.

She was hoping to have heard from Lewis herself. Even a

short letter inquiring whether she had arrived safely and that all was well. Preferably some mention of the plans he had for their future once they both returned to Munro. Ideally, a roguish reference to missing the taste of her body. Anything to suggest she was on his mind and that his thoughts were occupied with mending the distance that had crept in between them since the start of their marriage.

But there was nothing.

Jillian told herself he was probably very busy. He was no doubt throwing himself wholeheartedly into the causes he stood for in Parliament. And when the season was done, he would surely put his energy just as fully into their private cause.

She must be patient.

Still, a few lines to show he had not quite forgotten her would have meant much in the parched landscape of their relationship.

All the more reason to send a letter of her own. She would set the tone. *Here, see, I am thinking of you. I carry your interests at heart. These pages show my commitment. Please write back and do the same.*

Jillian grudgingly allowed Wallace to dress her before slipping from the house without breakfast. She would see to the needs of her stomach later. First, she would gain the answer she needed for her letter. The sooner it was sent, the sooner she would hear back from Lewis. She pictured his delight at seeing pages and pages of farming insights. He might even use some of his newfound knowledge in his arguments on the floor of the House of Commons. He would speak with confidence and carry the secret pride that his wife supported his endeavors. He would be grateful that he had married her, remembering all that she was to him. It would inspire him to do better by her. Perhaps he would inquire if the house he had first picked out for them was still available—a place where they could again be fully themselves.

Oh, how she wanted that! Every fiber of her being yearned for such a reconciliation. Anything less would be a betrayal of the promises they had made. After all, their marriage vows had not been the first declarations of commitment between them.

Fond memories of their visits at Munro House lifted her steps into a lightness she had not felt in ages. At least, not toward Lewis. In no time, and with the echo of a smile upon her face, she had reached the fallow field that was her intended destination.

As luck would have it, Mr. Boyd appeared on horseback, a cloud of dust surrounding him as he drew to a halt.

"Mrs. Bradford. I had not expected to see you here today. Have I forgotten an arrangement?"

"Not at all," Jillian called up to him. "I was really looking for anybody who might tell me which crop you intended for this unused land. You shared so much important information yesterday, and I admit that not all of it made it into my notes."

Mr. Boyd lifted his cap and scratched his head with the same hand before replacing the item atop his slightly unruly mop. "I am not surprised. I think I rather overdid the details of my lecture. However, since we only had the one opportunity, I could not think what might be unimportant enough to leave out."

"Oh," Jilly replied, perking up at the possibility of another morning with her old friend, "it was only limited to one meeting because I did not want to impose upon your time. But if you are willing to share more of your wisdom, I would gladly follow you on your rounds until your teachings are exhausted."

Mr. Boyd hesitated. "Perhaps we shall deal with your question today and you may send such knowledge as you have to Mr. Bradford. If he is desirous of more detail, he should feel free to ask me and I will reply when I have a spare hour."

Jillian, however, was not easily discouraged. "That is a generous suggestion." She caressed the long, velvety nose of the horse. "And yet I cannot help but feel that such correspondence would demand more of you than an easy verbal exchange between us while you are seeing to your duties. Besides, I enjoy learning." She cocked her head cheekily. "You would not deny me such a worthwhile education, I hope."

Mr. Boyd's habitual seriousness was deepened by a small frown. "Certainly not. Perhaps Mr. Bradford would share his and my correspondence with you? Then you may learn together. That would seem more acceptable to the public eye than his wife accompanying me on my rounds a second day."

"But we are friends!" Jillian's face screwed up into a shape she hoped matched her disgust. "And we have been such long before I even *met* Lewis." She stepped back and threw her arms out to encompass the entirety of their surroundings. "We are observed by scores of farmhands who follow all our movements across the estate. What better chaperone can we have? Not that I *need* one, as a married lady."

Simon Boyd lowered his eyes and shook his head slowly. "Alas, I do not make the rules. Children may play together in fields where adults may no longer walk with equal innocence. At least, not as innocence is perceived."

Jillian waved a hand about before thrusting it on her hip. "Then I shall invite Ellena to join us. Surely, the sobering presence of a viscountess will silence all doubts?"

Mr. Boyd replied with a calm and patience that was so much a part of his nature. "I understood that her ladyship has not been home since she was married nigh on two years ago. It would be strange, indeed, if she should choose to wander the estate neighboring the one she has actually come to visit, especially when she has her young son with her."

"You are far too sensible, sir," Jillian said, her mouth shifting into a sulky pout. "It appears I am to do without your enlighten-ment unless my husband deems it fit for me to read what you send him."

"I'm afraid we are bound by propriety, ma'am."

Jillian rolled her eyes. "Ugh! Not you, too! There seems to be no end to the number of people who will lecture me on the subject."

"I offer no lecture, Mrs. Bradford. I merely wish to protect your reputation. That is what a friend would do, is it not?"

"I suppose I cannot argue with that," grumbled Jilly. "But you shall not wriggle out of the dance we agreed to on Saturday."

He made a small bow with his head. "I would not dream of it. Those are far less formal circumstances, and the rigid rules of society will be somewhat relaxed. Only one dance, mind you," he added sternly. "I will not have you spoken of in slanderous tones."

"My boringly intact reputation thanks you, I suppose," Jilly said.

Mr. Boyd closed one eye and stared at her with the other. "I do not think the value of an unsullied reputation is to be scoffed at. Once lost, it is almost impossible for it to be restored. As your friend, I would urge you to remember that."

Jillian released a protracted sigh. "I know, I know. Contrary to everyone's opinion, I do not purposefully seek out ways to break the rules. But there are just so many of them! And they seem to have multiplied since I became Mrs. Bradford. I miss the simpler years of my childhood."

Mr. Boyd leaned back in his saddle. "Ah, so do we all. But I think you will find it is not so bad as all that."

"I have yet to see any advantages."

Mr. Boyd let his gaze flow along the length of the horizon. "All of this"—he indicated the activities within their view—"works smoothly because I have ensured that it does." A small, nostalgic smile snuck across his mouth. "I can no longer catch tadpoles in the afternoon after my lessons are done. I do not steal jam tarts when my mother isn't looking. My hours are long and the tasks never-ending. But I make a difference. That was not possible to the same degree when I wore a boy's britches and dreamed a boy's dreams."

Jillian's eyes were now firmly on the ground. The toe of her boot traced small furrows in the dry earth. "I would share your sentiment if such opportunities were also available to me," she said softly. "All that has changed since I became Mrs. Bradford is that my world has narrowed considerably. I am expected to find joy in idleness and great shows of wealth. Nothing has any real purpose. My life had far more meaning when I was helping my mother or playing with my brothers or saving Ellena from a life too similar to what I have now."

"These are notions you should confide to Mr. Bradford."

"He is aware of them."

A silence followed these words. Jilly did not know how to proceed from here and it seemed neither did Mr. Boyd. Their easy conversation had ground to a halt.

The gentleman cleared his throat. "Turnips," he said suddenly.

Jilly's head pulled up. "I'm sorry?"

"Turnips. That's what we'll be growing in the fallow field next season. A rotation of wheat, turnips, barley, and clover allows the soil to be fed what it has lost while staying productive."

"Er… thank you. I shall add it to my report. Lewis will be pleased."

"Good.

"Yes."

Mr. Boyd began to pull at the reins to turn his horse's head, then stopped and half-twisted back toward Jillian.

"It's not like you to give up."

Jilly's mouth slacked and she stared up at him, past his muscular thigh and tanned hand that held the reins with light control but full authority, into the face that she had known all her life. "Who says I have?"

"That is good, then. You know I only ever want the best for you."

He touched his free hand to his cap, which barely contained his thick, blond hair. His blue eyes rested upon her face for a moment longer before he clicked his tongue and urged his horse to walk on with a tuck of his heel.

Jillian watched him move onto the next field, which was only about a hundred feet away. There, he swung from the saddle to crouch and consider what a worried worker was pointing out to him in the cultivated furrow. She was all but forgotten. A common refrain.

She began to walk back to Trenton Grange, a path which would take her past Mr. Boyd—not that he would pay her any mind. She tried to carry herself tall and proud, as if not in the least interested in what he was doing.

As she approached the two men, Simon Boyd's head swung in her direction. He paused thus, seeming to wrestle with himself. Eventually, his solemn expression relaxed a little. He stood as she was about to pass by. "Don't women of your standing have a lady's maid?"

Jillian paused in her step and nodded.

"Bring her with you next time you stroll through the estate. She might learn something too."

Jilly brightened. "You mean…?"

It was his turn to nod. "If I'm not too busy. And it can't be too often. Even the presence of a lady's maid will not stop tongues wagging if the heads to which they belong put their minds to it."

Now he put his foot in the stirrup and heaved himself back into the saddle. He allowed himself the subtlest of smiles before moving on again. This time, he did not look back. But he did not need to. He had left a kernel of hope, something for Jillian to hold on to. Oh, there would be walks to the village and picnics in the meadow with Ellena and little Christopher, perhaps even Mrs. Trenton, and definitely a maid or footman tagging along. Joining Mr. Boyd on his rounds, however, gave her a sense of purpose. Something Lewis had never allowed. She was grateful that her dear, old friend had taken pity on her. How grateful she was to have renewed their connection!

Words echoed up from recent memory. *"The old will feel new."* The words of the fortune-teller, so easily discarded before, now rose up with the force of truth. What was the rest? *"The new will feel old."* That could only mean one thing: her marriage to Lewis. The spark was gone. So far, any change for the better was mere talk.

There had been a warning, too, she remembered with a small

shiver. What was it again? Something about starting anew. Ah, yes… *"Love will grow cold until you embrace new beginnings."* Well, that was a two-way street, was it not? She could not fan the embers into flames if Lewis did not make an equal effort.

One thing was certain. Mr. Boyd had reminded her how easy it was to make a compromise that suited both parties. Lewis had only ever wanted *her* to make sacrifices, to suppress everything he had once loved about her. How was she supposed to embrace all that had been thrust upon her if she did not have her husband's support and understanding?

How easily Lewis had slipped into his role as heir to the barony! How quickly he had set aside their shared dreams. He would have to put action to his promises before she trusted him again.

Meanwhile, Jillian was free to do all that had been denied her these past six months. It was like a spring shower after the barren cold of winter. Little buds of contentment were sprouting again. The weeks ahead would see her blossom fully into herself once more. Jilly felt the confidence of such certainty seep into her core and bloom outward until she fairly glowed with optimism.

Time for breakfast. And then a romp through the meadow. A daisy chain for Christopher. Deeper breaths. Broader smiles that stretched from her heart across the entirety of her face.

The letter to Lewis could wait. Let *him* write first, set the tone. She would match *his* efforts. Since there were currently none, she liberated herself from the need to produce any of her own.

No, indeed, all efforts would be spent on living more fully. And if Lewis wanted to join her on such a quest, she would welcome him.

If not…

A tightness clenched her heart. Jillian pushed it away violently with her mind. She would focus on that which she could control. As for the rest, it would happen no matter what she did today.

Onward, then. To a hearty meal, a day well spent in a field of flowers, and the company of those who loved her as she was.

And, on Saturday, the chance for real celebration, sans finery and meanness behind tilted fans. Just good friends and good fun.

Ah, yes, thought Jilly, *life is looking very good, indeed.*

CHAPTER TWENTY-ONE

L EWIS STUMBLED OUT of bed at noon. This had become the norm. Meetings, dinners, sessions, even dances filled his calendar, often ending in the small hours and leaving him worn out. There was no Jilly to come home to, no welcoming touch as he fell upon the sheets, exhausted. No wife to accompany him to functions, whether formal and unwelcoming and sure to lead to an argument, or intimate and friendly and rewarding in the way it lifted their spirits.

He had to admit, the latter sort had been rare. Far fewer of his friends had been as open-minded as he had thought them to be. He had believed that the London crowd would be more progressive in their thinking, more accepting of Jillian. In truth, they had only been more subtle in their rejection of her.

He had watched her shrink into a smaller version of herself and had been helpless to do anything about it. They were committed to see the season through. At least, he was. Having Jilly spend these weeks in Ermenbrough had been a relief to them both. No more snide remarks from his parents. No large dinners his wife could not bring herself to sit through. No need for him to try to split himself into two, even three versions of himself as he played whatever role was required of him.

And always their marriage suffered. There was little enough to nourish it.

He could see now how unfair he had been. He had made the necessary adjustments to fulfill Philip's role with relative ease. He had been consumed with doing whatever it took to keep his parents from nagging him. If Jilly had been able to rise to the challenge, they would have fared well. But he had promised her a life so opposite to what it now was, it had been like asking the moon to stop shining and become a stone.

He had never thought such a request would become necessary. He had pictured the sort of comfortable lifestyle he had enjoyed whenever he'd visited Howell and his lady—a dose of propriety along with a large helping of warm society. Jilly could have managed that well enough.

But the viscount and viscountess were an anomaly. Of course, he had known that. Lewis had believed he could emulate it. Then Fate had forced his hand. Now he was chained to a life of rigid expectation, and Jillian along with him.

The initial thrill of managing the estate, gaining his father's respect, and serving in the House of Commons had worn off. These could not make up for the atrophy in his relationship with his wife. They had planned a particular life together. And it looked nothing like the one they now merely endured.

It was up to him to find a solution. He must fathom a way to meet what society required of him without dragging Jillian into its clutches. And he had no idea how.

He should at least be writing to her. She needed to hear that these thoughts milled through his mind because she was important to him. That he acknowledged his failings. That he wanted to revive the hopes they had shared in the beginning. But he did not know how to back these words with deeds. If it had been that easy, he would have done so by now. And without a clear path forward, any words he wrote would sound empty, the hollow vessels of thoughts he could not carry out.

Because he knew not what to say, he did not write. Let her think him busy, for he was. Let her think his mind preoccupied, for that was true, too.

If only *she* would write, he would have something to reply to. He could say yes, he missed her also. No, London in all its splendor could not match the wonders of Ermenbrough, where the love of family and acceptance of friends surpassed any attraction held by theater or park or museum.

But Jillian did not write.

She was very likely in her element, back within the environment that best suited her. He must give her time to have her fill of it before she turned her thoughts to him.

And yet...

Did she not think of him *at all*? Had this decision to spend time apart been unwise? Was she so truly happy without him now that she was able to do all that gave her joy? Did she... Lewis swallowed. Did she regret having left it all to marry him?

Perhaps he *should* write to her. She would be forced to acknowledge his letter. He might gauge her mood from her response.

But did he really want to know? If Jillian spared no thought for him, was that something with which he wanted to burden his heart? What could he do about it here in London?

No, he must wait and trust. When they were reunited in little over a month, he would be free of all distraction from the season and she would have recovered somewhat from her frustrations with the *ton*. They would put their heads together. Even better, they would put their hearts together. This time, they would know what they must deal with. They would both be wiser. He would manage her needs better. Except... at this moment, he could not think how. And he was back to the reason why he could not write his wife a letter. Instead, he must pine for her in silence. And count on blind faith to present a way forward.

As an experienced barrister, this was not the way he normally handled things. There would be precedence in previous cases. Facts, logical arguments. Instead, what he had were the often-obsolete norms of society as passed down by countless generations versus the sheer will of a free spirit who refused to conform.

And, his conscience reminded him with painful regularity, he had promised Jilly she wouldn't have to. In fact, he had been looking forward to breaking the rules right alongside her.

Damn and blast it all! *Philip, you selfish wretch! What were you doing at that gaming hell? You're the one who wanted all this. The power and position. The barony and its privileges. The games of the ton and its infernal rules. You had no business being in a place like that. You had money and our parents' love, friends and a woman you wanted to marry. What more could you possibly have been seeking among the dregs of society? Look what your selfishness has cost me!*

But Philip could never answer. And if he did, it would likely be to say he had done it because he could. Because he had felt like it. And why was Lewis complaining, anyway? These were *his* privileges now. He could do just as *he* wished.

Lewis leaned his head into his hands. He simply wasn't made of the same stuff his brother had been. And if it did not come easily to him, no wonder it was that much harder for his dear Jillian. And she *was* his. Forever and ever. Yet "forever" could quickly turn from a blessing into a curse if he did not *do* something!

Lewis reached over and tugged the ribbon to call for his valet. Clothes. Food. And then a brisk walk to clear the cobwebs from his mind. Today, he must create at least the semblance of a plan. Maybe that would be a worthwhile something to put into a letter.

Except after Lewis had eaten, his father called him into his study. Lord Bradford wasted no time in getting right to the heart of what irked him.

"Rumor has it you and your associates are putting forward a motion to Commons to undo elements of the Corn Laws. You know it will never pass muster in Lords. Why waste your time on it? You are working against your own interests."

Once again, Lewis was reminded how differently he and his father approached such matters.

"I cannot vote against my conscience, Father. My constituents are ordinary folk whose lives are affected by these laws. And if they are suffering, it is up to us who have the means to change these circumstances to do so."

"But you must know such a motion will stall with Lords."

"Even so, an effort must be made. One day, the House of Lords may surprise us. We will persist until such a day comes."

Lord Bradford *harrumphed*. "I had hoped, with Jillian away, you might show more measured thought. But I see her influence remains."

Lewis heaved a deep sigh. "Father, I have thought as I do for much longer than even my first acquaintance with my wife. It is a sorry reflection on your and my relationship that you have managed to remain unaware of this. Perhaps it did not matter before because Philip always did as you wished and I was occupied in the courts, not Parliament. But this is who I am. This is how I would have thought and acted even if I had not married her."

The baron tapped an impatient finger on his desk. "Someone like Miss Sangford would have set you straight. She would have guided you to the right social circles. She would have coaxed you to make better decisions, as all wives do when they have their husbands' wellbeing in mind."

"I am sorry you feel that way." Lewis shrugged. "I happen to think Jillian has done exactly what you wish a wife to do. She has reminded me to consider others and not take myself too seriously."

"And yet you do not appear to be happy."

Lewis grew quiet. He lowered his gaze. "That is my own fault."

"Is it?"

Lewis stared into the palms of his hands. They were empty of answers. How many times hadn't he had these discussions with his parents? They could not, *would* not understand. He had allowed himself to be drawn into their world. The very world he had rejected so bitterly until six months ago. He had let their reasoning sour his own. And he had let it sour his relationship with Jillian.

Once again, he was spending his energy in a debate that would have the same outcome as every single one they'd ever had before. He should have been using his time to mend his marriage.

Lewis stood up abruptly. "I'm going for a walk."

"You're only running away from the truth," his father called after him as he marched toward the door.

Lewis ignored him. Or, at least, he tried to. But his father's words stuck in his mind. Lewis pulled the door of the study open and resisted the urge to slam it shut in frustration. He stalked past a footman, a maid, another maid, and, finally, the butler, disregarding their polite acknowledgements and seeing himself out despite the footman's race to reach the door before him.

If Jilly had been here, she would have stopped and talked to every single one of them. She would have known about any illness in the family, a sudden hardship, a recent baby. And he would have rolled his eyes impatiently because it Just. Wasn't. Done. When had he become so much like Philip? Why had he lost sight of the marvel that his wife cared so deeply?

Out in the street, he took a deep breath. The persistent smog drew into his lungs and he coughed it out, only to breathe it in again. It was exactly like the rules that governed his life: insidious, treacherous, and almost impossible to free himself from. Jilly had been his fresh, country air—an uncorrupted, life-affirming force for good.

If he could rather obey his instincts, he would step into the next hired carriage and take himself off to Ermenbrough. He would take Jillian in his arms and renew his vows to her. They would not leave the pastoral peace of that borough until they were whole again and knew the way forward.

Alas, he was bound to London until the end of the season. Corn Laws and riots would demand his attention. His parents would sigh and protest at anything for which Jillian would have admired him.

But. The minute he was done here, he would fly from this prison he had made for himself.

Until next season…

Argh! It was never going to end, was it? Not unless he resigned. But when he became baron, he would be serving in the House of Lords instead. Would he have to leave his wife for half of each year to spare her the misery of London? Or, if he served by proxy only, would he be able to make a real difference, being absent from all debates?

There were so many obstacles to happiness. Where to start in removing them?

As if symbolizing his answer, Lewis began to put one foot in front of the other. He did not know where he was going, only that each step took him further from the household where he had never been happy. He felt the tug of it, pulling him back. But he fought it. He leaned forward, as though against a wind, lifting his foot and placing it down a few inches farther ahead. It was like moving through treacle.

Lewis stopped. He turned toward the center of the road, raised a hand, and hailed a passing hackney.

"Where to, sir?" asked the driver.

"Out of the city," said Lewis, his foot upon the step as he hauled himself up.

"Anywhere in particular?"

"I'll know it when I see it."

"Right you are."

The horse snorted. Quite possibly, it did not like the smog any more than its human companions did.

The rhythmic rumble of wheels on cobbles was both soothing to Lewis's battered thoughts and bruising to his thighs. It was a long ride to escape the busy thoroughfares that crisscrossed London. It took a good half hour of avoiding shouting pedestrians and near-accidents between reckless vehicles that demanded right of way before the stone and brick of the city made way for open fields. They passed several farms and clopped over a bridge before

Lewis found what he had been looking for.

He tapped the roof with his cane. "Wait here," he told the driver. "I will be back in twenty minutes. You will be rewarded handsomely for your patience." And he stepped down onto the edge of a meadow.

As Lewis paced through the wild grasses, he realized he was not, in fact, suitably dressed for what he had in mind. And yet—he thought with the thrill of newfound freedom—he also didn't care.

Small birds took flight on tiny wings as his movements disturbed their hidden activities. Some took to the trees ahead and flitted from branch to branch as he approached the shady sentinels. Others swung low in their glide path and came to rest on the woody stalks of spent flowers. Between the trees and the dry, sunburnt hollows—in the zone where shadow and sunlight alternated as the day progressed—Lewis found a long stretch of wildflowers.

He threw a quick glance back at the hackney driver. The man had leaned back with his hat over his face. There wasn't another soul on the road.

Without further hesitation, Lewis sank into the lush growth of fresh grass and fragrant blooms, rolling onto his back, his arms tucking behind his head like a pillow. Above him, the bright blue of the sky seemingly stretched on forever.

It was the closest he had felt to Jillian in ages, even though she was currently two hundred miles away. If he closed his eyes, he could imagine her beside him. No nagging voices drummed in his head. No nameless echoes of expectation. Only the remembered softness of his beloved's skin, the sun upon their faces, laughter bubbling up from within.

Lewis could sense a gaping wound begin to close. He took a tentative sniff. Pollen tickled his nose, but no coal dust filtered into his lungs. He breathed more deeply. In. Out. A steady flux of good, pure air and a heady mix of scents.

He felt himself being knit back together. Ermenbrough was

surely doing much the same for Jilly. He reached out to her with his heart, a love letter of sorts. He imagined her now, stopping suddenly with whatever occupied her, a shudder of pleasure rippling through her limbs and torso as the tendrils of his thoughts wrapped gently about her. His body was a beacon, pulsing a signal of passion, of joy, of longing toward the one with whom he would be reunited in this moment.

He heard footfalls.

For a second, he believed it to be Jillian, brought here by the sheer will of his yearning for her.

The sound stopped.

"It's been almost half an hour," said a voice that was not Jillian's. "I'll be needing to get back. I have regulars who'll be looking out for me."

Lewis shielded his eyes. The hackney driver loomed over him.

He sighed. Back to reality. But the break had done wonders for his spirit. It had given him perspective, reminded him what really mattered. No more would he create distance with the one person who nourished his soul, or seek meaning with a host of people who only cared about the role they expected him to play and how it suited them.

Of course, he would still need to attend today's parliamentary session. He still had commitments for the season. But he had promised Jillian fields. And chickens. And, by gum, she was going to get them!

CHAPTER TWENTY-TWO

"A BSOLUTELY NOT! I simply do not belong there."
Ellena bounced Christopher on her knee with some agitation. He gurgled and flexed his small fists open into gleeful stars. "Hossie!" he cried, something he had taken to doing whenever he rode upon his mother's knees. It was no surprise that this had been his first word since he loved to visit the stables at Munro House and pat the muscled backs of the more patient steeds when his parents held him up to them.

Ellena's frown disappeared at once, replaced by a maternal smile and cooing encouragement. "Yes. Horsie. Clip-clop. Clip-clop." She added a fair attempt at a neigh and pulled back on invisible reins. "Whoa there, horsie."

"Hossie!" cried the delighted little boy again, and his mother obliged immediately by resuming the energetic bounce. The chair creaked beneath the ungainly activity, but Ellena did not seem to mind. Jillian knew her friend was determined to be a different sort of parent than her own had been.

"Fine," said Jilly. "Don't come to the roof-wetting. I'll take Wallace. And I'll add a footman for good measure. You know, to fend off all the men who would tarnish my reputation." She waited for Ellena to smile at her little joke. But no smile was forthcoming. "Thomas is going," she added. "He will do nicely. I'm sure they would both love a night of capering with the locals."

"You really shouldn't be going, either," warned Ellena. "You are no longer one of them, Jilly."

Jillian folded her arms across her chest. "Am I to throw away a lifetime of friendships because I married Lewis?"

"No, but these friends of yours cannot help a lifetime of trained thought, either. You are now one of the mistresses in their eyes. Someone to treat with solemn respect. Just because you haven't changed does not mean you are the same, as far as they are concerned."

"But Thomas was the one who suggested I join them! And Mr. Boyd has promised me the first dance. *They* don't seem to share your dull concerns."

Ellena pursed her lips. The bouncing stopped and little Christopher turned and looked expectantly at his mother. "Jilly, you know I love you…"

"Oh, dear." Jilly rolled her eyes. "This sounds like the beginning of a lecture."

"I'm sorry to say, but we do need to have a serious talk."

"All right. Get it over with. Christopher is getting bored and so am I."

Ellena drew her son up into her arms and stood quickly. She walked to the door and, pulling it open, gestured to the footman outside. "Take him to his nurse, please. I will fetch him again in a little while."

Empty-handed, Ellena returned to her chair. She clasped her palms together, interlacing her fingers. "Jilly," she began. "I can never thank you enough for offering me your wonderful, wild heart when I needed relief from the constraints of my childhood. The ease with which you moved through the world showed me it was possible to breathe more deeply, even when the pressure of so much expectation sat as a weight upon my chest. Honestly, if not for you, I would have been a shadow of myself. Rather like my mother…" She paused to steady herself. "You must therefore understand that I would never want to change you."

"However…" said Jilly, a wry smile flitting across her mouth.

"Yes, well…" Ellena stumbled in her little speech. "It wouldn't be a serious talk if there weren't a 'however.'"

"Out with it, then."

"I'm trying!" Ellena retorted. "Being the voice of reason is not a role I relish, you know."

Jillian waited in silence. Anything she said now would only make it harder for her friend. The sooner they had their talk, the sooner she could get back to organizing the necessities that made it possible for her to attend the country dance. For go she would.

"I understand Mr. Boyd is an old friend…"

The mention of the man caught Jillian off-guard. What did he have to do with anything?

"One of many friends here in Ermenbrough," she replied.

"And yet he is the one with whom you spend most of your time."

A twinge of guilt pinched Jilly's heart. Nothing untoward had happened. But, yes, she had savored his company. It was safe, for she would never betray Lewis, and Simon Boyd was far too noble to consider such a thing. Still, time with him had been a pleasure. A revisiting of her earlier life with its freedoms and ease. A life she did not currently enjoy with Lewis. Even the promised dance with him had nothing to do with some sort of private affection. Mr. Boyd was a means to an end. A gateway to an evening of laughter and fun.

Jilly shrugged. "Everyone has employment that occupies them by day. I have been banned from the kitchen in both your home at Munro House and at Oakwoods, so I have obediently refrained from venturing into the one at Trenton Grange. But Mr. Boyd allows me—and, more recently, Wallace—to tag along with him on his rounds. I'm gaining valuable insights into the running of your neighbor's estate, something I can share with Lewis. I have not been an absent friend, have I? My morning circuit with Mr. Boyd has not prevented me from spending time with you in the afternoon."

"I do not feel neglected, Jilly. But you must understand that your regular visits with an unmarried gentleman, even when the circumstances are clearly innocent, are not... How shall I put this?"

"Appropriate? Respectable? Sanctioned by society? Go on, take your pick. Add your voice to everyone else's." Jilly's lips grew tight. "I had hoped that Ermenbrough would be the one place I could be myself. I have taken precautions that my actions might be deemed acceptable, but I seem doomed to failure."

Ellena leaned toward her friend, a hand on her knee. "I do see you trying, Jilly dearest. You have shown commendable restraint in avoiding the kitchen and not running barefoot through my father's garden. I have seen you resist the urge to chat with the servants when they are going about their tasks." She leaned back, signaling the end to her encouragement. "But the regularity of your visits with Mr. Boyd has not shown equal discernment. As for tonight's roof-wetting of the barn, how did it come about that he should promise you the first dance? Do you not see that such conversation straddles the boundary of propriety?"

"He is showing me a kindness as a friend! It is *because* everything here is topsy-turvy and not as I left it and I cannot get my bearings that I have worried people might not know if they should dance with me or not. Mr. Boyd is willing to set the example so that others may follow and I do not end up spending the night watching everything from some sad corner."

Ellena considered her finely groomed fingernails in silence. Perhaps they were a reminder of her status. Perhaps she simply couldn't look Jillian in the eye. "I am so sorry that everything has become such a struggle for you." Her tone was soft. Her gaze, as it lifted, was almost mournful. "These were the very difficulties I feared for you when you chose to marry Lewis. And I have no cure for what troubles you. I can only say that it is not such a terrible affliction as you deem it. A challenge, certainly, but it is not all doom and gloom to give up some freedoms for happiness."

"I've never heard such nonsense!" Jillian blurted out. "My freedoms *are* my happiness! Stifle them and I am no longer *me*. How can I be content when I am not myself?"

Ellena bit down on her lip. "Jilly, I am sure you will agree that you are more 'yourself' than most people. You have known a very unburdened childhood and no sorrow at all. You have been able to enjoy a carefree existence, and that has been an enormous privilege. But did you really imagine the rest of life would require nothing of you? All these friends from your youth have found satisfaction in humble work and clear boundaries. They have not bewailed their circumstances a tenth as much as you. Quite frankly," said Ellena, the pitch of her voice rising, "if you do not stop acting quite so spoiled, I shall be very disappointed, indeed."

The bluntness of Ellena's speech hit Jillian squarely in the gut. What a terrible thing to say! And from her best friend!

"Perhaps I should stay with my parents, after all." She sniffed. "Then I do not risk offending your sensibilities."

All softness fell from Ellena's face. "You would shun my family and inconvenience your own just to avoid taking a good, hard look at yourself? Fie on you, Jilly! I thought more of you than that."

Jillian sat primly, her indignation puffing up until it flowed over into speech. "Well, you are just the last in a long line of people who deem me a disappointment. Apparently, it is a cardinal sin to be true to oneself. But I shan't kneel to any such bullying." She rose with a jolting suddenness and whipped around to make for the door.

"Jillian, wait!" Ellena cried. "If you don't listen, things might well end very badly for you. You can never be happy in your life with Lewis if you do not allow for some change. What you are clinging to is a childish dream when you could have the real thing."

Jillian stopped with her hand upon the doorknob. She turned slowly, rebellion burning within her. "My unhappiness has nothing to do with a lack of realism. I am disappointed with

Lewis because he broke promises he had made. And he wanted me to be the only one who compromised."

Ellena shook her head. "His brother's death brought challenges to you both. You did not make room for Lewis to catch his breath any more than he did for you. You both tried to squeeze your expectations into circumstances where they no longer fit. If you really loved each other, mutual support and understanding would have come before demands. But you loved the *idea* of marriage. It was all play and endless freedom. No marriage can survive such willful insistence that all should go according to plan, especially when such plans are counter to where you find yourselves. There is a reason we make an oath. Marriage is hard. If we did not pledge to be loyal, then times of struggle would easily undo our affection."

Jillian's lip began to tremble. "I don't want to hear any more." Nausea lurched up into her throat. She pulled open the door with gusto, fled down the corridor, and descended the stairs swiftly, driven to such haste by an urgent need for fresh air rather than the usual lively abandon.

Outside, she leaned forward, her forearm bent against the wall of the house as she sucked in deep mouthfuls of cool breath. The queasiness subsided somewhat but did not altogether disappear. Walking carefully like a landsick sailor, her steps feeling unsteady and the nausea threatening to rise again, Jillian maneuvered her way to her family home.

It was strangely quiet. The boys must have been busy elsewhere. Jillian sat down gingerly, then jumped up frantically and emptied the contents of her stomach into the flowerbed by the door.

"Jillian?" came the worried voice of her mother. She hastened forward, a basket of eggs swinging precariously on her arm as she did so. "Wait here. I will fetch water for you to rinse your mouth with."

Mrs. Kinsey hurried inside and came back with a jug of water and a cup, which she filled and handed to her daughter. "Rinse and spit," she instructed.

Jillian did so.

"Better?"

Jilly nodded.

"Come and sit down. I will make you some ginger tea." Her mother threw out the rest of the water over the befouled plants to cleanse them, then hurried to put the kettle on the stove. "Is the food too rich for you at the big house?" she asked, throwing a concerned glance Jilly's way while she bustled around collecting the ginger root and breaking a piece off into the cup.

"Ellena and I had a falling out," Jilly mumbled low, wary that any sudden move or exertion might trigger another trip to the flowerbed.

"All friends have disagreements. Why are you allowing it to upset you this much?"

"I don't know. I didn't think I was. One minute, she was scolding me for promising a dance to Simon Boyd at the shindy tonight. The next minute, I was ready to retch out my breakfast."

An "o" of realization formed on her mother's face. "Jilly, when last did you bleed?"

"I don't remember exactly. I'm a few weeks late with all the stress and the travelling and..." Jillian's expression shifted to match her mother's. "You don't think...?"

Mrs. Kinsey smiled in a knowing way. "I do."

"You think I am with child?"

Her mother laid her hand upon Jillian's shoulder. "I think you are with child."

Jilly cupped her own hand across her still-flat belly. If her mother was right, a little life was forming there, deep within the safe cocoon of her body. A little Lewis or Jillian. Her breath snatched. Something beautiful may have come from the unhappiness of the past months...

"Should I tell Lewis?" she asked aloud.

"Not yet," her mother answered. "Let us be certain before we give him hope."

Hope. This *was* a thing of hope, was it not? A little joyful bundle to love with all their hearts.

A possible heir.

Jilly's mood darkened.

A son or daughter to be trained in the ways of the Bradford family. A girl who must not run barefoot. A boy who must be baron one day.

The nausea rolled through her once again. Her mother ran and fetched a bowl. Jillian waved it away.

"I'm all right," she said. "But I think I might want to lie down a bit until this queasiness passes."

"Of course."

Jillian's mother helped her to the bigger of the humble beds, pulled off her boots, and brought a cool, damp cloth to lay across Jilly's forehead.

"I don't like feeling out of sorts," Jillian complained.

Her mother took her hand and wrapped it inside her own. "If there is a little one on the way, you may have to get used to it for a while."

"Little tyrant." Jilly smiled wanly and lay her hand across her belly. "I guess there'll be no more leaping about for a while. That should make everyone happy. Especially Ellena. She didn't think I should attend the barn roof-wetting tonight. It seems she will be getting her wish."

"Now, now," her mother scolded gently, "no one wishes you ill, you goose, or desires you to give up your happiness. But mothering is a solemn commitment. You will be thinking of the little one first now. Putting their needs before your own. There is a very special kind of happiness set aside for those willing to do that."

Jillian tried to lie quite still, but her thoughts tumbled through her brain. Yes, she would protect this baby… if she were indeed with child. It must never feel neglected as Lewis had been. Or be expected to live up to silly rules that had nothing to do with decency and kindness. She would fight for this little soul as no one had fought for Lewis. Jillian felt the mother tigress rise within her, a powerful instinct, enough to swipe fiercely out of the way all who would hurt this tiny, fragile life. The urge to bare her teeth and snarl at those who would wound the innocence of her little babe grew hot within her.

And then the nausea followed.

Jillian rolled over and released what was left of her breakfast into the bowl her mother had held out hurriedly. Mrs. Kinsey gently removed a stray strand of hair from her daughter's cheek and used the damp cloth to wipe her mouth.

"Can I stay here with you?" Jillian asked plaintively.

"For the day?"

"Until my return to Munro."

"Wouldn't you be more comfortable in that lovely guest room at Trenton Grange with maids to see to your every need?"

Jillian closed her eyes and fought the giddiness that now joined the nausea in torturing her. Her voice was small. "They will fuss over me." She took a shallow breath. "But not with love. I have had enough of that sort of attention." She opened her eyes again, focusing them on her mother's kind face. "Please, I can sleep on a straw mattress on the floor. "I just want my mum."

A tear formed and slipped down the side of her nose.

"There now," said her mother. "I think we could manage that. You just rest. I will go speak to Lady Howell and explain things to her quietly. Only as much as she needs to know. No need for us to make a big fuss. Now, close your eyes awhile. I will pull the shade. And when I come back, I will make you a new cup of ginger tea."

Jillian sighed out her relief. Her body, which had been a tight fist of fear and physical distress, released itself more fully into the soft embrace of the mattress. She would be all right now. She was safe.

In a few more days, if her bleeding had not resumed and the nausea did not abate, she would be able to tell Lewis the life-changing news that he was to become a father. There would be a letter at last. She smiled—a slow, weak version of her usual display, but a smile nevertheless.

She imagined Lewis reading the words, his eyes growing large, his heart, like hers, filling to capacity for the new life they would bring into the world. He would abandon his stiff ways, so recently acquired, and run down the hallway, waving the letter at anyone he passed and shouting, "I'm going to be a father!"

Much later, when he had calmed from the initial excitement, he would sit and write and share with Jillian all the plans he had for their new little family to be happy. She would receive it and hold the words to her heart. This would be the push he needed to make things right, once and for all.

Jilly's eyes grew heavy as her thoughts grew peaceful. Just a few more days…

CHAPTER TWENTY-THREE

London, early June 1816

THE SOLICITOR HAD just been shown from his study. Lewis sat back, arms crossed behind his head, feeling very pleased with the plans he had set in motion. He had even begun to hum a little ditty—something he had not done for many months—when his father appeared in the doorway, brandishing a letter, his face a thundercloud.

"That wife of yours causes trouble even when she's two hundred miles away!" he bellowed.

Lewis threw himself forward into a more formal posture, partly out of habit when in his father's presence and partly in readiness to defend Jilly's honor.

"What are you talking about?" he asked. Not that he wanted to know. It clearly wasn't good news.

"I've just received a letter from Henry Trenton." Deep frown lines appeared on his father's already serious face.

"Why would he be writing to you?"

"He is troubled by how Jillian has been conducting herself at Trenton Grange. I suppose I should not be surprised." Lord Bradford growled his deep displeasure. "Can she not even rein herself in for the sake of Lady Howell? They're supposed to be best friends. But your wife seems to have lost all sense of reason. Your mother and I are gravely concerned about the blight she continues to cast on this family."

Lewis's hackles rose. He knew what sort of man Trenton was. Controlling. Unyielding. If anyone lacked reason, it was more likely he, for he could not be reasoned with. It would have taken very little at all for Jilly to offend him.

Lewis's apparent lack of concern only fueled his father's rage. "What are you going to do about it?" the baron demanded.

"Perhaps you will allow me to see the letter for myself." Lewis held out an open palm to receive the inflammatory pages.

"Here." Lord Bradford thrust them into his son's hand. "And to think you could have married Miss Sangford."

Lewis chose to ignore the comment. If all went as planned, he would be hearing a lot less of these sorts of remarks in the near future.

He cast his eyes down to the painfully neat, small lettering that matched Mr. Trenton's exacting personality. The man had wasted no time in coming to the point. And his point, it seemed, was to declare Jillian an unsuitable character and to beg Lord Bradford's interference. And beg he would, for Henry Trenton had two weaknesses: an unhealthy love of money and a simpering awe for any personage of the nobility.

Your most excellent lordship,

It is with deep regret and no small embarrassment that I write to you for your assistance.

We have, as you know, your daughter-in-law as our houseguest for the next six weeks. However, it has taken less than a week for her to bring disruption to the calm and honor of my household and shame upon your fine name.

You should know that she has attached herself on a daily basis to Mr. Simon Boyd, the land steward of my neighbor, who, being away at present, is unaware of the behavior of his employee and therefore cannot rein it in. It would appear she has used the presence of her lady's maid to lessen the blatancy of her actions. But this only means that both young women are making fools of themselves, following the fellow on his rounds and dragging the viscountess's name through the mud by association.

Moreover, against our sound advice, Mrs. Bradford has taken it upon herself to attend a dance intended for the laboring class. Mr. Boyd, I understand, is to attend also. As companion, Mrs. Bradford intends to have her mother, a woman who has never taught her children anything of restraint and could therefore provide no guarantee for your daughter-in-law's reputation at the dance.

Finally, in a pique of rage, Mrs. Bradford this morning denounced her connection to my daughter, seeking to stay with her parents instead. As excuse, she offers that she is unwell and prefers to be tended to by her mother. But I suspect this is just another ruse to do as she pleases. Without my sharp eye or the milder intervention of the viscountess (her supposed friend), Mrs. Bradford may now apply her will to any manner of impulse that incites her. It is a most alarming state of affairs.

As you might imagine, your lordship, I have received her visit with us in good faith, but such courtesy has not been returned by our guest. I must humbly ask you to intercede. If there are words that may sway her actions, I beg you to utter them to her with immediacy. Otherwise, it is my dearest wish that you recall her to London, where you may take her under a firm hand before your good name is left in tatters.

Your servant,
Henry Trenton

Oh, dear.

Lewis could imagine all too easily the clash between the personalities of Jillian and Mr. Trenton, for two more opposite souls could scarcely exist.

Jillian would have felt herself freer to do as she once had—spending time with those who had been her peers and childhood friends. Boyd was a fine fellow, both in character and appearance. That much had been clear from Penelope's interest in him. But Jilly would not have allowed herself *that* much freedom, would she? The fact that she had thought to take a lady's maid along on her rounds with Mr. Boyd told Lewis she was trying to keep some semblance of propriety. Or did she not trust herself around him? Was it possible that an old friendship was bringing her more joy than Lewis had provided in some time? Her accompanying Mr. Boyd as he worked reminded Lewis how desperately she had wanted to be of use at Oakwoods, and how he had told her, time and again, that such roles were denied her. Jilly was no doubt loving her new freedom, yet she was certainly trying to act responsibly. Lewis could only admire that she was still trying. He needed to prove himself worthy of her. Especially if she was experiencing a daily reminder that Lewis did not provide the satisfaction to her soul that Mr. Boyd did.

As for the dance, the laboring class had once been all she had ever known. These were people whose company she would seek to relive some of the freedoms of her unmarried years. Joining them for an evening of fun... Ah, he could just imagine it. Her eyes dancing with delight. Her feet stepping lightly. Perhaps a strand of hair would come loose... But he would not be there to tuck it behind her ear. He would not have his hand upon his waist. He was missing out on seeing her at her happiest. But then again, it had been that way for some time.

Whether she had been invited there, he did not know, but it was likely she had hoped such an event would allow her to spend time with old friends in a way they could not do under more formal circumstances. Jilly would have wanted that more than anything. If she had been welcomed, he would be very glad, for it would be a balm for the wounds the *ton* had inflicted upon her. And he counted himself and his family among those who had added to her pain. He prayed she *had* been welcomed. He could not bear the thought of her suffering at the hands of those she considered her sanctuary.

Either way, it was hardly a shameful deed to join in a country dance or two, especially when it was a casual affair. Mr. Trenton was really grasping at straws to find fault with Jilly. And his insult to her mother was simply unforgivable. Mrs. Kinsey might have been a woman of humble origins, but her character lacked nothing. The Henry Trentons of this world had much to learn from her.

As far as Lewis was concerned, there were only two worrying elements to this letter. Why had two such dear friends fallen out? And what made his wife so unwell that she required the attentions of her mother? Jillian was the healthiest being he knew. This would not be a mere seasonal sniffle. It angered Lewis that Mr. Trenton had sought to write a tattling letter to his father instead of calling a doctor for his wife. The man had been more concerned with the minutiae of etiquette and had not even described what ailed his guest. He had even gone as far as to call her a liar! Lewis considered it a great mercy that Henry Trenton did not stand before him now, for he would have been hard-pressed not to punch the fellow on the jaw.

"Do you see?" Lewis's father tapped the pages with an irate finger. "She is making a mockery of you, fraternizing with this Boyd fellow. I mean, what is a lady's maid going to do if her mistress tells her to hold her tongue? And Jillian's mother would be no better. You see what Mr. Trenton has to say about her. It is a damnable state of affairs, Lewis!"

Lewis stared at his father. It would be equally wrong to punch the baron, but Lewis was finding it very hard to hear his father echo Trenton's ugly remarks.

"Mr. Trenton," said Lewis through a tight jaw, "is a kowtowing, mean-spirited bully. He thinks and says the worst, running to you with such vile insinuations simply to curry favor with a man of title."

Lord Bradford was unmoved. "You are willfully ignorant of your wife's behavior. She does as she wishes and the more you allow such freedoms, the more freedoms she will take. If you are not going to take her in hand, you will find yourself suing for divorce, for she will certainly cuckold you."

The insult was so offensive that Lewis would have been in his rights to make a scene. A hot fury rose within him, one that may have caused him to strike the man who spoke such evil if it had not been his own father. The fact that it was a man of dignity who had felt free to express these vulgar thoughts made it infinitely worse. So much so that Lewis plowed through the white-hot rage that burned in his skull and landed in a pool of deadly calm on the other side.

"It would appear," he said, the tone in his voice so mild as to be dangerous, "that Mother thinks Jillian to be going mad and you believe my wife incapable of faithfulness." The corners of his mouth turned down and his lips curved into a show of disgust as though he had caught a whiff of a foul odor. "And to think, all these months, I have asked Jilly to consider following your example." He puffed out a wry laugh. "I have been such a fool."

"Now see here!" Lord Bradford swelled with indignation.

"No, Father, *you* see. You see how Penelope does not want to marry because she dreads being bound by the shackles of a married woman. See how I had almost no relationship with you or Mother while Philip was alive. Note how I rose in favor quite suddenly upon your firstborn's death. Consider the character of Miss Sangford, whom you would foist upon me as the ideal candidate for a wife."

"What of it?"

"'What of it'? *This* is your answer? Well, then, I shall explain. Simply put, Father, none of your children have known parental love. All decisions have been borne of rigorous expectation. When Philip complied, you could turn a blind eye to your other offspring. Penelope and I were at best annoying, inconvenient. At worst, all but invisible. But even Philip did not gain your true affection. He merely won your approval. That is why you were happy for him to marry a cold-hearted creature like Miss Sangford. You did not seek his happiness, only for him to do what *looked* pleasing." Lewis shook his head, his hand to his brow. "Heaven help him. I believe *that* is why he took himself to such a place as led to his demise. *He was rebelling*." His voice sank as the reality of it hit harder. "Poor man. I did not think he had it in him."

"Stop!" bellowed Lord Bradford. "You will not sully Philip's good name because your own choices have been fodder for gossip! *He* was a son I could be proud of!"

"Really, Father? You are proud that he died outside a gaming hell? Why was he not at a gentleman's club, or riding with Miss Sangford, or meeting with Mr. Cooper, our steward? Why did he feel a need to be amongst such society, especially if he knew it would displease you?"

His father's shoulders slumped. "I do not know. It cost him dearly. It cost our whole family dearly."

"Ah, yes, because now this second-class son"—he indicated with his thumb to his own chest—"has had to play at being the heir. And, for a brief time, I *did* fill Philip's shoes." Lewis grabbed at his shirt as if it suffocated him. "Oh, how quickly I forgot myself and lapped up the attention you suddenly threw my way! What a good boy I was! And how soon I turned against my beloved!"

Lord Bradford pushed against his cane and drew himself fully erect. "That woman has done nothing but cause strife within this family! You should never have married her in the first place. Now look at the precipice to which she has brought us."

"What precipice, Father? Has our position suffered? Our lands? Our friendships? What, besides some ill-intentioned tittering and this malicious letter from Henry Trenton, has occurred to harm us? I see you do not even show concern for Jillian's wellbeing. You do not ask why she is unwell or what has been said or done for her to question her oldest friendship. You lay all blame at her feet. You only care for how you are perceived by society. What about how your own family sees you? While you wave your scepter about, do you even think whom you strike with it? How it hurts them?

"Jillian has brought warmth and lightness to my life. And you would have preferred I marry someone who ate with the right fork yet wanted nothing but the wealth and title that would one day be mine. Jilly has loved me simply and completely and did not seek anything more. Still, you have condemned her, berated her and, most importantly, learned nothing from her.

"Fool that I was, I followed your example. I first came to love Jillian *because* she is different. And then I expected her to change. I asked her to be something she is not and thought we would be happier for it. What madness! If she *had* become all you have expected of her, she would no longer resemble the person I fell in love with."

Lord Bradford turned a cold eye to his son. "You persist in your loyalty to this woman who will be your undoing. I have tried my best to bring you to your senses. I do not understand this hold she has over you. But you *will* send for her. She cannot be allowed to blacken our name. In fact, have her delivered to Oakwoods. Penelope can return home and they can keep their mischief limited to our private grounds. What I did to deserve such wayward offspring, I will never know."

"No," murmured Lewis, "I don't suppose you will. One thing is certain, Father, you will have little cause to speak to me of this again."

"Oh?"

"I will be fetching Jillian myself. And I will make sure that, once I have her secured, she stays put."

"Well, that, at least, is happy news. I had begun to think I had lost you entirely."

"Fear not, Father, I am returning to the place you have always kept me: on the periphery of your world."

"Now, Lewis, don't start this childish mewling again."

"It is quite the opposite," said Lewis blandly. "I have finally grown up. I no longer crave your approval. It carries no weight with me anymore. The price is too high."

"Really, Lewis, your mother and I…"

Lewis marched past his father, who spun around, flustered.

"Lewis! I am talking to you! *Lewis!*"

But Lewis had left the room. Moreover, he had left any thought of his father far behind. He would send Parliament his excuses—an urgent family matter—and leave London behind too. Time to reclaim his life, his freedom, his wife.

The footman jerked to attention as Lewis approached.

"Have my valet come up to my rooms," instructed Lewis. "And tell Cook I will be needing refreshment for the road. Then step 'round to the mews and have them ready the coach for a long journey. I will be heading north in an hour."

"Yes, sir," answered the footman, his long limbs quickly striding from the room so that he might perform the list of tasks.

Right. Time enough to scribe the letter to the Speaker of the House of Commons. And to update his sister on developments. He would not bother to do as much for his mother. She would only reiterate everything his father had said. Perhaps a short note could suffice. He really did not want another lecture. His mind was made up. His focus was on Jilly now and their future together.

Come to think of it, he should have all of Jilly's things packed too. He would never be bringing her back to this house. Wallace, her lady's maid, had gone with her to Ermenbrough. But one of the other maids could pack the few things she had left behind just as easily. He would arrange for it shortly. He just needed a moment…

Lewis would have loved to have stepped outside to catch his breath, but London air did not offer such a refreshing option. Beside him, the piano Jilly had never learned to play to his mother's satisfaction stood open and ready to make any sound it was bid. Lewis reached across with two fingers and began to play a simple tune. His rich baritone joined in.

> *"At ball or play, she flirt away, and ever giddy be;*
> *But always said, I ne'er will wed, no one shall govern me."*

Ah, Wild Thing, thought Lewis. *I am coming to claim you once again.*

Then he withdrew his fingers from the keys and shoved them into his pockets, humming the rest of the song as he made his way upstairs, shedding his worries as he went.

CHAPTER TWENTY-FOUR

W HEN, BY TUESDAY morning, Jillian had awoken once again with the urge to toss a breakfast she had not yet consumed, she was quite decided. She was with child. The past three days, she had felt exceedingly tired, although the nausea did lessen as the day progressed. She was growing used to her new pattern of existence, which was slower. And more fragile. Rather like the life she carried within her womb.

It also meant that, by early afternoon, she knew it was safe to leave the despised, ever-ready bowl behind and stretch her legs along the village road, even if it was at half the pace she was used to.

It was also why, when she saw Ellena, Christopher, and his nurse heading back from the village toward her, she did not have the usual strength and alacrity to nip across the field and dodge them.

They were currently pausing over a patch of daisies. Ellena was reaching down to gather a small posy. Perhaps she planned to make a floral chain for herself as the two of them used to do when they'd been nymphs together. Or maybe she intended to shape a wreath with which to crown her son and heir.

The sight of Christopher clutching a single flower in his chubby, little hand and jamming it clumsily up against his nose brought a surge of maternal feeling to Jillian's breast. Next year, it would be her own son or daughter who tugged so at her heartstrings.

It was wrong that Ellena was not part of her journey into motherhood. Their tiff had been silly. Jillian hadn't even gone to the dance that had led to the high feeling between them. They would certainly have talked it out the next day if Jillian hadn't been staying with her parents. And she had only done that because she was not feeling her best. Strange that Ellena hadn't even looked in on her. They had never behaved so badly to each other before.

Here, though, as if handed on a platter, was a chance to make things right. So, Jillian kept walking, closing the gap between herself and the best friend she had already begun to miss terribly.

At the sound of Jillian's boots crunching on the pebbly path, Ellena looked up. Uncertainty flashed across her features.

Jillian posted a brave smile upon her face to reassure her friend that she came in peace, but her own insecurity caused it to falter and fade.

"Lovely day for a walk," Jillian said, cursing herself that their close bond should now need the crutch of such platitudes.

"I see you are well enough to enjoy one," answered Ellena.

Was that reproach in her tone? Would she have preferred if Jillian were bedridden?

"You would have known how well I was if you had come to see me," she found herself saying. *No, Jillian! Don't be petty! You want to mend the rift, not widen it.*

But Ellena had already matched her lessened grace. "Seems to me you weren't so ill after all. Wallace, whom you appear to have abandoned along with the rest of us, has seen you out and about every afternoon. Sneaking off to see Mr. Boyd, were you?"

"Ellie! That is a terrible thing to say!" Jillian never thought she would hear such an accusation from the mouth of her best friend. How could she even think such a thing? It wasn't like her at all.

"Well, what am I to think when you banish yourself from my parents' home, say you are too ill to be tended to by anyone but your mother, and then hasten off across the field in the afternoons?"

"Anything but that! Think me infantile for threatening to abandon you, sulky that my friend should scold me so soundly for wanting the company of my humbler friends, foolish for wanting to hide away with my own family when I am a grown woman. But to accuse me of mischief behind Lewis's back!" She suppressed a moment of guilt. She *had* enjoyed Simon Boyd's company. Very much. He had made her feel whole again. But he had never been intended to replace Lewis. If anything, those hours together had been reminders of how Lewis had once been. And she would have *that* Lewis back in a heartbeat.

"But why lie, Jilly? Why pretend to be ill? We have never had dishonesty between us."

"I wasn't lying." Jillian's hand automatically reached for her belly. "I had no intention of staying with my parents. Not really. But when I went to ask my mother to accompany me to the roof-wetting, I felt very nauseous, indeed. I even had to lie down to rest while she made me ginger tea. Mother thought... and since these four days have passed, I am certain she is right..." Jillian looked shyly at her belly.

Ellena's eyes widened. Her mouth fell open. Then, like the sun breaking through clouds, a smile lit up her entire face and she threw her arms around her best friend. "A baby? You're going to have a baby! Oh, that is the Best. News. Ever!"

The two women hugged and laughed and completely dissolved four days of petty disagreement that should never have happened in the first place.

"I'm so sorry I said what I did about Mr. Boyd." Ellena had the good grace to look embarrassed. "I can't believe I let my father override my judgment."

"I should have known such a thought would not originate with you," answered Jilly. "The irony is, I didn't even go to the dance. I was feeling too wretched to be bouncing and twirling in a crowded area. It would not have been seemly to be sick on poor

Mr. Boyd's shoes." She grinned.

But Ellena did not join in the mirth of the comment. Her hand lifted swiftly to cover her mouth. "Oh, Jilly, I just remembered. Father sent a letter to Lord Bradford. He had taken such umbrage at you shifting to your parents' cottage, he quite considered it the last of a string of offenses of which he considered you guilty. He did not know you never went to the dance. Nor did he believe you truly ill. I'm afraid the letter would have been filled with unintentional falsehood and a good dose of Father's heavy-handedness. It will create a terrible impression on your father-in-law. I'm so sorry!"

Jillian considered the matter for a minute. Then she reached down and scooped up Christopher onto her hip. "Lord Bradford thinks little enough of me as it is. I can hardly sink further in his estimation. But today, we have sunshine. And the company of a sweet little cherub. Our friendship is restored." She nestled her nose against Christopher's soft neck. He giggled and grabbed a fistful of her hair. "I will write Lewis that he is to become a father," she said as she carefully unwound the strands from Christopher's fat, little fingers. "I will explain my side of the story, for his lordship will be sure to have burdened Lewis with the contents of the letter." Jilly kissed the boy's cheek and set him back down again. "Whether Lewis will need to have anything explained will depend upon his faith in me. At least I can add some good news to the bad."

"I shall write in support of you," Ellena added firmly. "Lewis knows I would never lie to him. If our correspondence is in step with each other's, he will know it is my father's viewpoint that is skewed."

With their plan thus forged, Jillian and Ellena set aside the serious business of letters and interfering fathers. They picked more flowers, plaiting chains, which they wore while walking back home arm-in-arm, chatting about the joys and challenges of motherhood.

As they neared the line of cottages, Jack came running down

the path toward them. He seemed to be in a great hurry yet stopped abruptly when he reached them.

"Jilly, Lewis has come! He waits for you at the kitchen table. Mum is making him a plate of bread and butter. He looks worn out, like he hasn't slept at all. He thought you'd be in bed, ill. But when I told him you were out walking, that did not seem to make him happy. You'd better come and explain things to him. He looks about ready to fall into a bed himself."

Jilly looked hesitantly at Ellena. "So, not a letter, after all."

"It's better this way," answered her friend with a gentle smile. "You can see his face when you give him the news."

"I don't know." Jillian was no longer so sure of herself. "If he has come, it is because of what your father has written. Perhaps he has believed it all."

Ellena took a firm hold of Jillian's arm. "I will come with you. We will put all suspicions to rest. Be strong. Lewis will not want to doubt you. Let us release him at once from all fears."

With Christopher and his nurse in tow, Jillian and Ellena walked the rest of the distance to her family's home. They did so in relative silence, with only the innocent babble of Christopher ringing in the air.

It was enough to draw Lewis from the house. He appeared in the doorway, gray-cheeked and exhausted, a worry-line folding into his brow. He stared at the approaching party, wrapped as it was in an atmosphere of tranquil togetherness. The worry-line dissolved, but the fatigue caused him to stumble as he stepped toward them.

At once, Jilly was three strides in front of Ellena and gaining speed. She pushed herself into her husband's embrace, both holding him up and held by him.

"Hullo, Wild Thing," he murmured into her hair. "We need to talk."

CHAPTER TWENTY-FIVE

JILLY SAT BESIDE Lewis on a bench in the Trentons' garden. It was the nearest semblance of privacy they could find. Neither the Kinsey family cottage nor the Trenton manor could provide a space for them to speak freely. And Lewis was far too worn out to walk and talk along a country path.

Jillian, on the other hand, was positively glowing.

"I believed you to be ill," Lewis said a little reproachfully, though the sight of Jillian once more her radiant self made him happier than he could possibly have imagined.

"I *have* been," she countered. "Maybe not bound to my bed all day, but certainly not well enough to seek the company of Mr. Trenton." She scrunched up her face at the mention of his name.

Lewis understood all too well. Perhaps she had exaggerated her symptoms somewhat to escape the man's unpleasant interference. Well, Lewis would cure that ailment easily enough.

"Are you well enough to come home with me?" He tucked her hand into his to show he meant it.

Jillian turned her head from him, the full measure of her delight at his arrival slipping from her face. "If I have been too ill to endure Mr. Trenton, I am certainly in no condition to return to London and be under your parents' roof once more."

"Ah," said Lewis, carrying the secret knowledge of his plan and eager now to share it with Jilly, "but we would not be returning to London. I have excused myself for the last few weeks of session."

Jillian shook her head. "Even if we were alone at Oakwoods, or in Penelope's company, I would still prefer to remain with my mother. She knows what I need."

Lewis tried to hide his disappointment. "And what do you need? You seem to be in excellent health."

"It comes and goes."

"Like a fever? Is it wise, then, to be walking about and tiring yourself?"

"No, not like a fever. Fits of queasiness."

Lewis was not ready to give up yet. If Jillian was only experiencing a tummy ache, it should be easy enough to treat. "What brings it on? Do you know the cause?"

Jilly turned to face him once again, the rosy glow returning to her cheeks. "*You* are the cause."

The accusation startled Lewis. "*I* make you sick?"

Why was she smiling? These were not humorous words.

"You make us a family." Jillian took the hand that held hers and drew it to her belly. "I am only unwell in the mornings…"

Lewis remained confused. He knew Latin and Greek and could argue his case in court, but he had no knowledge at all about women's bellies and why, if such a part of his wife was troubled, he should be to blame for it, especially when he had been all the way in London.

"I don't understand," he confessed after some thought and no success.

"Lewis, you ninny, you're going to be a father!" Jillian laughed.

Realization dawned in his bone-weary mind. "A baby?" he asked, his voice cracking.

Jillian nodded. "I was going to write to you today. I first wanted to be sure. But here you are. Perhaps I should thank Mr. Trenton for his letter. It is so much better to tell you in person, to see your face, to… Lewis, are those tears?"

He brushed the moisture briskly from his eyes. Then he folded his wife into his arms, holding her as if she had been rescued from the edge of a cliff, where one misplaced step would have cost them everything.

"I'm going to keep you safe," Lewis promised, his voice thick and rough. "You and this baby and any other children you may bless us with. You will see."

Jillian stiffened in his embrace. "Your parents will work against your good intentions."

Lewis leaned back so that she could see his face and know that he meant every word. "We will not be returning to London. Not until next season. And then we will be sharing accommodation with our friend the viscount. And Ellena, of course, if she chooses to join him. He seldom stays for the whole season, using his proxy so that he may attend to matters back home in Munro instead. But he has granted us the use of his townhome regardless. You will see my parents only if and when it pleases you."

"What about Oakwoods?" countered Jilly, though Lewis could see a flicker of hope in her eyes. "Even the servants are not truly mine that I may build a relationship with them. All of them, including Wallace, were chosen *for* me. And the weekly Sunday dinner is enough for your mother and father to chisel away at our happiness and teach our innocent babes their way of thinking. The very thought of such a fate befalling our children, especially if there is a son who will be your heir, crushes the breath within my breast."

"As it does mine, beloved," answered Lewis. "Oakwood must receive us again, but only to collect our belongings. We will return to the estate one day when we are both ready. If that means waiting until I am the baron and can dictate the manner in which we live, so be it."

Jillian now sat up straight, listening with rapt attention to her husband's every word. "Are we to live in Ermenbrough?"

"We shall certainly visit. But I do not like to be observed by Mr. Trenton and have more of his wicked letters reach my father, only to disturb his already ill-managed peace. No, I have something much better in mind."

Now Jillian leaned forward as if to draw the answer from Lewis with the force of her curiosity. "Where, then?"

"Do you remember a house on the outskirts of Munro? A shaded lawn? A private garden? We talked of chickens…"

"I thought you said…"

"Forget what I said. I acted in haste. Philip's passing threw me off-balance and, in trying to right myself, I made a mess of things. We had promised to find our own way, and I should have stayed the course. For a while, I lost my bearing and thought our plans beyond our reach. But they were always ours for the taking. I want them back. I want *you* back."

Jillian was silent at these words. Her lack of response ate away at Lewis's confidence. Did she not believe him? Was it too late? Had he done too much harm?

"I am still unsuited for the role of baron's wife," she said softly.

"No, my love, you are only unsuited for the role of the *current* Baron Bradford's wife. Mercifully, that position is already taken. But you… *ah, you…*" Lewis gazed upon his wife, who inspired him to dream beyond his limitations once again. "You will breathe life into that gray, old building and the musty norms by which it has been governed."

"Perhaps…" Jillian looked shyly at the hand that held hers, "I might add a little dignity to my step. And not confuse the servants with too much friendship."

"They will love you, anyway," Lewis promised her. "For you cannot help but be kind and generous and selfless. And if our children's mama likes to gambol with them on the lawn, so much the better. They shall learn to laugh as well as run an estate."

"Will your parents not be angry?"

"If that is how they wish to fill their time, they may do as they like. We shall not allow their chagrin in our home. They will soon choose whether to keep company with us or not. As for

Penelope, I hope we can have her stay with us if she wishes. She would make an excellent aunt, and a valuable companion for you."

"I should like that very much. Especially when we are in London."

"Ah, but you will be very busy in London." Lewis closed an eye in an exaggerated wink.

"I will?"

"Oh, yes, my dear. Our children, if they take after you, will run you ragged. And if you have energy to spare, you will be occupied with your personal project."

"My what?"

"I have arranged for you to serve on the board of trustees for St. Giles Asylum for Orphans. All it took was a small donation and their knowledge of your sincere devotion to their cause. You shall throw your natural passion into helping them change the children's lives for the better. You have told me over and over that your life lacks purpose. I am sorry it took me so long to hear you."

Jillian threw her arms about her husband's neck as she smothered him in kisses. He laughed and fended her off playfully. "Stop! Stop! What will people think?"

Jilly stopped abruptly. "So, that still matters so much?"

Lewis grinned. "Only if they think I really want you to stop."

Jilly relaxed a little, but her expression remained serious. "I thought I had lost you."

"I had lost myself," Lewis whispered. He leaned in and kissed her left cheek. "But I have been reminded why I loved you in the first place." He placed a kiss on her right cheek. "And I will never forget again." Now his lips found hers. Her mouth grew slack and wet as Lewis pressed against it with his own. Pulling back gently, he caught his breath and tilted forward again, their lips colliding, separating and bearing down on each other with feverish, heady relish.

Jilly ran her fingers through the back of his hair and drew him even closer, her own locks falling from her shoulders as she tilted her head back and offered him the soft nape of her neck. With nimble fingers, Lewis loosed the ribbon of her bonnet and freed her golden mane, the bonnet dropping to the end of the bench behind her. His teeth nipped the lobe of her ear. The tip of his tongue ran…

"Whoa, don't let Mr. Trenton see you at it in his garden," came Sam's voice across the sweet briar behind them. "He won't have the stomach for it. Probably chase you out as soon as look at you. Besides, I've got to prune this shrub and you'll get thorny cuttings all over you."

"Or you could be our lookout." Jillian grinned at the lanky twelve-year-old.

"No, thanks. Da won't like me shirking my duties. Anyway, aren't you too old for such antics? You're not a blushing bride anymore, Sis."

Sam ducked as Jillian jumped up and aimed a playful tap in his direction.

"Get her away from me!" he cried, laughing and bobbing to evade another swipe from his sister.

"Not before you pay for calling me old," puffed Jilly, lunging at the nimble sprite who easily maneuvered himself beyond her reach. After two more attempts, she gave up. "Our children are going to run circles around me," she complained to Lewis.

"I would expect nothing less if they're to take after you," said Lewis.

"Hmm, perhaps I should start walking more sedately, after all."

Lewis grabbed Jilly by her waist and tugged her toward him. He tucked the knuckle of his forefinger under her chin and lifted it so that they might look at each other, eye to eye. "You have a wild heart, my love. I would not see it tamed. You will teach our children all they need to know to manage in society. But, more importantly, you will show them what it is to be truly alive. And I would not have it any other way."

Jillian buried her face in her husband's warm embrace. "What am I going to do with all those copious notes I took for you about farming?" she murmured into his jacket.

"When we reach Oakwoods, you and I shall meet with Mr. Cooper, Father's land steward, and you will amaze him with the wealth of your knowledge."

"Really?" Jillian perked up at once.

"Really. And you shall choose your own cook and lady's maid, unless you have grown fond of Wallace. Choose whomever you like, someone who matches your personality and who has not been selected for you by my parents. Perhaps Ellena can make a recommendation."

"Oh! Do you think Ellena will mind if I leave after little more than a week? I haven't really spent that much time with her and I only seemed to have made things worse for her with her father."

"I was actually meaning to have a word with the fellow before we leave. Set him straight, as it were."

Jillian lowered her gaze. "You don't have to do that for me. I know I have your trust."

"I am glad of it. But my father, as you know, is easily perturbed. I would prefer to avoid unnecessary correspondence from this quarter in future. As for Ellena, she will not begrudge you a happy resolution to your troubles."

"Are our troubles resolved, though? Your parents will resent every decision you have made in this regard."

"My parents have chosen their path and we have chosen ours. If these diverge beyond what they can tolerate, then that, too, is their choice. I will no longer be hamstrung by their expectations of us. You are my future, Jilly. You and our children. That is enough for me."

Jilly subsided into his arms once more. Lewis savored the heat of her body against his.

"Ahem." Sam raised the shears and made a clipping motion in the air. "This shrub ain't going to trim itself."

"Oh, all *right*!" Jillian huffed. "We'll just have to take the carriage to the inn and continue our conversation there."

"I can think of other things I'd like to do rather than talk." Lewis's words breathed hotly into Jillian's ear.

"Ah, yes," she agreed, winking coyly at him, "I supposed you'd like to sleep. You must be *very* tired."

"You know," Lewis answered, "I seem to have found my second wind…"

EPILOGUE

Munro, March 1817

BABY NICOLA LAY against her mother's breast, sound asleep. Jillian's eyes began to close. There was nothing like a shared nap to refresh the drowsy duo.

At the edge of her hearing, she detected the soft step of someone entering the room and halting, no doubt unwilling to disturb mother and child. The housekeeper had the afternoon off. And Pen, who was now sharing their home, was out riding, as was still her habit. The thoughtfully quiet presence must therefore be Lewis. Her eyes opened enough to see him hesitate, look back toward the corridor, then bite his lip.

"Is something the matter?" Jilly asked, though the answer was obvious.

"My mother is here," he said quite suddenly, as if he needed to get the words out before he lost courage. "She wishes to speak with you."

Jillian's heartbeat accelerated. She had neither seen nor heard from either of Lewis's parents since their return to Munro. Nicola was already a month old. What had changed? Was Lord Bradford unwell? Was his wife here to blame them for it?

Nicola stirred, her sleep disturbed by the tension flooding Jillian's body.

"It is not like her to break with etiquette," pondered Jillian. "Isn't it the done thing to write and announce one's intention to visit? These matters are usually important to her."

"I know it is unexpected." He seemed to waver. "I can send her away…"

"But you don't want to."

Lewis's shoulders drooped. "She looks… worn down."

"The proud and fierce Lady Bradford? Worn down?" Jillian wanted to feel sympathy, but nine months of being ignored had not silenced the knowledge that this woman had believed her to be verging on madness.

"Will you see her?" asked Lewis. "Please? I can stay. If she behaves badly, I will send her on her way at once."

Her husband's face was so woeful, Jillian could not possibly say *no*. There was almost nothing she wouldn't do for him. He had given her everything she needed, fought everyone and everything for her. Now it was her turn. "If there is any chance she wants to do right by you, I am willing to try."

Lewis lit up at these words. He disappeared quickly behind the door. Jillian could hear him tell the footman, "Send her up."

He waited out of sight on the landing. Jillian, too, waited, curiosity and apprehension vying for supremacy. Their baby settled once more, unaware of the momentous scene that unfolded around her.

The door swung open and Lewis entered the room with his mother leaning on his arm. It was strange to see her no longer wearing black. Had Philip really been gone so long? Despite her moss-green dress, the matriarch seemed as much in mourning as ever. Her hair, previously streaked with gray, was now entirely white and many more lines crisscrossed her face. Lewis had not been exaggerating. She *did* look worn out.

However, the moment Lady Bradford saw little Nicola, her face softened. She took a step forward toward her granddaughter, but Lewis indicated a settee farther from his wife and babe. Lady Bradford, clearly disappointed, complied and sat where she was told.

Silence lingered awkwardly. Lewis looked from his wife to his mother and back, but neither initiated the conversation. He sighed.

Jillian's heart went out to him. None of this was easy for any of them. Lady Bradford had called on them and should say what was on her mind, but she was not good at apologies. Jillian was the hostess and was obliged to make her welcome, but she did not know if their guest *was* welcome yet. And Lewis was caught in the middle, as always.

Across the room, their visitor's eyes were locked on the bundle of sweetness in Jilly's arms. Honestly, it was obvious why she was here—whether she deserved it or not. *No*, thought Jillian, *whatever I decide to do now, I do for Lewis, not her.*

Having made up her mind, Jilly stood carefully, scooping Nicola up and cradling her head. She crossed the space between herself and Lady Bradford and asked, "Would you like to hold her?"

The woman whom Jilly had only ever known as stern and unbending now melted into doting benevolence. Her arms reached out eagerly to receive her grandchild. Her only grandchild.

"She has your eyes," she told Lewis as Nicola opened them at the unfamiliar touch of her not-mother. "And your hair." She looked up at Jilly.

"Well, the beginnings of it, at any rate," said Jilly with half a smile. "She really is only a downy, little chick at present."

"You will need a son, too," said Lady Bradford automatically. "Oakwoods must have an heir."

Jillian pinched her lips shut. Not everything could be undone in a day. Perhaps it never would be. But Lady Bradford had swallowed her dignity to come. Jillian would allow a little wiggle room, even if it meant simply saying nothing.

"All in good time, Mother," Lewis cautioned, ready to defend his little family.

Lady Bradford looked up at him as if she had just realized what she had said. "Oh. Oh, yes, of course. This is a good start, certainly. Er… you have done well, Jillian." The sentiment sounded uncomfortable in her mouth, but she uttered it nevertheless. And Jilly noticed.

"Is this why you wished to see me? You want to know your granddaughter?"

"I had hoped…" A tear formed in the corner of Lady Bradford's eye. "Philip is gone forever. And Penelope is determined never to marry. Your children are the only grandchildren we will ever know."

"We will raise them as we see fit," Lewis said firmly.

His mother stiffened. "That much, you have made clear." She said nothing more, though Jilly imagined she resisted the saying of many things.

"If you will love Nicola," said Jillian, the warmth of her voice promising that her words were intended with kindness, "and enjoy your time with her instead of trying to shape her to your views of the world, then I would be happy for you to visit here. Lord Bradford too."

"He will come around, you know," said Lady Bradford, her attention diverted once more to the cherublike cheeks of baby Nicola. "Especially because you have been gracious to me."

Jillian watched Lewis sag deeper into his chair, as if he had just released a heavy weight he had carried for too long. She had not fully understood how much he had wanted this. He had always rebelled against the neglect he had experienced and had sought happiness along a completely different path than the one his parents had trodden. But even now, aged thirty-one and a father himself, he was still a boy who wanted his mother and father to care.

"We will be patient," Jilly reassured Lady Bradford, but her eyes were upon Lewis, the man who had chosen her above his own family. How deeply he loved her! It was heartbreaking that he had ever had to choose at all.

"Perhaps, if we are truly to be family, you can forgive your son for wanting this." Jillian indicated herself, their home. "And love not only his daughter, but Lewis, too? He was once a babe in your arms, just like this little life you hold. And he still craves your affection. I ask, not for myself, but for him, your flesh and blood."

Lady Bradford stared at Jillian, her jaw slack, a crease deepening between her eyes. "We have always loved him!"

"Then," replied Jillian, "I urge you to find a way for him to know it. A gentle word. A conversation without reprimand. Tell him you are proud of him. Spend time with him for its own sake—no lesson to be learned."

"I… This is not… We don't…" Lady Bradford halted in her flustered speech. She took a deep breath. It shook a little as she exhaled it. "I will try. We will try."

Jillian resisted the instinctive urge to throw her arms around her mother-in-law and squeeze her with all her might. Such an embrace would create more alarm than pleasure. Instead, Jilly reached down and placed a light kiss upon the woman's brow. "Thank you," was all she said.

Then she fetched Lewis by the hand and led him across the thick rug, pressing his shoulders down firmly so that he was obliged to sit next to his mother on the settee, sharing a space more closely than they had done for the better part of thirty years.

"There!" said Jillian, stepping back to take in her handiwork with satisfaction. "Now the two of you can coo over our daughter together. I will go fetch us some tea." She laughed as Lady Bradford raised a quizzical eyebrow yet wisely said nothing. "It is the housekeeper's day off," she explained. "Besides, I make a very good cup of tea. I have acquired a fine blend that Mrs. Trenton likes to make. So, you see, you and I are learning new things together."

Lady Bradford nodded. "So we are." She reached a tentative hand and patted her son on the knee. "So we are."

Baby Nicola gurgled at her grandmother and wrapped her tiny hand about the lady's finger. In the doorway, Jilly paused to drink in the scene of delicate domestic bliss. *One day, she thought, those little hands will plait a daisy crown for her grandmother. And it will be the proudest jewel the white-haired matriarch has ever worn.*

Then she skipped down the stairs of her home to make tea, humming a tune as her shoes thumped a merry beat all the way to the kitchen.

Acknowledgements

Because the heroine of this story has such a challenging relationship with her mother- and father-in-law, it might be easy to assume I have drawn from personal experience. However, nothing could be further from the truth. And so, I would like to thank Berel and Leila for welcoming me wholeheartedly into their family, treating me like a daughter, and leading with love in their sixty-plus years of marriage. Thank you, Leila, for being a fan of my writing and encouraging me to publish decades ago, long before my first book, when you said my family newsletters were like chapters from a novel.

Amy McNulty, my editor, bless you for pushing me to give my best and doing it with a warm heart.

Thank you to the knowledgeable members of the Regency Fiction Writers organization, who answer my urgent questions when a vital plot point depends on getting the historical facts right and I need the answer yesterday.

But you, my readers… Ah, you are my favorites, hands down. Thank you for taking a chance on my books and an especially big thank you if you leave reviews, even if it's just a star rating. I spend months behind my keyboard for each book-baby and just one word of encouragement can keep me going. These books are for you. I hope they bring you joy.

About the Author

Elizabeth Donne writes sweet Regency romance, a natural outpouring of a lifelong love affair with English literature.

She has spent most of her life in Cape Town, South Africa. In 2015, she moved to Iowa with her husband, their two children, two cats, and their African bush dog. When she's not writing, or discovering the secret wonders of the Midwest, she is enthusiastically introducing her visitors to the joys of drinking *rooibos* tea. With a biscuit, of course.

www.ingramcontent.com/pod-product-compliance
Lightning Source LLC
Chambersburg PA
CBHW072059300726
48975CB00003B/639